THE PREY

TOM ISBELL

HARPER
Voyager

HarperVoyager
An imprint of HarperCollinsPublishers
1 London Bridge Street
London SE1 9GF

www.harpercollins.co.uk

A Paperback Original 2015
1

A catalogue record for this book
is available from the British Library

ISBN: 978-0-00-752818-9

Printed and bound in Great Britain by
Clays Ltd, St Ives plc

To Pat and Pam,
Sisters

PART ONE
LIBERTY

Wild animals never kill for sport. Man is the only one to whom the torture and death of his fellow creatures is amusing in itself.

—JAMES ANTHONY FROUDE

from *Oceana, or, England and Her Colonies*

PROLOGUE

Blood drips from fingertips, splashing the floor. A mosaic of white hexagons, outlined in black, now splotched with red. Droplets, then a puddle, a pond, a lake.

Blood. Purpling. Coagulating before his eyes.

Darkness presses against the outer reaches of his periphery, narrowing his vision. The world grows dim.

He reaches out a hand against the blood-smeared wall. Fingers squealing on tiles. Tries to call for help but the words get strangled in his throat. He collapses to the floor.

Eyes land on a knife, its razor edge trimmed in red. Blood. His blood.

Darkness closing in. The world reduced to a pinprick. Fatigue washes over him like a summer storm.

My final moments, *he realizes.* All come down to this.

He does not hear the door swing open, the swift stomping of feet. The ripping of fabric. The improvised tourniquet. Being lifted and carried, swept out the door, leaving behind a world of black and white and red.

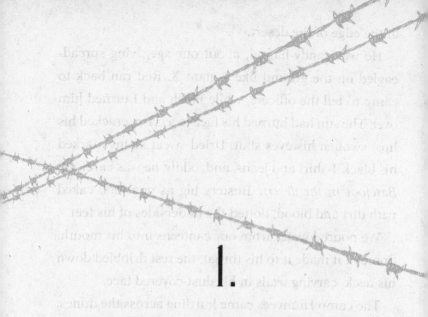

1.

WE FOUND HIS BODY on a Sunday morning. Three circling buzzards, their black silhouettes etched against a blazing blue sky, clued us in that *something* might be down there. Down in the gullies where the foothills gave over to desert.

At the very edge of the No Water.

We thought a possum. Perhaps even a wolf. Certainly not a kid fried like an egg, stretched out in the meager shade of a mesquite bush.

He wasn't dead, but if we hadn't found him when we did, he would've been. Maybe within the hour. Then this story never would've happened. There'd be nothing to write about because it all changed that late-spring morning, the day we found him dying of dehydration at the edge of the desert.

He was sandy-haired, about our age, lying spread-eagled on the ground like a giant X. Red ran back to camp to tell the officers, while Flush and I turned him over. The sun had burned his face to a crisp, cracked his lips, swollen his eyes shut. Dried sweat stains marked his black T-shirt and jeans, and, oddly, he was barefoot. *Barefoot in the desert!* Blisters big as quarters, caked with dirt and blood, dotted the undersides of his feet.

We poured water from our canteens into his mouth. Some of it made it to his throat; the rest dribbled down his neck, carving trails in his dust-covered face.

The camp Humvees came hurtling across the dunes. The boy stirred, his eyes opening into a squint.

"He's alive!" Flush shouted. Master of the obvious.

He mumbled something neither of us could quite make out. I bent down, stretching my gimp leg out to the side so I could press my ear close to his mouth.

"What was that?" I asked.

I gave him another slurp of water. He tried to speak, the sounds painful to listen to. Like stepping on broken glass, all crunch and scrape.

Red jumped from the Humvee, Major Karsten right behind.

"Th-th-there," Red said, with his tendency to stutter.

"Stand back," Karsten said. No one didn't obey an order from Major Karsten.

6

Wearing desert camouflage, he marched across the sandy terrain, his boots leaving massive footprints in the earth. He knelt by the boy's side, picked up his right arm, and examined it. There was a thick burn mark there: a ridge of red scar tissue oozing pus. Karsten inspected it a full twenty seconds before feeling for a pulse. By then, other vehicles had arrived, disgorging brown-shirted soldiers.

"Get him to the infirmary," Karsten commanded.

The soldiers loaded the boy onto a stretcher and slid him into the Humvee like a pan of dough going into an oven. The vehicle roared back to camp.

"Who found him?"

Major Karsten was looking right at us, his anvil-shaped face skeletal in appearance. The sun cast a deep shadow on the scar that angled from left eyebrow to chin.

"We all did," Flush said.

"Ever seen him before?"

"No, sir."

"Did he say anything?"

Flush was about to answer but I beat him to it. "He tried. Nothing came out."

Karsten's eyes settled on me. I knew that gaze. *Feared* that gaze.

"Nothing?" Karsten asked.

"No, sir," I answered.

7

His eyes narrowed as though gauging whether I was being truthful or not. "Come see me when you get back, Book. I want a full report. You LTs return to camp," he said over his shoulder. "That's enough CC for one day."

Black smoke belched from the exhaust and the remaining Humvees made doughnuts in the desert before ascending the ridge.

"I saw him first," Flush said, his pale, round body sinking in the shifting sand as he and Red plodded up the hill ahead of me. "Why didn't Karsten ask me for a report? Why Book?"

"Do you want to m-meet with Karsten?" Red asked.

"Well, no," Flush conceded.

"Then shut your p-piehole."

That's the way it was—people talking about me as if I wasn't even there. Sometimes I felt utterly invisible. Like if I turned around and took a suicide walk into the No Water, no one would notice. I guess that's why I buried myself in books. There was comfort there. Security.

As the heat seeped through the soles of my shoes, a sense of dread settled in my stomach. The prospect of facing Major Karsten was enough to send a wave of nausea through me. Of all the officers in Camp Liberty, he was by far the most feared.

But it was more than that—I had lied. The boy *had* said something. Words I alone had heard. Words that raised the short hair on the back of my neck.

"You've gotta get me out of here," he said, seconds before the first Humvee pulled up. And then, for good measure, he repeated it once more.

You've gotta get me out of here.

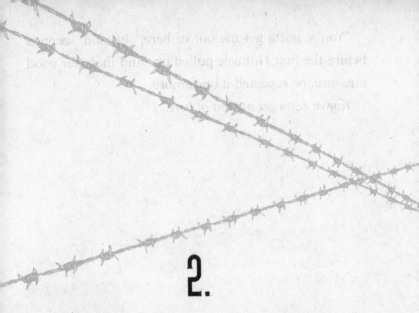

2.

HOPE BENDS HER EAR to the cave's entrance, her body tense.

She's convinced she's hearing sounds. Not the noises she's grown accustomed to—scurrying rats, the flap of bats' wings—but something else entirely. A rustle of leaves? Something . . . human.

She fears the soldiers are getting close.

"Hope," her sister whispers.

"Shh."

"Hope," Faith says again.

Hope motions her sister to be quiet . . . and then sees the reason for her distress. Lying on black bedrock, their father's head lolls listlessly from side to side. Hope leaves the mouth of the cave and hurries to his side.

In flickering candlelight, she sees his cheeks are badly sunken, his normally robust face pale as chalk. When she places a hand on his forehead, it's scalding.

"He's burning up," Hope says. She turns and sees the tears welling in her sister's eyes. Hope points to a small pool farther back in the cave. "Go soak a rag and we'll place it on his forehead."

"What rag? We don't have anything." Faith's voice borders on panic.

While it annoys Hope that Faith can't solve problems on her own, she's right about this: they don't have a thing. The last few weeks have been a desperate scramble from one hiding place to another. They've been forced to leave nearly all their possessions behind, burying them in remote patches of the wilderness. They'll have no need of them once they reach the Brown Forest and cross into the new territory.

If they reach the Brown Forest.

Hope rips the bottom off her shirt and hands the filthy wad to Faith. "Here. Now go."

Faith scuttles to the cavern's dark recesses.

Hope takes her father's hand. It's rough and callused, more like sandpaper than skin. She studies his left foot, now nearly twice as big as his right. It's purple and inflamed, with red lines shooting up the calf. All because he stepped on a jutting nail, its tip scarred with rust and radiation. After all they've been through, to have it come down to something as simple as a little infection.

Which has grown into a big infection.

She stares at the cave's entrance, still not sure if she heard something. Drifting clouds obscure what little moon there is.

A voice startles her.

"Go easy . . . on your sister." Her father, his words gravelly.

Hope grows suddenly defensive. "I do."

Her father grunts. "She tries, you know."

"Yeah, well, sometimes not hard enough."

He forces a smile, the wrinkles creasing beard stubble. A corner of his black mustache angles up. "Sounds like *my* words."

Of course they're his words. Where else would she have learned them?

His eyes close. Then he whispers, "You're your father's daughter. And she's . . . her mother's daughter."

It's true, of course—no denying it—and it always strikes Hope as odd that two siblings, born mere minutes apart, can be so utterly different. It's obvious that she and Faith are twins. Both sport matching black hair, identical brown eyes, the same tea-colored skin. The only physical difference is weight; Faith is perilously thin . . . and getting more so by the day.

But in all other respects they are wildly different. Faith is shy, introverted, afraid to take chances, while

Hope is just the opposite: fearless, athletic, bold to the point of reckless. As far as Hope's concerned, they may as well have sprung from separate mothers entirely.

Hope remembers the day they raced sticks in the stream behind the house. What were they then, five or six? Although it was obvious Faith would rather have been inside attending to her dolls, she agreed to play, and they ended up shouting with delight, rooting for their tiny twigs tumbling down the mountain creek.

But when the soldiers showed up and the sound of bullets echoed off the surrounding hills, Hope and Faith forgot racing sticks. Forgot how to smile and laugh. The girls' last memory of that childhood home—and their childhood itself—was their mother lying dead, blood pooling from her forehead onto the warped boards of the front porch.

Hope dragged her sister to a hollow log and there they stayed for two whole days. When their father returned from a hunting trip, the three of them took off, not even daring to return home to bury their mother or pack supplies. They feared the Republic's soldiers were staking out the house.

That was ten years ago. They've been on the run ever since, rifling through abandoned houses, living in trees and caves. They even spent one winter in a grizzly's den, praying the bear wouldn't return.

Out of necessity, Hope has grown more tomboyish

with each passing day, learning how to start fires, how best to throw a spear. Her only vanity is her hair, which is black and long and silky—resembling her mother's. A way of honoring her fallen parent.

"One thing," her father says. "You have a choice to make."

Hope stares down at him. What's he talking about? "All we've been doing these last ten years is making choices," she says.

"This one's different." His voice is a raspy whisper. "There's a reason the government's after us."

"Yeah, because you didn't sign the loyalty oath."

He gives his head a shake. "That's just part of it."

What is he about to tell her? And why does she feel a sudden dread?

"Go on," she says.

"You're twins."

Hope sighs in relief. "Gee, I had no idea."

He continues, "And the government wants twins."

Hope cocks her head. Where's her father going with this? Is he delirious with fever or is this for real? "I don't get it. What's so special about twins?"

He grimaces. "You have a choice to make. Either stay together . . . which means you'll be hunted the rest of your life . . ."

"Or what?" she dares to ask. She realizes she has ceased to breathe.

"Or separate."

His words are like a thunderclap. *Separate?* It's true, Faith can be irritatingly slow and often holds them up. But separate? The thought has never crossed her mind.

She peers toward the cave's interior; Faith is wringing water from the rag. Her skeletal silhouette looks ghostlike. Draped around her shoulders is their mother's pink shawl. It's tattered and torn, singed from fire.

"Why would we do that?" Hope asks her father. "Faith wouldn't last a day."

"If they catch you . . . neither of you will."

Hope wants desperately to find out what on earth he's talking about—but at that moment Faith returns. She places the damp cloth on her father's forehead. His eyes close and he's asleep within seconds.

"What was he saying?" Faith asks.

"Nothing," Hope answers a little too quickly. "Just nonsense. Fever and all."

Hope crawls back to the cave's entrance, staring into the dark through a curtain of dripping snowmelt. Her father's words bounce around her head. *Separate from Faith? Abandon her?* What an absurd idea.

As the black night presses against her, Hope can only pray it's a decision she'll never have to make.

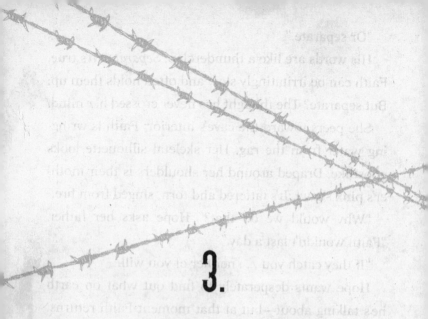

3.

I TYPED UP MY report using one of the camp's bulky typewriters. Although we'd heard of cell phones and computers and something called the internet, all that was fried by the electromagnetic pulse that accompanied the bombs.

Omega, they called that day. The end of the end.

One enormous burst of electromagnetic radiation and everything that was even remotely electronic was fried to a crisp. Computers became the stuff of legend. Most cars were no longer drivable. And although I'd read about them, I'd never seen an airplane in the sky. And figured I never would.

Not that Camp Liberty was without luxuries. Every Friday night we gathered in the mess hall to watch movies, the film projector powered by the camp's generators. The problem was, only a handful of movies survived, all oldies, and so we saw the same ten films all year, every year. *Stagecoach*, *Shane*, *To Kill a Mockingbird*, that kind of thing.

I stripped the paper from the typewriter's roller. For obvious reasons, I neglected to mention the boy's whispered message. I walked the report over to Major Karsten's office and left it with Sergeant Dekker.

"Slice slice," he said with a sneer, enjoying the in-joke that—thankfully—only a couple of us understood.

My face burned and I got out of there as fast as I could.

Days passed. Rumors flew. Some claimed the boy in the black T-shirt was a convict on the run. Others said he was no outlaw, merely an LT from an adjoining territory.

What I couldn't figure out was why he was in the middle of the No Water in the first place, on the outskirts of an orphanage.

That's what Camp Liberty was, although in official Republic jargon it was called a "resettlement camp." There were several hundred of us, all guys, most with birth defects brought on by Omega's radiation. Those toxic clouds remained floating above the earth like Christmas ribbon encircling a present, just waiting for someone to tighten the bow.

Our poor mothers had been doused with so many gamma rays or alpha particles or whatever it was, that they brought us into the world with one too many fingers or one too few or shriveled arms. Or, in my case, one leg shorter than the other. And then they died shortly after giving birth.

It was never clear how it all began. Some say a group of no-goods on the other side of the planet got hold of weapons of the nuclear kind. Others claim our own allies were to blame, attacking countries who then counterattacked. However it started, a dozen nations ended up shooting off nuclear warheads like it was the Fourth of July, until every major city in the world was obliterated. Utterly wiped out.

Of course, since all this took place a good twenty years ago, we had to rely on what the soldiers told us. Which wasn't always accurate.

It was the other camps I wondered about. They had to be out there, right? There were rumors, of course—grisly tales of torture and atrocities—but who really knew what was true and what was made up.

"John L-183?" A Brown Shirt was standing by my table in the mess hall.

"Yeah?"

"The colonel wants to see you."

My fork lowered. Whenever Colonel Westbrook asked to see an LT, it usually meant one thing: punishment.

18

Was it the false report? Had the colonel somehow figured out the boy had told me more than I let on?

"Maybe you're going through the Rite early," Flush suggested. I shook away the notion. No one graduated until they were seventeen. I still had another year.

"That'll teach you to read so many books," Dozer said, snorting. He was a barrel-chested LT who could *never* be accused of reading books.

The acne-scarred soldier waited for me to get up. Like all the soldiers in camp, he wore a uniform of black jackboots, dark pants, and a brown shirt. That's why we called them Brown Shirts. We were clever that way.

I left the mess hall feeling like I was headed to my execution. Sunlight blinded me as we crossed the camp's infield. Above us, the flag atop the pole cracked in the wind like a whip. *Snap. Snap.*

We approached the headquarters, an ancient, rotting log building that sat in the middle of camp like a festering sore. An older Brown Shirt sat hunched over a sheaf of papers, a sweaty sheen covering his face.

Three straight-backed chairs lined the wall. To my surprise, one of them was occupied. It was the boy from the No Water.

Even though I'd helped save the guy's life, he didn't offer a word of thanks. Didn't even acknowledge my presence.

The door to an inner office opened and out stepped

Colonel Westbrook. He was of medium height with an unimposing face, his dark brown hair styled in a kind of comb-over across his skull. Like all the officers, he wore a dark badge on his left sleeve. It sported the Republic's symbol: three inverted triangles.

I must've seen the colonel a thousand times, but never up close. For the first time I noticed the blackness of his eyes. There was not a bit of color in them at all. My heart was in my throat as I followed him to his office.

There were two others in the room as well. Sergeant Dekker, wearing his customary smirk beneath his oily hair, and Major Karsten, sitting ramrod straight by the window. Perspiration trickled down my side.

Westbrook's eyes focused on a manila folder opened before him. His finger traced one line of information after another. "You're John L-183," he said at last. "The one they call Book, yes?" He said my name as though it was something unpleasant tasting.

"That's right."

"Nothing to be ashamed of. We need more scholars. They're the future of the Republic." His tracing finger halted, and I knew exactly where he'd gotten to in my life history. Blood rushed to my face.

"Liberty has a new member," he said, his coal-black eyes boring into me. "We want you to show him around. Any problem with that?"

"Um, no, sir."

"Get him situated. The sooner he's one of us, the better for all concerned."

"Yes, sir," I said, relieved. This wasn't a punishment after all.

"And, Book?" Colonel Westbrook leaned in, his fingers splayed on the desk like talons. "See what you can find out. Where's he from? He's got no marker and we don't know much about him. After all, if he's in need of help we have to know what he's been through. You can understand that, can't you?" A pointed reference to my own past.

"Yes, sir," I said. "But I don't want to rat on people."

"It wouldn't be ratting. It'd be *informing*." He smiled grimly. "It's very simple, Book. You help us, we help you. And who knows? A year from now, when you go through the Rite, we might look into making you an officer."

Put that way, it didn't seem so bad. And it was true: I did know a thing or two about secrets. "Okay," I said.

"It's settled then. I'll have Major Karsten check in with you from time to time."

I looked up at the major. The scar that edged from his eyebrow to his chin seemed to pulse like a living, breathing thing.

I couldn't get out the door fast enough.

4.

HOPE KNOWS HE'S DEAD the moment she returns from watch. Faith is tucked into the curve of their father's body, her tears soaking his shirt.

Hope places her fingers against the crook of his neck. Cold to the touch. No hint of a pulse. It hits her like a punch to the gut.

"Come on," she says, pulling her sister off.

"We have to bury him," Faith says, eyes red.

"I know."

"How're we going to do that? We don't have a shovel."

"We'll think of something."

"But what? We can't leave him like this."

"I know that . . ."

Faith is screaming now. "We have to do something!

22

What're we gonna do?"

Hope slaps her sister hard across the face, regretting it instantly. Faith's head snaps to one side, the red imprint of Hope's fingers tattooing her face.

"I'll take care of it," Hope says, finding a reason to look away. "We'll cover him with rocks. That way the animals can't get him."

"Is that a proper way to bury someone?" Faith whispers.

"Proper enough. You go take watch. I'll do this."

Faith drags herself to the cave's entrance, running the back of her hand across her runny nose. Hope feels a stab of guilt for the way she treated her. *Still, someone has to be the strong one,* she tells herself.

The first thing she does is retrieve her father's few belongings. A knife. A leather belt. Flint from his front pocket. It feels like an invasion, going through his clothes, but she has to do it. Flint means fire. A knife means survival.

There's something else there, too. A small, gold locket, attached to a thin, tarnished chain. As soon as Hope's eyes fall on it, she has a distant memory of it dangling from her mother's neck. And when she undoes the clasp and opens it, she knows what she will see before she sees it.

Two miniature oval photographs. One of her father, one of her mother. From younger days. How innocent

23

they look. And happy. Now encased in a locket's tomb, facing each other for all eternity. No wonder he carried it with him all these years.

She slips it into her pocket.

The process of dragging rocks is tedious, and she carefully places them atop her father's body as though—even in death—he can feel the weight. Faith weeps steadily by the cave's entrance. Hope's eyes are as dry as sand. There is no time for tears. Her father taught her that.

Live today, tears tomorrow.

Hope has crossed her father's hands atop his chest when she notices the curled, clenched fingers of his right hand. They are stiff with death and it's no small struggle to straighten them. More surprising than the effort itself is what she discovers within his gnarled grip.

A small, crumpled slip of paper.

Hope tugs the paper free from her father's hand. She sees one word written there, scrawled in charcoal.

Separate.

Hope shakes her head and crumples the note back up.

When she finishes the burial mound, both girls gather by the body. They have never been to a funeral before. Or a wedding. Nothing.

In lieu of a prayer, Faith says, "I heard what he told

you. About separating."

Hope tries to hide her surprise. "He was delirious," she says. "Out of his head with fever. I'm not thinking of it if that's what you're asking."

"I'm not." Their eyes run up and down the grave of rocks. "But I think we should."

"You think we *should*? Separate?"

Faith nods. "If he was right about that twins stuff, it sounds like you'd"—she pauses to correct herself—"*we'd* have a better chance on our own."

"Faith, you wouldn't last a day out there. No offense."

Faith bristles. "I'm not as helpless as you think."

"Uh, yes you are."

Hope can see she's hurt her feelings. If Hope isn't slapping her sister with her hand, she's doing so with her words.

"I'm going to get some food," she says, impatient and angry all at once.

Faith doesn't respond.

At the edge of a swampy bog Hope spears half a dozen plump bullfrogs. She brings the meat back to the cave late that afternoon and it cooks up good. They wolf it down without a word. After dinner, they settle on their makeshift beds, still not having spoken since the morning. Hope falls into a deep sleep, dreaming of everything and nothing.

When morning sunlight wakes her, there's no sign of

her sister anywhere.

"Faith," she calls, first inside the cave, then out. The only answer she gets is birdsong. "Faith!"

Still nothing.

No extra footprints pattern the ground. No sign of wild animals. But Faith's few possessions are gone. No canteen, no backpack, no shawl.

Hope curses not so silently to herself. She isn't sure who she is angriest at: Faith, for thinking she can make it on her own, or herself, for basically daring her to go.

Or her father, for bringing up the notion of separating in the first place.

Although Faith's body is light and her footprints barely dent the ground, Hope will have no problem trailing the flattened grass, the snapped twigs. After ten years of tracking prey at her father's side, she knows the signs.

Hope finds the trail and determines which way Faith has gone . . . then promptly goes the other direction. To hell with her sister.

26

5.

I EXPLAINED THE BASICS: chores in the morning, classes in the afternoon, CC—Camp Cleanup—on the weekends. The boy in the black T-shirt didn't ask a single question, but I got the feeling nothing escaped his attention.

When we exited the mess hall, I realized I hadn't introduced myself. "I'm Book," I said, trying to sound tougher than the name. "Who're you?"

"L-2084," he murmured.

Sometime after Omega the government made the decision to label all the boys John. Our last names were what distinguished us: a series of numbers matched with a letter for our camp—L for Camp Liberty, V for Camp Victory, etc. Our "identities" were tattooed on our right arms.

Apparently, all girls were called Jane, but that was only a rumor. We'd never actually seen any for ourselves.

"Not your official name, your nickname," I said. "Like I'm Book because I read a lot, and there's Red because he has a red splotch on his face and Twitch because he does and Flush because he doesn't."

The boy in the black T-shirt said nothing.

"What'd your friends call you back where you came from?" Then, in an awkward attempt to follow the colonel's orders, I asked, "Where'd you say that was again?"

"I didn't," he growled.

We toured the rest of the camp in silence. Finally, I asked, "What'd you mean in the No Water? About getting out of here?"

"Just what I said," he answered tersely. As if it didn't need explaining.

"Why? This is a decent camp. And our grads do really well."

A small sound escaped Black T-Shirt's mouth. A grunt? A scoff? But when I turned to look at him, I didn't get any reaction at all.

Neither of us spoke as we made our way across camp. As we passed two LTs, one of them knocked into me and I nearly lost my balance. The LT shouted out, "Who's your boyfriend, Book *Worm*?"

They laughed. So much for making a good impression on the new guy.

28

Beneath the arched ceiling of the Quonset hut, a hundred-some bunk beds stretched out in long rows. At the base of each bed was a wooden trunk, storing all our worldly possessions. In my case: books. Dozens of them.

Black T-Shirt stopped, pointing to the very last bunk in the room. "This one taken?" He clambered effortlessly to the top and lay on his back like some Egyptian sarcophagus.

Apparently, the tour was over.

"You don't get it, do you?" he said.

His words startled me. "Get what?"

"This." He gestured vaguely to the barracks, the camp itself.

"I get as much as I need to get," I said, suddenly defensive.

He shook his head. "You have no idea."

I turned on my heels and stormed out, angry I had ever bothered to help save L-2084's life in the first place.

I walked to the southwestern edge of camp. Below me lay endless desert; above me a jagged range of mountains. The cemetery itself was soundless. I made my way through a labyrinth of sun-bleached crosses until I found the marker I was searching for.

L-175. Known to us as K2.

A series of eerie images danced through my brain like fireflies.

Giant trees crashing to earth. Startled shouts. A final, haunted expression.

Pounding on a door. Red on white. Blackness darkening the edges of my periphery.

My face grew suddenly clammy. I squeezed my eyes shut and gave my head a violent shake, as if it were that easy to chase away demons.

It didn't work, of course. Never did.

I opened my eyes to blinding sunlight and reached out a hand to the wooden cross, rubbing my fingertips over its weathered ridges. I tried to speak, but the words got stuck in my throat. Those twin demons, guilt and grief, clamped my mouth shut.

Poor K2.

I noticed a yellow school bus heading up the hill below me, trailing a white plume of choking powder from the gravel road.

I knew who was in it, of course. Orphans. Headed for the nursery, where they'd be raised by surrogates until—one day—they'd become LTs.

There were fewer and fewer buses these days. I didn't know if that was a good thing or not. All I knew was that I'd go through the Rite and be long gone before these kids could even read or write.

The bus came up the rise. On its fender were three

crudely drawn inverted triangles. Inside the vehicle were row after row of boys, some so young they were held in nurses' arms. Others slightly older, their faces pressed against the window in a mix of fear and wonder. Years from now they wouldn't be able to recall their mothers or fathers; what they'd remember was the day they arrived at Camp Liberty . . . and be grateful it wasn't someplace worse.

I spun around and returned to camp. Gone for the moment was the shame of my past, the guilt I carried, replaced instead with those mysterious words uttered by Black T-Shirt.

You've gotta get me out of here.

6.

ORANGE LIGHT FLUTTERS ON Hope's face. She pulls a gutted rabbit from the spit and eats every last morsel, sucking the bones clean. As she pokes the embers, thoughts of Faith swirl in her head. It's been nearly a week since they went their separate ways and Hope knows her sister has no flint. Has she been without fire this entire time?

But it was Faith's decision to go off on her own. Besides, their father said they should make this choice. The thought of him makes her pat her pocket and feel the small gold locket. Also the crumpled bit of paper with that one word: *Separate*.

No. I can't think about it.

What she thinks about instead is the boy with the

piercing blue eyes. He'd come traipsing through just a few weeks past, looking for a night's shelter from the rain. Her father allowed it, on the single condition that he stayed at one end of the cave and his two daughters at the other. Hope remembers how she and Faith stared at him long through the night: his sandy hair, the embers' dull orange light sculpting his face, the rise and fall of his chest as he slept.

He was the first guy her age she'd ever seen, and she often wonders who he was and where he came from. Wonders if she'll ever see him again. Or if she's destined to be by herself her entire life.

She tries to sleep, and when she wakes just a few fitful hours later, Hope knows what she has to do. She douses the fire, packs her belongings, and heads out, her route reversed from the day before—she must find her sister.

Faith is ridiculously easy to track. She might as well have left painted arrows on the ground. Did she learn nothing from their father?

Hope suddenly stops. Something has caught her eye.

She retraces her steps. All around her, spring wildflowers poke through the earth: shimmering royal blue, egg-yolk yellow. And a carpet of miniature blossoms, the petals white as snow.

But one is stained with a single dot of red.

Blood. Fresh blood.

Other drops on blades of grass. Faith is bleeding.

Hope takes off in a jog.

Her father's message echoes in her brain: *Separate*. What he failed to understand was that she doesn't have a choice. Faith is her sister—her *twin*. As different as they are, there's no separating them.

Late that afternoon, Hope finally spies Faith from a great distance: a solitary figure wading through waist-high weeds. She zigzags back and forth. Is it delirium that pushes her from side to side? Or loss of blood?

Hope has two options: race straight across the valley or hug the tree line and circle around. Her second option will take longer, but it's obviously safer. A body walking through a barren meadow is just begging for trouble.

Despite her best instincts, Hope chooses the quicker route. Faith is in trouble. She needs Hope *now*. Hope begins to run, her heart hammering in her ears.

When she finally reaches her, Faith's words are accusatory. "What're you doing here?"

Hope is taken aback. "Coming to find you, what do you think?"

"I don't need to be *found*. I'm just fine on my own."

"You're bleeding . . ."

Faith clenches her right hand into a fist, but not before Hope sees the thick slice across her palm. "It's

34

nothing. Knife slipped."

"Let me see."

"It's nothing."

Hope feels a surge of anger. Here she's gone to the trouble to find her sister and put her life on the line and Faith wants nothing to do with her.

"Faith, you can't do this. You won't make it on your own."

"I can make it on my own just as well as you," she says over her shoulder.

"Oh, come on . . ."

Faith wheels on her twin, nostrils flared. "Why don't you think I can make it? Because I'm helpless without you? Because he wanted us to separate so you could live and not me?"

"That's not true and you know it."

"I heard him, Hope. He was telling you to go your own way. He wanted you to live. Well, guess what? I'm giving him what he wanted."

Bug bites cover every inch of Faith's face, and her eyes are nearly swollen shut. But even more painful for Hope is the haunted expression Faith wears. A look of genuine sadness. Hope doesn't know what to say. What words can possibly ease her sister's pain?

When Hope is finally about to speak, she's interrupted by a low rumble. The earth shakes beneath their feet. Their father told them about earthquakes, but

35

they've never experienced one. A flash of movement out of the corner of her eye swings her around.

It's not an earthquake but a thundering of hooves. Horses. Dozens of them, headed straight for the two girls. Atop each of them is a Brown Shirt hoisting a semiautomatic rifle.

It only takes Hope a second to react.

"Run!" she screams at the very top of her lungs.

Hope drags her sister as best she can, tearing through the tall grasses. But there's no place to hide. Their only hope is to reach the trees and pray the woods are thick enough to keep the horses from following. Then the Brown Shirts will be forced to dismount and lug their heavy weapons.

It's a long shot, but better than none at all.

The rumble of hooves grows louder. The roar swells like a thunderstorm, hailstones slamming into the ground.

Both girls are sucking wind. Faith's lungs make harsh, raspy sounds with each inhalation.

"I have . . . to stop," she wheezes.

"No!" Hope says.

Faith bends over, clutches her knees. "Go," she coughs. "I'm done."

"You're not done. We can do this."

The horses are gaining speed. If the sisters leave

right now, they stand a chance. But only if they leave *this very instant*. "Come on!"

Faith shakes her head. "Go," she says. "It's what Dad wanted." She meets Hope's eyes. "It's what I want, too."

Hope looks at her sister. And at the approaching Brown Shirts.

"H and FT," she says.

Faith doesn't respond.

"H and FT," Hope repeats.

It's their secret code. Has been since they were kids, since that awful day when their mother was shot before their eyes.

H & FT. Hope and Faith Together.

Finally, Faith says it back. "H and FT."

Hope guides her. In her one hand is Faith's arm; in the other is her spear. She veers straight for the sun, forcing the Brown Shirts to squint into the sunset. Forcing them to slow down to navigate creek beds and boulders.

The tree line grows closer and Hope can make out the dense underbrush. It's all shrubs and thick tangles of vines. Good for hiding. Living hell for a horse. No way the Brown Shirts can navigate this maze. Hope realizes they've caught a break. They should just make it after all.

The first gunshots blast the trees in front of them. Bark explodes. Small birch trees are sliced in half. Faith slows.

"Don't stop!" Hope yells.

"But they're shooting at us."

"And we'll stop if they hit us!"

They're a mere twenty yards from the woods when a lead horse circles around and cuts them off. Then another. And another. There's suddenly no way out.

Still, when a Brown Shirt draws a pistol, Hope reaches back with her spear and sends it flying. It sails through the air, entering the soldier's chest, the pointy end sticking out his back. A dazed expression paints his face as he tumbles off his horse.

A dozen other Brown Shirts raise their M16s and target them on Hope.

"Don't shoot!" a voice cries out.

A trailing Humvee comes to a sudden stop and a man waddles forward. He is heavy to the point of obese, with thin, almost invisible lips. Unlike the men on horseback, he doesn't wear the soldier's uniform of the Republic, but a black suit with a white shirt and a thin black tie. His most striking feature is the soiled hanky he grips in his hand, which he uses to dab at the corners of his eyes.

"Don't shoot," the pudgy man says again, and rifle barrels lower. He appraises the twins with leering eyes. His sausage fingers cup Faith's chin. "We've been looking for you two," he says in a nasally voice. "Oh yes, we've been looking for you for quite some time."

7.

THERE WAS A FUNERAL to attend. There were *always* funerals at Camp Liberty. Another LT had succumbed to the lingering effects of ARS. Acute radiation syndrome. It was a lanky kid named Lodgepole who'd developed a tumor in his neck the size of a softball. Frankly, he was lucky to die when he did.

I didn't know Lodge well, but had a feeling I would've liked him. Which is exactly why I *didn't* get to know him. What was the point of making friends if ARS was just going to pick them off?

Another reason why I immersed myself in books.

I read everything I could get my hands on. History, biographies, fiction. If it was on the dusty shelves of our little library, chances were I'd checked it out.

But that wasn't all. Someone was giving me books as well. It wasn't uncommon to open my bedside trunk and find some new volume. None of the other LTs got books—just me—and I couldn't figure out who was doing it.

As for Black T-Shirt, I still hadn't found out anything about him, other than the fact that he was incredible at everything athletic. Whether it was shooting arrows or kicking soccer balls, he was drop-dead good. Yet another reason he pissed me off.

Now that he wore the camp uniform—jeans, white T-shirt, blue cotton shirt—his old name no longer cut it. So we called him Cat, because he was athletic and mysterious and half the time we didn't hear him sneak up beside us.

"Lemme ask you a question." There he was again, standing beside me at the mess hall door. "You're called LTs, right?"

"That's right," I said.

"Why?"

"It's short for *lieutenant*. A military abbreviation. 'Cause we're the future lieutenants of the world."

"Says who?"

"The camp leaders. Westbrook, Karsten, Dekker, all of 'em."

Cat shot me a look of disbelief. "Seriously?"

The hair rose at the base of my neck. What was

40

it about this guy that rubbed me the wrong way? "Seriously," I said.

He tried—not very hard—to stifle a laugh. "So what happens when they leave here? The graduates?"

"You mean after they go through the Rite?"

"Yeah, tell me about the *Rite*," he mocked.

"There's a big ceremony where all the seventeen-year-olds pledge allegiance to the Republic, then they're bussed to leadership positions elsewhere in the territory. It's a pretty big deal."

This time Cat didn't bother trying to hide his laughter. It was a harsh, mocking laugh, and I couldn't take it anymore. I brushed past him and stepped outside into the pouring rain. Cat was beside me in a second.

"You don't have to get all pissy," he said. "I'm just trying to help."

"Yeah, well, maybe I don't need your help."

"Fine. Your funeral."

Something about his tone pushed me over the edge. I turned and gave him a shove.

"Who the hell do you think you are?" I demanded.

His expression was blank. Icy rain plastered his hair to his forehead.

"I've lived here nearly all my life," I went on, "but you're the one who acts like he knows everything. Well, screw you!"

"I don't know everything . . ."

41

"Well, you definitely act that way."

". . . but I know *some* things. Like you're crazy to think they call you LT because it's short for *lieutenant*."

"So if you're so smart, what is it?"

"You really want to know?" His words cut through the rain like a knife. "It's short for Less Than. Which is exactly what all of you are: a bunch of Less Thans."

I felt like I'd been sucker punched. I was too stunned to respond.

Cat went on. "When you were a little kid, the Republic decided your fate. They determined where you were going to go, what you were going to be. Soldier, worker, Less Than, whatever."

"Then how come none of us have ever heard that?" I asked.

"Probably 'cause the Brown Shirts didn't tell you."

I struggled to form thoughts. "How do they decide who's a . . . Less Than?" Just saying the words made me uncomfortable.

"Handicaps, obesity, skin color, politics, who knows. They don't announce the criteria, but it's pretty clear. I mean, look around."

I thought of the two hundred or so guys in Camp Liberty. Some of it might've been true, but that didn't mean anything. Sure, I had brown skin, and Twitch and June Bug had black. Dozer had a withered arm, Red a splotch on his face, and Four Fingers, well, four fingers on each hand. But all that was just a coincidence. Right?

"Politics?" I asked. "What kid knows anything about politics?"

"Not you, your parents. If they're dissidents, then you're branded Less Thans for sure."

"But why?"

"Because if the normal people want to survive the next Omega, we can't have a bunch of Less Thans holding us back."

My head was swimming. Not only was he suggesting we weren't normal but that we might not even be orphans. "This is an orphanage," I managed.

"Who said?"

"The Brown Shirts."

"You don't think they'd lie, do you?"

My knees felt weak. Was it even remotely possible he was telling the truth? That we'd been ripped from our mothers' arms and sent here because we were considered "less than normal"? I felt the sudden need to get away.

"What's the matter?" he called out. "Can't face facts?"

That did it. I spun around and leaped toward him and we tumbled hard on the rain-soaked ground. My fists began pummeling him. Roundhouses and jabs and uppercuts, one after another, landing first on one side of his face and then the other.

The other LTs made a halfhearted attempt to break us up, but they seemed all too happy to watch. And then I realized: Cat wasn't fighting back. He was *letting* me hit him, barely blocking my punches. It made me all the angrier.

"That's enough," Cat finally said, and he sent a fist in my direction. I fell to the side.

I pushed myself to a sitting position, blood trickling from my nose. Cat's one punch had drawn blood; it had taken me a couple dozen to do the same to him.

"You showed him," said Flush.

But I knew I hadn't. The LTs drifted off to the barracks.

"Why didn't you fight back?" I panted.

"I only beat up people if I have reason to. I don't have a good reason to beat you up." He sipped a breath. "Yet."

He pushed himself up until he was sitting in the mud, his face near mine.

"If you're so smart, let me ask you this," he said. "What do you know about the men outside camp?"

"You mean the Brown Shirts?"

"I mean the *other* men."

I could've bluffed my way through an answer, but I was too exhausted for lies. "Nothing," I conceded.

"I figured as much." Then he said, "They know about all of you. And if you don't do something about it, you'll be dead within the year."

44

Although I tried to hide it, my eyes widened. "Prove it," I said.

"What're you doing tomorrow afternoon?"

That night I couldn't stop thinking about what Cat had said, his words jangling around my head like pebbles in a tin can. When I finally fell asleep I dreamed of her again: the woman with long black hair. She existed in some distant memory of mine, but who she was and how I knew her were details forever lost. All I knew was that she'd been appearing in my dreams more and more often until I no longer knew what was memory and what was imagination.

In the dream, we were racing through a field of prairie grass, my child's hand encompassed in hers. Although she was far older, it was all I could do to keep up with her—two of my short strides matching one of hers.

Behind us came a series of sharp pops, like fire-crackers. There were other sounds, too. Shrill whistles. Shouting. Barking dogs.

The land sloped downward to a hollow and we drifted to a stop. She put her hands atop my shoulders and stared at me. Wrinkles etched her face. Crow's feet danced at the edges of her eyes.

I realized the pops were bullets; I could hear them pinging off the rocks and whistling past my ears.

Someone was after us. Someone was trying to *kill* us.

Even though the woman seemed about to tell me something, I didn't want to hear it—I didn't want to *be there*—so I jolted myself awake, the blackness of the Quonset hut pressing down on me, my breathing fast.

It was another hour before I fell back to sleep, wondering who the woman was and what she was about to say.

8.

HOPE AND FAITH ARE jammed into the back of the
Humvee. The convoy makes its way across nonexistent
trails until they reach something resembling an actual
road.

It's the first time they've ever been in a vehicle. Well,
a *moving* vehicle. They've slept in plenty of abandoned
ones during their years on the run, but this one is actually in motion. Nothing could prepare them for the
sheer speed of it.

The sun sets and an eerie calm settles over the landscape. The Humvee's twin headlights cut two jagged
holes in the darkness.

Hope wonders where they're being taken. Every so
often, the heavyset man swivels his thick head and

peers back from the passenger seat. He says nothing.

In the distance, Hope catches a fleeting glimpse of structures. Listing log cabins, tar-paper shacks, old wooden buildings with peeling paint. All surrounded by a ten-foot-high fence, topped with an unending coil of razor wire. Anchoring the four corners are guard towers with Brown Shirts poised behind machine guns.

Hope's mouth goes dry. After sixteen years, ten of them on the run, she and her sister are about to be imprisoned.

"Camp Freedom," the obese man says cheerfully. "Your new home."

The camp's colossal gates shriek open and the vehicle rolls to a stop. A soldier pulls open the passenger door. There are Brown Shirts everywhere, each wearing the Republic's distinctive dark badge with three inverted triangles. But it's the others who draw Hope's attention.

Girls. Scores of them. All wearing the same coarse, gray dresses that hang limply below their knees. Faded, scuffed boots adorn their feet. Based on their expressions, they seem to regard Hope and Faith as a couple of feral cats.

A tall, stooped man with a tidy mustache and a balding pate emerges from a cinder block building.

"I see you've met Dr. Gallingham," he says. "I'm Colonel Thorason." He pauses briefly, as if expecting the girls to bow or otherwise show how impressed they are to meet the camp overseer. "Life here is very simple: you abide by the rules or face the consequences. Is that clear?"

Hope and Faith nod.

"In that case—" He interrupts himself when he spies a woman walking their way. She is tall, with straight blond hair and enormously round cheekbones. An ankle-length coat is draped atop her shoulders. Thorason takes a deferential step backward as she approaches.

"Which one threw the spear?" she asks. Her tone is as sharp as the razor wire atop the fence.

"I did," Hope says.

Hope waits for a reaction. A slap. A punch from a soldier. Something to teach her a lesson. Instead, the woman reaches forward and fondles Hope's hair, letting the silky strands run between her fingers.

"Such pretty hair," the woman murmurs. "It's obvious you take good care of it." The woman forces a brittle smile and begins to walk away.

"Do what you need to do," she says over her shoulder to Colonel Thorason. "But that one"—pointing her finger in Hope's direction—"gets shaved."

Hope and Faith are taken to a bathhouse, where they're stripped and showered with a white powder.

"Delousing," the female guard explains in a flat

monotone. She has a square block of a face that seems incapable of smiling. She throws two dresses at them: ill-fitting gray things. A pair of dirty combat boots finishes the ensemble. When the guard turns her back, Hope retrieves her father's locket from her pants pocket and stuffs it in her boot. That and the scrap of paper.

The woman turns back around, brandishing a large pair of scissors, the blades nicked with rust.

"Don't move," she orders, "unless you want this through your eye."

She snips the scissors twice, then seizes Hope's hair. Watching her long strands of hair ribbon to the ground, it's all Hope can do not to cry.

Live today, tears tomorrow.

When the woman finishes, she grabs a broom.

"Here," she says, thrusting it in Hope's hand. "Clean up your mess."

Hope grits her teeth and does as commanded, but not before running a hand over her bald, patchy head. She feels as naked as a plucked bird. But it's more than that; it's almost as if—somehow—she's lost a piece of herself. A piece of her mother.

A male guard with a jutting chin enters. In his hand dangles an odd-looking tool with a pointy end. His gaze lands on Faith.

"Right arm," he commands.

When Faith doesn't move, the Brown Shirt sighs

50

noisily and yanks up Faith's sleeve. He turns on the device, tattooing a number on the outside of her arm. Tears roll down Faith's cheeks as *F-738* is branded into her skin. The guard motions for Hope. She pulls up her sleeve without being told. Her skin prickles as *F-739* is engraved.

F-738 and F-739—their new identities.

Photographs are snapped, and then the Brown Shirts usher them back outside to a tar-paper shack. On the front, painted in garish yellow, is a large letter *B*. A thick chain snakes between the door's handle and a security bar. The guards open the lock and shove the twins inside.

"You're in luck." Jutting Chin smirks. "We have a vacancy."

Once their eyes adjust to the gloom, Hope and Faith see a series of cots crammed too close together.

And girls. Around twenty or so, all approximately their age. Their expressions are openly hostile.

No one bothers to say anything. "I'm Hope. This is my sister, Faith." No response. "We're new."

"No shit," someone mutters.

Finally, one of the girls asks, "What happened to your hair?"

Hope runs a hand over her head, still not used to the stubbled absence. "They cut it off."

"Why?"

"I don't know. Maybe 'cause I killed a Brown Shirt."

If Hope thinks that will impress the others, she's wrong. The girls don't react at all. They just climb into their narrow cots and prepare for sleep.

"Come on," Hope says to her sister. "Maybe they'll be more talkative in the morning." She leads Faith to two empty beds jammed into the corner.

"I meant what I said back there," Faith says, her first words in hours. "About Dad wanting me to die."

"No you didn't," Hope says.

She cleans her sister's wound as best she can and helps her get ready for bed. They haven't slept on anything resembling a mattress in ten years, and Hope can't get comfortable. Only when she lies on the floor is she able to find a position that's right.

Stretched out on raw, warped pine, she can't get her mind off these girls. There's something odd about them that Hope can't put her finger on. Something deeply . . . disturbing.

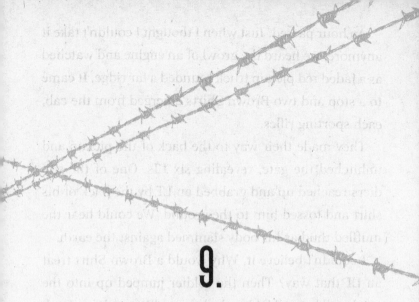

9.

C AT TOOK TWO OF US: Flush and me.

It was midafternoon when we exited the north side of camp. A couple of Brown Shirts watched us with mild interest; there were no fences at Camp Liberty, and in its twenty-year history, no one had bothered to escape. Where would you go?

After a thirty-minute climb, we veered west, heading up Skeleton Ridge. Finally, we came to a stop, lowered ourselves to the ground, and poked our heads above the ridge. Far below us lay a quiet valley: a meandering stream, dozens of scattered boulders.

"Why are we here again?" Flush asked. He was a few years younger, and not as patient as some of the others.

Cat just gave him a look. *You'll see.*

An hour passed. Just when I thought I couldn't take it anymore, we heard the growl of an engine and watched as a faded red pickup truck rounded a far ridge. It came to a stop and two Brown Shirts emerged from the cab, each sporting rifles.

They made their way to the back of the pickup and unhitched the gate, revealing six LTs. One of the soldiers reached up and grabbed an LT by the back of his shirt and tossed him to the ground. We could hear the muffled thud as his body slammed against the earth.

I couldn't believe it. Why would a Brown Shirt treat an LT that way? Then the soldier jumped up into the truck and began kicking the boys, yelling at them. Each time a boy tumbled to the ground, the soldiers laughed. I wondered why the LTs didn't fight back—until I saw their bound wrists.

Cat fished a pair of binoculars out of his pack and handed them to me. I adjusted the focus . . . and nearly lost my breath.

I recognized the LTs. They were a year older than me and had gone through the Rite the month before. One I knew very well: Cannon. The athlete we all wanted to be. And here he was, wrists lashed together, pleading with the soldiers. One of them sent a boot into his ribs. We heard the crack from a quarter mile away.

"I don't understand," I mouthed.

"Just watch," Cat said.

Once all six LTs were on the ground, the pickup driver whipped out a large knife and cut the ties that bound Cannon's wrists. Cannon rubbed his wrists gratefully.

The soldiers got back in the pickup and drove off.

"What's going on?" Flush asked. "Is it like a test? Do they have so much time to get back to camp or something?"

Cat barely acknowledged us.

When Cannon untied the other LTs' ropes, they scrambled to their feet and began to run. In the quiet of the early evening I could nearly hear the whisper of their legs parting grass . . .

. . . soon drowned out by the whine of motors. From the same bend where the truck had exited, four ATVs appeared. I'd seen four-wheelers around camp, but these were different. These had been outfitted with metal plates so they resembled some unearthly cross between military machine and triceratops. While the man in the lead wore an orange vest, the others were clad entirely in camo, dressed like it was hunting season.

Which, in a sense, it was.

Slung on their arms were black assault rifles. But somehow different from the M16s the Brown Shirts sported back at camp. Cat read my thoughts.

"M4s," he explained, "can do everything an M16 can, but with shorter barrels and stocks."

The Man in Orange stopped, shut his engine down to an idle, and waved a *Be my guest* gesture. One of the other three took off, exhaust trailing from his ATV. He stopped when he was within a hundred yards of the LTs, whipped up his rifle, and fired. A tendril of smoke plumed from the barrel.

One of the boys stumbled forward, arms flailing. I squeezed the binoculars until my knuckles shone white. But something was missing.

"No blood," I said, confused.

"Rubber bullets," Cat explained. "Not meant to kill. Not at first, anyway."

It was a game: four men with assault rifles versus six LTs with none. Predators vs. prey.

With Cannon supporting his injured friend, the LTs continued running. When they'd covered a good quarter mile, the three men revved their engines and took off. They weren't letting the LTs go; they were merely giving them a head start. *For sport.*

Far behind them sat the Man in Orange, arms crossed, observing from a distance. He was their guide. The hunt master.

The men steered the ATVs to the outer rim and corralled the six LTs, shooting wildly. Another boy went sprawling, clutching his face. When he pulled his hands away I saw a slick coating of blood dribbling down his cheek. A bullet got him in the eye.

The ATV whizzed away in search of moving targets. More challenging game.

One Less Than jumped into a stream. He lost his balance and fell face-first into the water with a splash. A four-wheeler followed, coming to a stop directly on top of him. The LT's arms flailed as he struggled for air, his head below water. The driver laughed.

Two more were brought down in quick succession. *Pop! Pop!* They lay motionless on the ground.

One of the remaining LTs ran for a scraggly pine, leaping for its outstretched limbs. He swung his legs up over the branch and began to climb.

The men treated him like target practice and riddled him with bullets. When the LT fell, his body sailing through twenty feet of air, he landed hard atop his head. There was no mistaking the sickening sound of his neck snapping in two.

Only two were left: the boy with the missing eye, and Cannon, standing by his side, shielding him from further bullets.

The men seemed intent on prolonging the moment, orbiting the two LTs in ever-closing circles. The heaviest of the group reached into a back compartment and pulled out a jug. They passed it around, each taking deep gulps from whatever homemade brew it contained. Only when the sun settled behind the far ridge did the shooters put away the jug to finish off the LTs.

But when one of them lifted his rifle, Cannon cocked his arm as though making that familiar throw from third to first and gunned a rock forward. It hit the rifleist square in the face. Blood gushed from his nose like a fountain.

While his two companions looked on in a drunken stupor, Cannon raced forward, kicked the wounded man off the ATV, and hopped on himself. He picked up his injured friend, and the two of them went zipping across the pasture, wind sailing through their hair.

When the two other shooters finally understood what was happening, they began to fire wildly. The alcohol made them too unsteady to get off a decent shot.

Cannon and the wounded LT inched closer to the far edge of the valley. They were going to make it. It took everything in my power to refrain from cheering.

I had forgotten about the Man in Orange.

He gave his head a weary shake, and uncrossed his arms. Removing his rifle from its scabbard, he placed Cannon squarely in his sights. From a distance of half a mile he pulled the trigger. Smoke plumed from the barrel; the crack of the rifle shot followed a full second later.

The bullet struck Cannon in the back of the head and both LTs went flying.

By the time the other two men raced forward—now no more than ten yards from their quarry—Cannon had pushed himself to a standing position and round after round landed in his abdomen, his arms, his legs.

He remained standing longer than any human could under such circumstances. He refused to be brought down. Finally, a bullet exploded in his face and he flew backward, landing hard on the ground. This time he did not move.

The Man in Orange joined the others. When he was a couple of feet away, he finished off Cannon and the other LT himself. We could see the bodies quiver with each shot.

The shooters made their way to Cannon's corpse. One of the men posed with the body as though it were big game he'd brought down on safari. His friend snapped a picture—the camera flash a miniature lightning strike.

When the four ATVs rode out of the valley, their sport completed, they left behind the corpses of six Less Thans, each only a year older than me.

Then the red pickup returned, jostling to a stop when it reached a corpse. The two Brown Shirts went to the body and swung it back and forth until they had enough momentum to fling it into the truck's bed. *Thud!* They drove to the next bodies and repeated the process—*thud! thud!*—their movements weary and nonchalant. As if they'd done this a hundred times.

When all six dead LTs were loaded in the back, the

truck bounced back the way it'd come, its red taillights shining like devil's eyes before disappearing into the darkness.

Just like that the valley returned to its peaceful self.

"Who were they?" Flush demanded as Cat led us back to camp.

"Hunters," Cat said.

"But why'd they do that?"

"'Cause you're a bunch of Less Thans." He said it like it was the most obvious thing in the world. "You're not only less than normal, you're less than human."

"So what'd those LTs do that got them punished?"

Cat stopped. "You're not listening. You all are prey, and your camp is one big hatchery. Those six LTs did nothing more than have the bad luck to get sent here. Period."

"A hatchery?" Flush repeated.

"A place where fish are raised, then released into rivers so fishermen have something to catch. You're just a bunch of Less Thans—being raised to be hunted."

"So why teach us anything at all?" I asked.

"'Cause otherwise it'd be like shooting fish in a barrel. If it's too easy, it's not sport. There's gotta be *some* challenge."

In its own sick way it made a kind of sense.

For the next hour no one spoke. We descended

through dense woods, moving as quickly as darkness allowed. Skeleton Ridge was no place to be at night. I don't think I took a breath until we caught sight of the camp far below, its lights sparkling.

"How do you know all this?" I asked.

"Because I've been on the run. I've seen people. I've talked to them." His eyes grew suddenly distant. "Before I came here, I stayed with a man and his two daughters. They put me up in their cave. They told me things—like how afraid they were of the Republic and its Brown Shirts. They were running from soldiers. *Everyone's* running from soldiers."

"But that doesn't—"

"Listen," he said, his piercing blue eyes cutting through the dark. "All of this is true—the proof is right under your nose. Or under the *Brown Shirts'* noses. You rescued me in the desert, I told you about the Hunters. That makes us even. What you do with this is up to you—I don't give a shit. I'm getting the hell out of here and going to the next territory."

With that, he turned and scrambled down the mountain.

That night my mind was reeling. I dreamed of her again: the woman with long black hair. We were running through the field of prairie grass, the air so pungent with gunpowder it wrinkled my nose. Behind us came

61

the same awful sounds as before: screams, explosions, the sharp crack of bullets.

Only this time there were others running, too. Cat. My friend K2. Cannon. All running for their lives.

The old woman pulled me low to the ground, and when she opened her mouth to speak, I didn't force myself awake. This time I let her talk.

"You will lead the way," she said.

I waited for more.

"I—I don't know what you're talking about," I stammered. "*What* way? And who on earth will listen to *me*?"

She smiled briefly and then disappeared, vanishing into the gunpowdery haze.

I woke with a start, my T-shirt clinging to me from perspiration. All around me, LTs slept soundly. I wondered if any were haunted by dreams as I was. Wondered too if I would ever begin to understand mine.

As I tried to get back to sleep, I thought of what Cat had said as we descended the mountain.

Right under the Brown Shirts' noses.

Something else, too. The stuff about that dad and his daughters. I wondered where they were now—if they'd escaped the soldiers and made it to freedom. Wondered if I'd ever find out.

10.

HOPE NOTICES THE OTHER girls seem oddly subdued. Repressed. *Haunted*, even.

The only thing that's clear is that Hope and Faith aren't the only sisters. In fact, as Hope looks around the mess hall at the hundred or so other girls, it seems as if the vast majority are related.

"What's with all the twins?" she asks the girl opposite her. She's tall with red hair and there's something in how the other girls look at her that makes Hope think she's in charge.

"You'll find out," the girl says.

"You're not going to tell me?"

The girl's eyes narrow. "What's to tell? Everyone's experience is different."

Grabbing her tray, the red-haired girl rises and rushes out. She's followed by another who has identical facial features but is shorter and more fragile-looking. This frailer version of Red Hair hesitates, seems about to say something, then changes her mind. Hope shrugs it off. Another unanswered question.

Roll call follows breakfast. On the grassy infield, the girls line up by barracks in perfect geometries of rows and columns. Colonel Thorason removes a sheet of paper from a binder and calls out a series of *Participants*. The girls cringe when their numbers are called. Once the announcement is complete, the Participants are met by the pudgy Dr. Gallingham and marched off.

Hope has no idea where they're being taken. It's all a nightmarish blur.

She's assigned to work in the barn; Faith is put on a cleaning crew. Milking cows and shoveling manure reminds Hope of when she used to help her father. Before they were on the run. Back in happier times. The barn is also outside camp, on the other side of the fence, which makes it feel that much closer to freedom.

When she returns to the barracks at the end of her shift, she is met by the same hostile glares.

"Don't bring that barn stink in here," one of the girls says. "Latrine's in back."

Hope grits her teeth. A number of other girls stand at

the metal trough. They grow quiet when Hope enters.

"Can I get in there?" Hope asks, motioning toward the running water.

She's so focused on scrubbing the dirt from her nails that when she turns around, she's surprised to see she's surrounded by a circle of girls, over ten of them.

Hope feels a stab of panic. While her instinct is to run, there's no possible way she'd make it to the door. Instead, she remembers her father's advice about not showing fear when facing wild beasts. And what wilder beasts are there than the girls of Barracks B?

Red Hair steps forward.

"Where'd you come from?"

"Out there," Hope answers, shaking the water from her hands.

"All these years?"

"That's right."

"No one could evade the Brown Shirts that long."

Hope shrugs. "We did."

Red Hair leans in until their noses are practically touching. Hope doesn't notice the girl behind her—not until she yanks Hope's arms back. Hope struggles but it's no good. The girl who has her arms is one giant slab of muscle.

"You better not be working for the Brown Shirts," Red Hair says, sending a fist into Hope's stomach.

Hope's lungs collapse. Red Hair grabs Hope's chin

and hits her hard across the face. Pain explodes from Hope's jaw and she crumples to the cold cement floor, tasting the metallic tang of blood.

Through swollen eyes, Hope sees Red Hair bending over her.

"We were just fine until you came along," she hisses. "And don't you forget it."

The girls exit, leaving Hope bruised and bleeding on the latrine floor.

That night at dinner, the other prisoners seem slightly more talkative than before.

But there are two exceptions.

The stub of a girl who grabbed Hope's arms; her bowl cut of black hair frames a permanently grim expression. And the frail sister of Red Hair. She averts her eyes and doesn't look at Hope once.

One by one, the girls finish their meager rations and leave the mess hall. When the frail girl walks by, she drops something next to Hope's plate. A piece of fabric. Hope regards it warily. When she unfolds it, she discovers it's a head scarf. She fashions it atop her bald head, grateful for the covering.

Back in the barracks, it's as though Hope and Faith don't exist. The prisoners go about their routines without the slightest regard for them.

Everyone has climbed into their cots when they hear

a loud rattling sound: Brown Shirts stripping the chains from the door. A moment later, a girl appears, haloed by moonlight. Once she's inside, the door is shut, the chains and locks refastened.

With halting steps she shuffles forward, seemingly unaware of her surroundings. She speaks to no one. *Sees* no one. She has wet herself and the sharp aroma of urine fills the room.

Red Hair gets up, placing her hands on the girl's shoulders. "You're back here now, Diana. We'll take care of you."

Diana, a tall, willowy girl with angular features and auburn hair, nods vacantly.

"You're safe now, Diana."

"Safe?" Diana echoes.

Her voice is distant, otherworldly.

In the pale moonlight Hope can make out Diana's eyes. They are glazed and faraway, focused on some remote horizon. It's like seeing the shell of a person only—a human being without a soul.

Hope shudders.

Too many questions run through her mind.

What's going on here? she wonders. *What kind of world are we in?*

Later that night when she uses the latrine she notices a prisoner standing in the back hallway, leaning against the wall as if keeping watch.

Stranger still is the ticking sound she hears as she returns to bed—a metallic clink. As she drifts off to sleep, fingering her father's locket, she swears she can hear it in her dreams.

Clink. Clink. Clink.

11.

THE NEXT MORNING CAT was gone.

His bed was made, his trunk empty. There was a good deal of speculation about where he might have gone—abducted by Crazies, recruited by Brown Shirts—but no one could say for sure.

I was out on the field when Sergeant Dekker came marching over.

"The colonel wants to see you," he said.

"Now?"

"*Right* now."

For the second time in a week, I felt my stomach bottom out at the prospect of meeting Colonel Westbrook. With the eyes of every LT—every *Less Than*—on me, I followed the oily Sergeant Dekker to the headquarters.

Instead of being led inside, I was ushered into the back of a Humvee.

"Where am I go—"

"You'll see," he answered, cutting me off.

Sweat trickled from my armpits as I sat waiting. Colonel Westbrook and Major Karsten emerged from the headquarters and climbed in the Humvee with me, neither saying a word. We took off. It wasn't until we'd left Camp Liberty that Westbrook turned around in the passenger seat, his coal-black eyes drilling into me.

"We're in search of a missing LT," he said, "and we thought you might be able to help us find him."

"M-me?" I stammered. "I just met the guy. I don't know where he is."

"So you know who I'm talking about."

"Well, sure, I mean—"

"And that wasn't you leaving camp with him yesterday afternoon?"

My face burned red, and it was all the answer he needed. The rest of the drive was long and silent.

The roads we followed were gravel and narrow, trailing the foothills of Skeleton Ridge and cutting through dense forests of spruce and pine. All at once we reached a clearing. There before us was a prison.

While it bore a certain similarity to Camp Liberty, there was one glaring difference: the entire site was encircled by a tall barbed wire fence. Guard towers anchored each of the four corners, with Brown Shirts poised behind machine guns.

I wondered who these inmates were who demanded such high security. I could only guess they were the most ruthless of prisoners, the most vile of criminals.

At just that moment the door opened to the tar-paper barracks and out streamed the inmates, all dressed in plain gray dresses and scuffed work boots.

Girls. Dozens and dozens of girls.

The only females I'd ever seen were two-dimensional ones from the movies. To finally see them in the flesh—and my own age, no less—took my breath away. A part of me felt like some ancient explorer encountering tribes from a far-off land.

All around me, girls in drab uniforms marched wearily from one side of camp to the other. But there was something I didn't understand. How was it these girls—these *prisoners*—were so highly guarded, while the Less Thans of Camp Liberty could come and go? What had these girls done that made them such dangerous criminals?

Also, there was something about how they moved—something about *them*—I found oddly disturbing. With downcast eyes and feet shuffling through the dust, they seemed almost . . . haunted. Like their physical bodies were present but their minds were a thousand miles away.

Colonel Westbrook seemed to read my mind. "So

you see, Book," he said, swiveling in his seat, "there are places in this world worse than Camp Liberty."

He climbed out of the vehicle.

"Don't move," Major Karsten added, fixing me with a skeletal stare.

He and Westbrook disappeared into the headquarters building and I sat in the stifling backseat, trying to make sense of what they had said, of what I was seeing.

Four guards escorted a handful of prisoners past the idling Humvee, marching them through a side gate to a barn on the other side of the fence. As I watched them, my eyes were drawn to one prisoner in particular. She was of medium height with light brown skin—skin the color of tea—and her hair was covered in a head scarf. There was something about her that caught my attention. It wasn't just that she was good-looking, although there was no doubt about that. There was some undefinable quality that drew me to her. It was almost like we had something in common—like there was something about her I already knew. Even from the distance that separated us I could make out the expression on her face . . . and I knew that expression. Had seen it countless times staring back at me in the mirror.

If anyone could help me understand what was going on, I knew it would be her.

12.

HOPE STACKS HAY BALES in the barn's loft. The work is hard and repetitive, but she doesn't mind. The intoxicating scent of fresh hay reminds her of the home she left ten years earlier.

A home with a mother and a father and life free of Brown Shirts.

A flash of movement out of the corner of her eye steals her attention, but when she peers through the loft window, all she sees are trees and the jagged cliffs of Skeleton Ridge. Strange. She could have sworn she saw something. Some*one*.

A moment later, it's the sound of footsteps that causes her to stop midlift, muscles straining. A Brown Shirt races through the fields.

When she turns around to stack the bale, she's shocked to see someone standing directly in front of her. He's about her age, with light brown skin and dark hair. The bale falls from her hands with a thud.

"Who are you and what—"

"Shh," he whispers. "I won't hurt you."

She takes an involuntary step backward but there's nowhere to go. The heels of her feet peek over the edge of the loft. "You shouldn't be up here." She eyes the pitchfork that lies a couple feet away. If she's quick enough, she can dive for it, reaching it before this stranger.

"I won't hurt you," he says again, palms raised.

Her fists clench. "What do you want?" He doesn't answer, so she asks again. *What do you want?*"

He opens his mouth to speak, but at just that moment the Brown Shirt comes stumbling into the barn, badly out of breath. The guy—the *intruder*—ducks behind the pyramid of hay bales, crouching in shadows.

Down below, the soldier circles in place, then raises his eyes until they land on Hope. "Did you see him?"

"Who?"

"An LT—a boy. Came running through. Just a moment ago."

Hope is about to speak but stops herself. She has no reason to trust this intruder—no reason at all—but she has even less reason to trust the Brown Shirts. Why

74

should she help them? All they've done is make her life a living hell.

But if she covers up the fact that she's hiding someone and the boy is found, she'll be the one who's punished. Why should she help him out—a perfect stranger? For all she knows, he's the enemy. One of the Crazies her father warned her about.

"Well?" the Brown Shirt prompts.

Is it her imagination or does she feel the boy's eyes boring into the back of her head?

"I didn't see anyone," she says at last.

"Then where'd he go?"

She shrugs.

The soldier does another circle, then makes a step for the ladder. "You sure he's not up there?"

Hope spreads her arms wide. "Come see for yourself if you don't believe me."

The Brown Shirt stares at her, unsure whether to climb up. Finally he hurries away and exits the barn.

Hope doesn't move. Now that the soldier has gone, it's just her and this intruder. If she's made a mistake— if she's misjudged him—she'll pay for it.

She slowly pivots in place. At first, she thinks he's disappeared—his departure as abrupt and secret as his arrival. Then she finds him—peeking through a crack between hay bales. His eyes flick anxiously from one side to another.

"He's gone," she says. "You may as well come out." Just to be safe, she picks up the pitchfork. Her damp palms grip the wooden handle.

The boy eases forward, brushing hay from his arms. He walks with a slight limp.

"Thank you," he says. "He would've killed me."

"He would've killed *me*," she responds, not hiding her irritation.

A look of regret sweeps across the boy's face. "I'm sorry I put you in that—"

"You shouldn't have. I'm in enough trouble as it is."

"I'm sorry. I just thought—"

"It's bad enough the other girls want to kill me, now the guards will as well."

"I said I'm sorry."

They stand there, facing each other, saying nothing. Separating them is a slice of sunlight, dancing with dust.

"Can I just ask one question and then I'll get out of your hair?"

She nods curtly.

"What is this place? What's going on here?"

"Camp Freedom," she says.

"Why are you here? Why're there guards and barbed wire? Are you all criminals or orphans or what?"

She doesn't know how to answer that—not in any brief kind of way.

"Look, I don't have much time," he says, "and I know I shouldn't have bothered you . . ."

"I'll say."

". . . and I'm sorry if I've gotten you in trouble, but I'm a Less Than from Camp Liberty and—"

"A Less Than?"

He waves his hand dismissively. "It's what they call us. We're looking for an escapee and we thought he might've come here."

She gives her head a shake. "Here? Why on earth would someone come *here*?"

"What I'm really asking is: If someone wanted to get to the next territory, what's the fastest way?"

For the longest time Hope doesn't speak. Ever since she and Faith came into camp, they've been ignored by everyone. Now, finally, someone is talking to her. *Needing* something from her. And that someone is this boy, whose honest expression and probing eyes set her heart racing.

"Can you help me or not?" he asks.

That's when she realizes what she recognizes in him. It's not like she's met him before—it's not like that—but there's something in his eyes. Kindness. Maybe even warmth. She doesn't mean to stare, but she can't look away.

"The Brown Forest," she blurts out.

"What about it?"

77

"That's where you want to go."

"Where is it? How do we get there?"

Hope leans the pitchfork against the hay bales and wipes a section of floor with her hand. "This is where we are," she says, hastily sketching a map.

He crouches next to her. She can feel the heat from his body. Smell traces of sweat and musk and woodsmoke. Masculine smells.

"You need to get east of the mountains," she says, her fingertips tracing the outline of Skeleton Ridge. "Until you hit the Flats."

"The Flats?"

"A white desert. Cross it and you'll reach the Brown Forest. Somewhere on the other side of that is the next territory."

"Have you been to the Brown Forest?"

"Once. A long time ago. My father took us."

"Is it safe?"

"Safer than here," she says.

They happen to lock eyes at the same moment, and Hope feels the blood rushing up her neck.

"Thank you," he says.

She nods. Her breathing is unnaturally shallow.

"I'm Book," he says, extending a hand.

She hesitates. A long moment passes before she reaches forward. "Hope."

They shake. His grip is surprisingly strong, and it's

78

like a jolt of electricity shoots up her arm. She pulls her hand back.

From outside comes the sound of footsteps. Book shoots a glance toward the barn door.

"If we ever escape," he says, "I promise we'll come for you."

"Don't. Not if you want to live."

A moment later, the Less Than named Book scrambles down the ladder and out the barn. Long after he's gone, Hope can still feel the touch of his hand, the heat of his skin. For reasons she doesn't understand, it's the first time she's felt alive since she and Faith were captured.

13.

ALTHOUGH THE BROWN SHIRT chewed me out for disappearing, more than anything he seemed relieved I showed up before the colonel found out. That way both of us avoided punishment.

Westbrook and Karsten didn't say a word the entire drive back to Camp Liberty, but I swear they looked at me differently. With a new kind of suspicion.

The feeling was mutual. After witnessing the gruesome slaughter in the mountains and the inmates of Camp Freedom, I was more convinced than ever the world was not what I thought it was.

As for finding Cat, the colonel never once asked for my assistance. It was almost as if he was more interested in threatening me with what I could expect if I didn't play along.

When we returned to Liberty, I didn't return to my barracks—not right away. I needed time to think, to process everything I'd seen. Like the girl.

The girl named Hope.

I couldn't stop thinking about her—especially those eyes. They were two brown pools. She didn't so much look at me as *through* me.

There was something else swimming in my brain—something Cat said on the way down the mountain. *Right under the Brown Shirts' noses.*

That night, once lights-out was called, I waited. When all the other LTs were snoring with a kind of clocklike efficiency, I tiptoed to the latrine. The cistern's edges scraped when I removed the lid, revealing a lone object taped beneath it. A flashlight. Not many to be found these days, but Red had managed to sneak one off a Brown Shirt months earlier.

I snuck outside. The night was cool, the grass stiffening with frost.

I made my way to the Soldiers' Quarters—a large rectangle of brick barracks where the officers and Brown Shirts lived, with soccer fields and a softball diamond in the very center. There was also an enclosed tennis court and an area for free weights. Barbells littered the ground, moonlight catching metal.

But there was nothing to be found—just some ball fields and workout equipment. What was Cat talking about? What was suspicious about all that? The

81

windscreen surrounding the tennis court flapped in the breeze and I decided to give it one last look.

The door was partially ajar and I turned my body sideways to slip inside. My eyes roamed from one corner of the court to the next. It was exactly what it appeared to be: a tennis court with a frayed net and fading green pavement. There was nothing there.

I was gliding back to the entrance when my foot sent something clattering across the court. I froze, praying no one had heard.

My hands fumbled on cool pavement until they landed on something small and round. A button. A measly button.

I cocked my arm and was ready to toss it over the fence when I gave it another look. My thumb nudged the flashlight on, producing a fuzzy, weak beam. There was nothing special about the button. Small. White. Four tiny holes for thread.

But when I held it against my shirt, I saw it matched the ones on my camp uniform. There had to be a lot of shirts out there with white buttons, but still . . .

From across the fields I heard the sounds of Brown Shirts leaving a party. I had to get out of there before they discovered me.

I let the flashlight's yellow circle guide me across the court. Metal caught light and glimmered back at me. A brass ring, set flush into the court. I let the light play on the surrounding area . . . and nearly lost my breath.

A rectangle was cut into the court, like a storm cellar door. Without thinking, I slipped my fingers beneath the cold metal ring and lifted. The door swung up, revealing a black chasm . . .

. . . and the reeking stench of BO, vomit, and urine. It nearly made me gag.

I poked the flashlight's beam into the hole, where it caught a ladder and black concrete walls. It was some kind of underground bunker. Then the light fell on pale, upturned faces—prisoners chained to walls. Their eyes were wide with terror; rags protruded from their mouths. They recoiled at the light, blinking and pressing themselves against the wall like vampires.

I started to move the light away when suddenly I recognized one of the faces. It was Moon, a round-faced LT who'd gone through the Rite earlier that spring. Now here he was, tethered to a bunker wall, unwashed hair plastering his forehead, his pants stained and soiled.

"Moon?" I asked, kneeling by the side of the hole. He squinted into the beam. "It's me: Book."

"Aagk?" he sputtered through the gag in his mouth.

My flashlight swung to the prisoner next to him. His face was jaundiced, eyes bloodshot, sores covering his half-naked body. I recognized him, too: Double Wide. And next to him was Beanie. And there was Pill Boy.

And Towhead and One Eye and all the other LTs who'd just gone through the Rite.

Why were they here? Weren't they supposed to be officers somewhere else? It didn't make any sense.

Unless Cat was right: we were nothing more than prey—raised in a hatchery for someone else's sport.

I tried to speak but nothing came out. No words, not even sounds. What could I possibly say to ease their pain?

My eyes squeezed shut and the images returned. *Dripping crimson on a tiled floor. The press of darkness. Shortness of breath.*

Raucous laughter broke the spell; Brown Shirts were approaching. I lowered the door back in place and hurried away, praying I hadn't been spotted. As I hustled back to the Quonset hut, my mind refused to let go of what I'd just seen. It was like K2's death: I knew if I didn't do something—soon—those faces would haunt me the rest of my life.

14.

EACH ROLL CALL IS the same: names are called in groups of two. Sometimes four, sometimes six. Always in pairs.

This morning, only two names are called. Jane F-738 and Jane F-739.

Faith and Hope.

While the others rush gratefully back to the barracks, Faith and Hope stand alone in the middle of the parade ground. Hope feels her legs go wobbly. A glance at her sister tells her she's in a kind of shock, the blood draining from her face.

"Coming, girls?" Dr. Gallingham asks, dabbing his watery eyes with a soiled hanky.

Although it's no more than a hundred yards to the infirmary, it feels like a hundred miles, each step worse than the one before. Hope hears a rattling sound and realizes with a start that it's Faith. Her teeth are chattering as though it were the dead of winter, even though it's a warm spring morning, sunlight stroking their faces.

"H and FT," Hope whispers.

Faith doesn't seem to hear. She shuffles forward like a sheep to slaughter.

Hope can't take it. First there was her father's death, then their capture. Now this. Any moment she expects to wake up from this nightmare.

The infirmary stands two stories high, with peeling white paint and bars covering the second-floor windows. Like a prison . . . or an insane asylum.

Dr. Gallingham leads them into a front reception area. A Brown Shirt tugs a key from his key ring and unlocks a door. Faith shakes uncontrollably as they're herded upstairs. Before them lies a long hallway. White-coated technicians hurry from one room to the next.

Hope glances into one of the rooms and sees a dead girl lying motionless on a stainless steel table, her lifeless eyes boring into the ceiling. A man in a white coat slices through her chalky skin with a scalpel, removing organs and plopping them in a bowl. In the next room, another man is powering up a portable handsaw, preparing to cut through a corpse's clavicle. Hope hears but does not see the scrape of metal biting into bone.

The smell is like burning hair.

"Eyes forward," Hope commands her sister, trying to spare her.

The two girls are led into a small room near the end of the hall. Water stains tattoo the ceiling. Before them are two beds, the white iron splotched with rust. Dr. Gallingham makes a grand motion with his damp hanky, indicating the girls should lie down.

"Good," Hope says. "I wanted to take a nap."

"And if you're lucky," Gallingham responds, "you might even wake up."

As soon as they're horizontal, two middle-aged female technicians begin attaching leather manacles to their wrists and ankles.

"What's this?" Hope asks, fighting against the straps. "Think we're gonna run away?"

"You'd be surprised."

At just that moment, the techs hold up syringes and tap the plastic cylinders. Small bubbles of hazy liquid dribble from each needle's end.

"Now then," Dr. Gallingham says cheerily, "is everyone ready to serve the Republic?"

"Just take me," Hope blurts out. "Leave my sister alone."

The doctor shakes his head. "You're missing the point. We need *both* of you. You have the same genetic makeup, so you're perfect for evaluating our drugs. You can help us determine which ones work"—he pauses dramatically—"and which ones don't."

"But we're not sick," Hope says.

Gallingham's thin lips part in a hideous smile. "Not yet."

One of the techs passes him a syringe, and before Hope can say anything else she feels the prick of the needle as it penetrates skin. Dr. Gallingham's fat thumb pushes against the syringe's plunger. "Good to the last drop," he says with a chuckle.

Hope doesn't know if it's her imagination, but she swears she can feel the poisons invading her blood-stream, spreading up her arm, her chest, racing through her entire body.

"What if it kills us?" she asks.

"That's why we have vaccines."

"What if they don't work?"

"Why do you think there are so many singles run-ning around?"

Hope finally understands: the haunted expressions, the lack of trust, the sense of despair. The girls all came here as twins. Thanks to Dr. Gallingham, many are now sister-less. Exactly what her father was warning her about.

"Finally get it, do you?" Gallingham asks.

As Hope tugs at the leather manacles, a wave of nausea rolls through her. Whatever they've been given works fast.

"We'll be back later," the doctor says in a cheery tone. "Sleep tight."

When he's gone, Hope swivels her head toward Faith and tries to say, "H and FT," but she only makes it to the first letter. Her eyes roll back in her head. Her last thought before blacking out is the boy in the barn, the touch of his hand, the press of his skin.

15.

MY WORDS WERE MET with silence. The five LTs—Flush, Twitch, Red, Dozer, and June Bug—all looked at me like I was crazy. We sat on the eastern outskirts of camp, hidden behind a heaping mound of rusted cars. "You really expect us to believe this stuff?" Dozer scoffed. "A massacre in the mountain? LTs in a bunker? A girls' camp surrounded by barbed wire?"

"I'm not making it up," I said. "Any of it."

Dozer laughed derisively and spat on the ground. His name was short for Bulldozer, as he had a tendency to bulldoze his opinions on everyone else.

"So what are you suggesting?" June Bug asked. Unlike Dozer, there was no hostility in his voice. Even though Omega's radiation prevented him from growing taller than five feet, it hadn't dampened his spirits. Which was probably why he was our unofficial leader. It was impossible not to like the guy.

"Head for the next territory. It's what Cat said he was doing. Maybe it'll be different there. In any case, we can't stay here."

No one spoke. Hard enough to just draw breath.

"How would we get to the next territory?" Red asked. "The mountain and desert are bad enough, but then there are those *p-people*."

He didn't need to say their names. The cities were inhabited by roaming gangs of criminals, referred to as Crazies. Even scarier were the Skull People, a tribe of primitive militants who killed anyone who dared approach their compounds.

"Yeah, and what're we gonna do?" Dozer chimed in. "Wander in the wilderness for years like frickin' Methuselah, trying to find some Promised Land?"

"Moses," June Bug murmured.

"Huh?"

"It was Moses who wandered in the wilderness. Not Methuselah."

"Whatever."

"I'm not saying we wander through any wilderness," I said, "just that we have to escape."

"Yeah, but *where to*?"

"Dozer does have a point," Twitch said, blinking.

He'd been born with a nervous condition that caused his facial features to spasm. Still, that didn't prevent him from being crazy smart. "We don't know which direction to go. There're no maps."

Ever since Omega, all maps had been confiscated. We only knew that we were somewhere in what had formerly been the western United States. Where, specifically, we had no idea. All the Brown Shirts told us was that we were now part of the RTA—the Republic of the True America—and our specific territory was the Western Federation Territory.

"We choose the only logical direction," I said. "East." They looked at me like I was crazy. "Think about it. We're surrounded on three sides by desert, but the south and west are nothing but sand. And we can't go north because of Skeleton Ridge. If the altitude won't kill us, the wolves will. So that leaves just one choice."

When they didn't respond, I went on. "Also, that's the direction of the Brown Forest. The girl in Camp Freedom said the new territory was just on the other side."

Dozer scoffed, but the others nodded quietly.

"Although it's desert, at least it's high desert," Twitch conceded. "There might be springs out there."

"And I know where the keys are kept in the vehicle compound," Red said. "What's to prevent us from taking some Humvees?"

Dozer sensed the tide turning against him. "And when we run out of fuel?"

"Then we hump it."

"Are you crazy?" Dozer asked, horrified. "We can't walk across a desert. Look at us. Look at *Book*." He pointed his sausage fingers in my direction. With my limp, I wasn't the fastest.

I had to admit: the realities of the plan were sobering. Miles of sage-covered desert. A dreary landscape as barren as the surface of the moon. And yet, what was the alternative? Stay in Camp Liberty and wait for the day to be imprisoned in a bunker? Or, worse, slaughtered by Hunters?

"We'll have to be smart," June Bug said. "Not just take enough supplies, but the *right* supplies."

"We'll stuff our packs with anything we can get our hands on," I said. "Crackers, jerky—anything that'll keep."

"And fill up canteens whenever we spot a water source."

Soon, everyone was throwing out ideas and a plan took shape. It was scary. *Beyond* scary. But staying at the camp—the *hatchery*—was no longer an option. Even Colonel Westbrook's promise to make me an officer was not tempting enough to make me stay. I didn't know who to trust anymore.

An uneasy silence settled among us. There was only

one thing missing, and we all knew it.

"We need someone who knows the geography," June Bug said. "Someone who can be a guide."

No one had to mention Cat's name for us to realize we were all thinking of the same person.

"Too late," Dozer said. "That coward's done gone and run. And I say fine. Let the sonofabitch die for all I care."

We headed back to camp, each going a different way so as not to arouse suspicion. As I made my way back, one question rattled around in my head over and over: How on earth could a measly bunch of Less Thans escape from Camp Liberty, elude an army of Brown Shirts, and make it halfway across the wilderness to a new territory? It seemed nothing less than impossible.

16.

HOPE DOESN'T KNOW HOW long she's been lying there. It could be hours, it could be days. She has vague memories of stirring, shivering from cold. Now she's burning up. Her dress is soaked in sweat; her entire body throbs with pain.

She looks over at Faith. Perspiration beads her forehead and her cheeks are flushed a bright red. Still, she is alive. Sleeping heavily with jagged, halting breaths.

Hope's eyes scan the room. On one wall is an enormous poster with the heading: *What Makes Someone a Less Than?* She remembers it's what Book called himself and studies the poster more intently.

Beneath the heading is an elaborate chart. A column

95

adorns one side, with the heading *Forbidden Categories*. The list includes Radiation Deformities, Homosexuality, Incompatible Skin Color, Political Dissidents, Nonapproved Religious Affiliations, Mentally Infirm. And goes on from there. Hope doesn't know what to make of it.

"Here. Drink this."

A prisoner bends over her, clad in the same gray dress that all the girls wear. Distinguishing her from the other inmates is a black eye patch covering one eye. She holds out a cup of water. Hope recoils.

"It's okay," the girl insists. "I work here."

Hope turns away. "I'm sick because of people who *work here*."

"It's not like that. I'm here to help. I'm a prisoner just like—"

Hope doesn't want to hear it. She sends an elbow into the girl's arm and the cup of water goes flying.

The girl with the eye patch sighs but says nothing. When she picks up the cup and refills it from the sink, Hope notices how bone-thin she is. Nearly skeletal. Like Faith. She offers the cup to Hope once more. "Just a sip," she says.

Something about her expression convinces Hope that maybe she's not as bad as the others. After a long moment Hope lets the emaciated girl slide a spoonful of water into her mouth.

"You girls in Barracks B sure don't trust others much," the prisoner says. She gets a rag and begins wiping up the spill.

"Why should we?" Hope says, even though she doesn't disagree.

"Because sometimes people help others out."

"And sometimes they do just the opposite." Black Eye Patch doesn't respond; she just finishes wiping the floor.

Hope studies the girl. If she harbors some ulterior motive, she hides it well. The girl brings the cup forward and Hope takes another sip. The water is cool and soothing. "From what I can tell," Hope says, "I didn't think anyone trusted anyone here."

"True, but it's worse with you all." The girl leans in and whispers, "It's almost like you're hiding something."

Her words echo Hope's suspicions. But what can her fellow barracks-mates be hiding?

"What do you think that is?" Hope asks.

The girl doesn't get a chance to answer.

"Good, you're up," says Dr. Gallingham, entirely too cheerfully. Black Eye Patch hurries out of the room.

Hope squeezes her eyes shut. She has already come to hate everything about him: his nasally, grating voice; his smug, lipless smile.

"And what was it you were saying earlier?" he asks with a smirk. "That you weren't sick? I trust that's

97

changed since last we spoke."

Hope has no desire to talk to Dr. Gallingham. She wants nothing more than to curl up in a ball and sleep. Still, there's something she wants to know. "What'd you give us?" she asks.

His face brightens. "An interesting question, and you'd be surprised how few of the girls ask. A rare strain of staphylococcus. Entirely treatable by vaccine, of course, but in today's world, there's little hope for developing one on such a grand scale. No CDC these days, sorry to say. But we can still create enough basic medicines for those we intend to save."

"And do you intend to save us?"

He forces a smile. "I intend to save at least one of you."

A thick heaviness spreads through Hope's chest. "How dare you," she manages to say, straining against the straps. How she would love to wrap her hands around the doctor's fleshy throat and squeeze the air right out of him.

"Now, now. No reason to be upset. But if you'd rather I not administer the antidote . . ."

He pretends to make a move toward the door.

"No!" Hope says. She can't let her anger endanger Faith.

"As I was saying," the doctor continues, "I'm sure one of you will survive. And *possibly* the other. As Ovid

98

once wrote, 'Medicine sometimes snatches away health, sometimes gives it.'"

Hope notices the two female techs are back. Each is staring at the monitors and jotting down information.

"But there is one thing I need to know," Dr. Gallingham goes on, peering at her with watery eyes. "Where's your father these days?"

Hope feels herself stiffen. "What're you talking about?"

"Your father. That's one of the reasons we've been after you, you know. Once we found the daughters, we knew we'd find him. Tic, tac . . . toe."

Hope's mind races. How could Dr. Gallingham possibly know her father?

"Well?" the doctor asks again. "Are you going to tell me?"

"Our father's dead," Hope murmurs.

"A very convenient answer. And one I'm sure he taught you to say. The only problem is . . . I don't believe you."

Hope feels like she's been slapped. "You think I'd make that up?"

"I think the daughters of Dr. Uzair Samadi would do anything to protect their father."

Hope flinches at his name. It's been forever since she's heard it. "I'm telling the truth."

"Hmm. You know, the longer you lie, the more I'll

be forced to bring you in here." Then: "So which of the two of you is feeling brave?"

Hope doesn't hesitate. "I am," she says.

"You sure?"

She nods fiercely.

"Fine. Then one full dose to this one"—he motions to Hope—"and half a dose to the other."

"Wait! That's not fair! Give Faith the full dose and me the half!"

"I would, but I think I'd rather keep you around. And then maybe you'll tell me what I want to know."

He nods to the techs, and they pick up two syringes— one full, one half full—and move toward the beds.

"You can't do this!" Hope screams, thrashing against her restraints.

"I think we just did," the doctor responds.

The needle jabs Hope's arm and she senses the cure— the full dose of it—entering her bloodstream. She feels utterly powerless to help her sister.

The medicine's coolness spreads down her arms like a drifting fog, and before she knows it she can no longer tell what's real and what's a dream. She thinks of Faith, and her mother and father, realizing that none of them can help her now. She has a memory of the boy in the barn, remembering the strong grip of his hand, the powerful kindness in his eyes. Maybe he can come to her rescue, she thinks. Maybe he will magically appear and cut through these bindings and lift her up, her body pressed against his chest as he carries her to safety. Maybe . . .

She falls into a deep and satisfying sleep.

17.

I WAS ON MY bunk reading *The Art of War* when I heard the shriek of whistles. Flush came dashing in.

"Emergency roll call!" he cried out.

Guys were scrambling to get in place and I ran to my assigned spot on the infield just as Sergeant Dekker strolled down my row, checking names off a clipboard. I glanced at June Bug and Red, their chests heaving, doing their best to hide the fact that they'd been up to something. Dekker stopped, eyed us coldly, then continued on his way.

What was going on? Were they on to us?

Sergeant Dekker assumed a pose of attention. No one spoke. Fifteen minutes passed. Then an hour. Then two. Dinnertime came and went. LTs shook from standing so long.

Banks of floodlights were suddenly switched on, bathing us in harsh, white light. Perspiration edged down the small of my back.

When Major Karsten and Colonel Westbrook finally emerged from the log cabin fortress, they were followed by someone I had never seen before: a tall, blond woman with high cheekbones and a severe gaze. An ankle-length coat hung from her shoulders. Westbrook leaned on the porch railing, his fingers biting into wood.

"As you all know," he began, "there is one road to freedom. And on that road are the following milestones: Obedience, Self-Sacrifice, and Love of the Republic. The three sides to the triangle." He pointed to his badge. His voice was cool, emotionless, as hard to read as his coal-black eyes.

"It has come to our attention that some LTs have not been as . . . obedient . . . as they could be. This we cannot tolerate. Is that understood?"

Each of the LTs gave his head an enthusiastic nod.

His gaze swept across us. Was it my imagination or did he linger an especially long time on me? The door behind him swung open and two Brown Shirts stepped out. In between their muscled arms was a limp LT, his head lowered like a rag doll's. When Westbrook grabbed the LT's hair and jerked his head upward, we saw who it was.

Cat.

103

He was nearly unrecognizable; his face was puffy and bruised, eyes swollen shut, and splotches of dried blood stained his cheeks. It looked like he'd been beaten within an inch of his life.

"As you may know, L-2084's been missing from camp these last few days, and only recently were we able to track him down. We thought he might want to share with us where he's been. We also thought he might tell us where he came from, because so far . . . we've learned absolutely nothing."

This time, when Colonel Westbrook looked out, I *knew* he was staring at me.

The colonel pinched Cat's face between his fingers. "I want you all to look at this LT. We call him 2084, but of course we don't know his original number, because he burned it off." A tiny smile played across Westbrook's face. "That's why I want you to see what happens when LTs don't abide by the rules."

A Brown Shirt emerged from the building. In his hand was a tool not much bigger than a screwdriver. It was plugged into an orange extension cord, which snaked into the log structure.

"Since L-2084 lacks a marker, it seems he needs a new one—one that won't come off." Westbrook gave the tall, blond woman a smug look—*This is how we do it here*, the expression said. Then he turned to Major Karsten.

"Major, would you do the honors?"

"My pleasure," he growled, his stare more piercing than the devil's.

As he took the tattoo engraver, I realized it wasn't what it seemed. It was a wood-burning tool, its shaft glowing red. They weren't going to tattoo Cat's number on his arm; they were going to *burn* it in.

"So now you know what happens when your marker mysteriously disappears," Westbrook said.

At that moment the bigger of the two Brown Shirts yanked Cat's right arm to the side while the other strapped it to the railing. Major Karsten stepped forward and pressed the red-hot tip into Cat's flesh, etching the first letter. A thin plume of smoke wafted upward, permeating the air with the nauseating odor of burned skin. Some LTs threw up on the spot.

Cat barely even flinched.

It seemed to take forever, Karsten pressing the searing metal tip into Cat's arm as he delineated each number. Blood dribbled down, striking the wooden floor like raindrops. Cat stood there with teeth clenched.

At last, when it seemed like Cat could take no more— when *we* could take no more—Karsten finished the final digit. He stepped back, the tool's metal tip glowing fiery red like a poker. The Brown Shirt undid the strap and flung Cat to the floor. Even from a distance I could see the rise and fall of his chest as he struggled for breath.

Colonel Westbrook let the silence lengthen. "Perhaps now," he said, loud enough for all to hear, "you'll tell us who you are and where you've been."

Cat looked up, his arm dripping a river of red. He had no intention of speaking.

"Fine," Westbrook said through gritted teeth. And then he hissed, "But don't think we're done."

He did an about-face and disappeared into the building. The woman followed, then Karsten and the Brown Shirts.

The LTs couldn't get out of there fast enough, scurrying back to the barracks like cockroaches, until it was just me. I took several steps toward Cat. He'd barely moved since the Brown Shirts tossed him to the floor.

"Are you okay?" I reached out a tentative hand but he swatted it aside.

"I don't need your pity," he said.

"Are you sure you're all right, because—"

"I said I don't need you," he said again.

Fine, I thought. *Have it your way.*

I walked back across the infield. And as I did, I had the strange but certain sensation I was being watched.

18.

HOPE FEELS THE FULL dose of the vaccine within a day; her aches recede, her fever ebbs. But Faith deteriorates further and further into a world of feverish nightmares—her body twisting in a series of grotesque contortions. In her delirium she mutters, "Why, Dad? Why?" over and over.

Hope wants nothing more than to cover her ears and block out the words. Her arm restraints prevent it.

When Faith's fever does finally break, Hope almost gets the feeling Dr. Gallingham is disappointed.

"Well," he says, dabbing a moisture-laden eye, "now we know to only administer half a dose." He waddles out of the room.

As soon as Hope and Faith are well enough to walk,

they're escorted down the stairs and shown the door.

"How did he know?" Faith asks.

Hope looks at her sister. "How did who know what?"

"That doctor know about Dad?"

Hope gives her head an angry shake. "He's just saying that. He didn't know him."

"But he knew his name."

"That doesn't prove anything."

"But he said—"

"And I'm telling you that doesn't prove anything." Faith looks like a dog that's just been kicked. Hope regrets her outburst almost at once.

"Look," Hope says, "go easy today, okay? You're still weak."

Faith nods a trembling chin.

"H and FT."

Faith musters a weak smile.

The days are remarkably the same. Silent breakfasts. Tense roll calls. Work details in the afternoon followed by muted conversations over dinner. Each night, Hope wakes and hears the steady *clinking* sound. Each night she thinks of the boy named Book.

Through it all, Faith clings to her sister's side—practically attaches herself there—so when Hope returns from barn duties one afternoon to find Faith is missing, she feels a stab of panic.

"Has anyone seen my sister?" Hope asks.

The other girls just laugh.

Hope searches everywhere: the barracks, the mess hall, even the tiny smokehouse. It isn't until she gives a sideways glance toward the storehouse that she spies a pair of thin, pale legs dangling from the top window.

Hope makes her way up the creaking stairs to the third floor, then edges through a labyrinth of pallets and cardboard boxes.

Faith sits on a wooden crate. Draped over her shoulders is her ever-present pink shawl—the one their mother knitted way back when. She faces the woods on the far side of the barbed wire fence.

Hope plops down beside her sister.

"What're you doing up here?"

Faith doesn't acknowledge her. Instead she says, "I found it."

"Found what?" Hope asks, but when her eyes drop to Faith's side, her heart gives a lurch. There sits the crumpled piece of paper, the word *Separate* scrawled in charcoal. The note found in their father's dying hand.

"It fell out of your pillow," Faith says, her voice flat. "Is it Dad's handwriting?"

"You know it is."

"When did he give it to you?"

"He didn't. I found it in his hand after he died. If anything, he gave it to both of us."

109

"Then why didn't you show it to me?"

Hope has no good answer.

"So I was right," Faith goes on. "He wanted us to separate so you could survive."

"So we could *both* survive," Hope corrects her.

"It was you he wanted to live. You said it yourself: I wouldn't last a day in the wilderness on my own."

Hope picks up the scrap of paper and rips it into tiny pieces, angry she didn't do it earlier. Extending her hand, she lets the fragments flutter to the earth like confetti.

"Do you remember the goats?" Faith asks out of the blue. Her gaze is suddenly miles away.

It takes a long moment for Hope to figure out what her sister is talking about. "Sure," she says.

"And the chickens?"

"The ones that pecked your shins?"

"And those pigs?"

"I swear I still smell 'em."

In earlier days, the memory might have prompted a laugh. The problem is they've long forgotten how. Smiling and laughter are no longer in their vocabulary.

Then Faith asks, "Do you remember the boy? The one who stayed in our cave?"

"Of course."

"Where do you think he is?"

"No idea." *Far away from here* is what she wants to

110

say. *Not stuck in this godforsaken territory.* But even as she thinks it, she has to hide her annoyance. What's the point of wallowing in self-pity? It only brings heartache and sadness. Besides, it goes against everything their father taught them: *If you want to change something, change it. Yesterday was yesterday; today is today.*

They are both quiet. From the woods comes the sound of a thousand croaking frogs. Then Faith says, in a voice that is barely a whisper, "Sometimes they come back alone. Without their sisters."

"I know, but it's not going to happen to us."

"You promise?"

"Promise."

A sudden weariness descends on Hope. It's tiring being the one in charge, the comforter, the provider. Even though she's only twenty minutes older than Faith, it's always been her role.

"Come on," she says. "We need to get to dinner."

Faith nods absently. They rise and make their way downstairs and out the door. For a mere instant, walking through the grass to the mess hall, Hope can almost forget where they are. She can almost trick herself into thinking they're back in the house in the mountains: Mom making breakfast and teaching them their lessons, Dad telling stories by the fireplace, his rich bass voice inspiring laughter and wonder. Afterward, their mother would play the out-of-tune piano in the parlor and teach them hymns.

> *"Come, Thou Fount of every blessing*
> *Tune my heart to sing Thy grace;*
> *Streams of mercy, never ceasing,*
> *Call for songs of loudest praise."*

For a brief, transcendent moment, it is Hope and Faith returning to their home and adoring parents, hearing the strains of songs and laughter, far away from this strange, cruel place.

But once they round a corner and see guard towers, the coils of razor wire and gun-toting Brown Shirts, the dream vanishes. This is their reality.

Yesterday was yesterday; today is today.

19.

"WE'RE PLANNING AN ESCAPE and want you to come with us," June Bug said.

We were standing in the latrine—all white tiles and dripping faucets, reeking of sour turds.

Cat eyed us curiously in the mirror but said nothing. His bruises had faded from black and blue to green and yellow. Only slightly less gruesome. If he was surprised by June Bug's words, he gave no indication. He continued to rinse his arm in the sink. The water dribbled past his wound and down the drain, tinged with blood red and pus yellow. "I'll be long gone before you all finish tying your shoes," he said.

"We'll pull our own weight," June Bug said.

"I'll take my chances."

"What if we paid you?"

Cat actually laughed. He turned, his eyes roaming from one of us to the other. "With what?"

"I don't know. We'd think of something."

He gave his head a shake. "Not interested. I left the YO Camp to save myself—no one else. Period."

We were shocked. It was the first bit of history Cat had revealed about himself.

"You were a Young Officer?" June Bug asked.

Cat nodded.

"So if things were so good there, why'd you leave?" Dozer said.

Cat didn't answer. He flicked off a piece of burned skin and flung it to the floor.

"Look, we go through the Rite next spring," June Bug said. "Which means if we don't leave now, we never will. And if you don't help us, I'm not sure we can reach the next territory on our own."

The dripping faucet was suddenly as loud as a cannon boom.

"Sorry," Cat said. "Not interested." He brushed past us and made for the door.

Before he got there, Dozer blurted out, "You know what, Cat? I don't know how you know all this shit—like where that massacre was going to be and the bunker in the tennis court—but why should we trust you when you're in on all these secrets?"

Cat hesitated. He turned. "Because I have a source," he said at last, and his words hung in the air like smoke. A source. A *spy*. The kind of thing Colonel Westbrook had wanted me to discover.

"Who?" June Bug asked.

"I can't tell you."

"How convenient. Why should we trust you then?"

"I never asked you to trust me. You're the ones who approached me." The door shut behind him, and we stood there in stunned silence. Eventually, we dispersed, tiptoeing back to our bunks.

As I slowly drifted off to sleep, I wondered about Cat's source, trying to figure out who it could possibly be. And I thought of what Cat *hadn't* said: without him, we'd have a snowball's chance of surviving that desert.

That night I dreamed of her again—the woman with long black hair.

But this time I was seated on her lap surrounded by flickering candles. She was reading—tales of Star-Belly Sneetches and a pig named Wilbur—her voice soothing me. Utterly comforting.

"Get up," a voice whispered.

Cat's face was inches from mine. I rolled to the side, hoping to reenter the dream.

"Get dressed," he whispered. "We need to leave now."

I bolted upright and tried to shake off my confusion.

Now? Was he crazy? We still had work to do, supplies to gather.

"We've been compromised," he explained. "We have to wake the others."

I jumped out of bed and slipped on my jeans. They were cold and stiff, deepening the shivers that shook my body.

Compromised? What was he talking about?

While Cat woke Flush, Red, and Twitch, I went to the beds of June Bug and Dozer. All around us guys snored heavily. The seven of us shuffled to the latrine.

Cat turned the dead bolt and got right to it. "Someone talked to Westbrook."

Everyone was suddenly wide-awake.

"Who?" Dozer asked. The muscles in his nonwithered arm grew tense.

"Don't know," Cat answered.

"So how do you know someone talked?" He clenched and unclenched his fist as if preparing for a fight.

"I just know."

"You woke us up for that?" Dozer asked. "Some vague possibility that *someone* might have said *something* to Colonel Westbrook? And I suppose this was your *source* who told you this?"

"Yes, as a matter of fact. Someone went to Westbrook and Karsten this afternoon and told them there's an escape planned for a few nights from now."

The air was sucked out of the room. All our hard work and planning—for nothing.

"So what do we do?" Twitch asked, blinking rapidly.

"Leave tonight," Cat answered. "It's our only option."

I inhaled sharply.

"But we're not ready," Dozer said. "We haven't finished gathering supplies. And there's no way we can retrieve the ones we have."

For once, I agreed with him. Everyone began talking.

Cat cut us off. "According to my source, the whole camp'll be on lockdown starting tomorrow morning. If we don't get out of here now, we never will."

We? I asked Cat.

"I'm coming with you," he said. There was no pleasure in his voice.

"Okay," June Bug said, "so let's meet at the storehouse in ten minutes. We'll load supplies into the Humvees and drive the hell out of here."

"Not possible," Cat said. "Westbrook's posting guards at the vehicle compound. There's no way we'll get a single Humvee past them."

June Bug looked stricken. Everything depended on being able to drive the first few hundred miles.

"Then how do we escape?" Twitch asked.

Before anyone could answer, we heard sounds from the bunkhouse. Shriek of whistles. Smashing of trunks.

"Soldiers," Cat said. "Searching for evidence."

117

"What do we d-do?" Red asked.

"Out the window. *Now*."

As we raced to the far end of the latrine, Twitch asked, "Do we meet at the storehouse?"

"There's no time," June Bug answered. "Not now."

"But we have to have supplies." There was no way we could survive a trip across the desert without food and water.

"Forget the desert," Cat said. "They'll track us down before we get a mile from camp."

"So where do we go?"

"Skeleton Ridge," I blurted out. Everyone looked at me like I'd lost it.

Cat nodded curtly. "He's right. We'll get some horses from the stables and head up the mountain. We can lose 'em if we're fast."

The fear of Brown Shirts was nothing compared to the absolute terror of Skeleton Ridge with its dizzying altitude and roaming wolf packs.

"There's an office by the stables," June Bug said. "There're packs and canteens. Probably some jerky. Not much, but enough to get us going."

"How about the bunker?" I asked. "We need to free those LTs."

The corners of Cat's mouth tugged downward. "They're not there, Book. Westbrook sold them off this morning." I remembered those terrified faces: Moon and Double Wide and all the others. The thought of them getting slaughtered by Hunters turned my stomach.

The door banged. "Open up in there!" Major Karsten called out. It was all too easy to imagine his skull-like face on the other side.

LTs scrambled out the window. More whistles shrieked. It was like a bad dream—everything happening too fast and out of control.

"Open up, I say!" Karsten yelled. The door buckled under the weight of his pounding.

Cat and I were the last to leave. He tossed me through the window and leaped out a second later. Just as we landed, we heard the dead bolt snap open, followed by a crunch of footsteps. We pressed ourselves against the building, hiding in shadows.

"What happened, Major?" a voice asked. Colonel Westbrook. His calm tone had a deadly venom to it.

"We broke up a secret meeting," Karsten answered. "Looks like they escaped out that window."

There was a moment's pause, then the dull echo of footsteps. From our hiding place in the shadows, Cat and I saw Westbrook thrust his head out the bathroom window. A moment later, he retracted it.

"I want every one of those Less Thans rounded up and brought back here," he commanded. "No exceptions."

"My pleasure," Karsten growled.

The footsteps receded and I tugged Cat's arm. "We'd

better get out of here," I said.

He shook his head. "Meet you at the stables." He took off before I had a chance to stop him.

I got up and ran, my one good leg carrying me as fast as it ever had, a part of me wondering if I'd ever see Cat again.

The stables were separated from camp by a quarter mile of pines and firs. By the time I got there, the office door was splintered open and the five LTs were stuffing backpacks with supplies.

As we worked, slipping pads and saddles on the horses, we heard shouts from camp. Banks of floodlights snapped on. Twitch buckled the cinch around the belly of my horse and helped adjust the stirrup because of my one short leg.

"Cat better get here soon," he murmured.

We led the horses out to the corral. From camp came the faraway sounds of muffled gunshots. It was hard to believe only an hour earlier I'd been fast asleep, dreaming of the black-haired woman. Hard to believe one's life could change so quickly.

There was a sudden scurrying off to one side and Red and Dozer fumbled with their bows. Cat burst through the woods before either nocked an arrow.

"Where were you?" Flush demanded.

"Had to do an errand. Come on. Let's get out of here."

We grabbed our packs and headed for the horses. A voice stopped us cold.

"Wait."

Faster than a snap, Cat had an arrow nocked and the bowstring pulled back tight. So that's how it was done.

"W-who is it?" Red asked.

Stepping through the undergrowth was a younger LT named Four Fingers. He was Flush's age and I didn't know him well. Just enough to realize that for such a big guy, he had a surprising baby face.

"Don't shoot," he said, hands in the air.

"What do you want?" Dozer demanded.

"I want to go with you."

We looked at each other. "Who said we were going anywhere?" June Bug asked.

Four Fingers's eyes took in the saddled horses. "You're escaping, aren't you? I want to come with you. I can earn my keep." He picked up one of the packs, hoisting it on his broad shoulders. For a fourteen-year-old, he was pretty damn strong. The whistles of the Brown Shirts grew closer.

"No room," Dozer said. "Now beat it."

We started to walk away. A small part of me felt for the kid.

"Fine," Four Fingers said, "I'll tell the colonel."

We froze. It was pure blackmail—but he had us good and everyone knew it.

121

Dozer raised his fist and took a threatening step forward. "You say one word, you little freak, and I'll rip off your head and feed it to the wolves."

Four Fingers didn't back down. The two locked eyes.

"Okay," June Bug finally relented, "but keep up. We don't wait for anyone."

Four Fingers's face broke into a ghoulish smile.

"Are you serious?" Dozer asked, outraged. "This jerk-off hasn't been on a horse in his life. All the Brown Shirts have to do is follow us up the mountain on their ATVs."

"Not if their ATVs don't work." Cat reached into his pocket and fished out a handful of keys. "Tough to start an engine without these."

From the sounds of the whistles, we knew the Brown Shirts had reached the other side of the woods. A flare rocketed skyward, bursting into a spitting blaze of green light. There was no time to waste.

We saddled an eighth horse and began making our way up the steep trail that led to the top of the dark, distant mountain—Skeleton Ridge. As our mounts picked their way up the rocky slope, I questioned if we were right to bring Four Fingers along.

Wondered, too, if I could work it to see the girl named Hope again. To find out more about her, who she was and how she'd ended up at Camp Freedom. For reasons I didn't fully understand, I couldn't get her out of my mind.

PART TWO
ESCAPE

but please turn around
and step into the future
leave memories behind
enter the land of hope
—ZBIGNIEW HERBERT
from "A Life"

20.

With a special inspection scheduled that night, Hope's been ordered to clean the barn. An important visitor is coming to Camp Freedom and everything has to look its best. Like Hope cares.

All that concerns her is living—trying to survive Dr. Gallingham and her fellow inmates so she and Faith can get out of there. And maybe find Book.

Even now, stacking hay bales, she swears she can smell his masculine scent: that pleasing blend of sweat and musk. It surprises her how much she thinks of him. How cruel it was to meet him that one time only and then . . . gone.

Laughter breaks her spell. Mean-spirited chuckling.

Hope inches to the edge of the hayloft. Below her,

at the far end of the barn, stand three inmates. They surround a fourth girl—Hope recognizes her as the strawberry blonde, the frail twin of Red Hair. Where the Brown Shirts have drifted off to is anybody's guess.

The girl tries to walk away, but the heavyset bully pushes her to the ground. The girl lands smack in a juicy puddle of mud and manure.

"I'll ask you one more time," the leader says. "What were you doing back there?"

"I wasn't doing anything," Strawberry Blonde says, her voice quivering.

"Just kicking dirt for the fun of it?"

The heavyset prisoner takes a menacing step forward. There's something off-kilter about her face—lopsided, even. "You all are up to something, aren't ya?"

The small girl's chin trembles. "I don't know what you're talking about."

"I think you do." She begins slamming her fist into her palm. *Smack. Smack.*

"Hey!" Hope suddenly yells. "What's going on down there?"

The three girls look up and exchange a glance. "Who the hell are you?" Lopsided Face asks.

"I'm Hope."

"Yeah, well, I'm Reality"—her two friends crack up—"and I say leave us the hell alone."

Hope climbs down the rickety ladder without a second thought, knowing she has little chance with these odds. Not three against one. Still, she reaches the ground and extends a hand to the frail girl, intending to help her to her feet.

Before she gets the chance, Lopsided Face spins her around. "I said leave us alone."

It takes everything in Hope's willpower not to throw a punch. "I am leaving you alone. It's her I'm helping."

Lopsided doesn't hide her disgust. "What's with you girls from B, anyway? What makes you think you're so special?"

"We just look after each other, that's all."

Hope's words surprise even herself. Here she is including herself in Barracks B as though she's lived there for years. As though the other girls accept her.

"Maybe you do, maybe you don't, but you're up to something. Kicking at the dirt. Searching in the gardens. It's like you're looking for buried treasure."

It's what Hope thinks, too.

A distant whistle shrieks. Time for the inspection.

Lopsided Face gives an irritated glance, then leans in until her nose is mere inches from Hope's. "We're not done here." She and her friends lumber away and Hope waits for them to disappear.

"Come on," Hope says to the frail girl. "Let's get you cleaned up."

127

"But the inspection—"

"Can wait. Come on."

Hope pulls her to her feet, mud and manure clinging to her legs.

"You won't tell, will you?" the girl manages between sobs.

Hope is irritated by the tears and confused by the request. "It wasn't your fault those bullies picked on you."

"Please don't tell Athena—about any of this."

"Fine. As long as you stop crying." Then: "So your sister's name is Athena, huh? What's yours?"

"Helen," she says with a nervous smile.

"Okay, Helen. Then get out of that dress and we'll clean it."

Helen covers herself. "But what will I wear?"

Hope lets out a long sigh; she has no time for tears, even less for modesty. She whips off her own dress and holds it out to Helen.

Helen just stares at it. "But that's yours."

"Exactly. Now take it." They exchange dresses and Hope fills a bucket with water. She begins to scrub. "Why'd they pick on you, anyway?"

"Some of the other barracks don't like us. They think we're up to something."

"Are you?"

Helen seems on the verge of speaking but stops

128

herself. "We'd better hurry," she says.

Hope wonders what it was Helen was about to say. "Go on if you'd like, I'm almost done here."

"But it's a special inspection. If you're not there, you'll be punished."

"What're they gonna do? Put me in prison? Go."

"Thank you," Helen murmurs, then hurries away.

Hope wrings out the dress and puts it on. Its dampness raises goose bumps and she rubs her arms to warm herself up. As she does, she thinks of the Less Than—Book. Although their encounter seems like a distant dream, she lets herself pretend it's Book who strokes her arms. She imagines him holding her firmly against his chest, the heat from his body mingling with hers.

Don't be a fool, she tells herself, and shakes away the thought.

Still, why is it that just thinking of him makes her feel less alone? Makes her want to escape from Camp Freedom this very moment?

By the time Hope returns, the inspection is under way. An entourage parades from one barracks to another. Hope slips inside her tar-paper shack through the rear door. The other girls are standing stiffly by their cots.

"Thanks for joining us," Athena says as Hope shuffles to her place in line.

129

"Don't mention it."

"Next time you put us all in jeopardy, let us know ahead of time, okay?"

The door swings open and in steps the tall, blond woman—the same one who demanded Hope's hair be cut off. *So that's who the special inspection is for.* As before, the woman wears an ankle-length coat that hangs off her shoulders. Colonel Thorason and half a dozen Brown Shirts single-file behind her, down one aisle and then another.

Suddenly the blond woman stops. "What's that *smell*?"

The entourage comes to a halt.

"There," one of the Brown Shirts says, pointing at Hope's feet.

Water drips from the hem of her dress, creating a small brown puddle on the pine floor.

Colonel Thorason stomps forward, grabbing Hope's arm to read her tattoo. "What's the meaning of this, 739?"

"I had an accident," Hope mumbles.

"And you didn't think it necessary to clean up for our honored guest?"

"I tried."

"Not hard enough," he sputters. "And just for that, I'm going to double your work duties, and then—"

The blond woman with the high cheekbones cuts

him off. "If I may," she says, her voice so sugary sweet it's painful to listen to.

"Of course." Thorason takes a deferential step backward.

The woman faces Hope directly. Her smile is brittle, her eyes icy. In a move so fast it startles even Hope, she rips off Hope's head scarf, revealing a patchy fuzz of short black hair.

"I thought it might be you," she says, deliberately tossing the head scarf into the puddle of brown muck.

Hope's cheeks burn red.

"Care to tell us how you got into this mess?" the woman asks.

Out of the corner of her eye, Hope sees Helen about to open her mouth. Hope beats her to it. "I fell in the barn shoveling manure," she blurts out. "I tried to clean up. Guess I didn't do a very good job."

"No, I guess you didn't. But then again, you know what they say. You can take the girl out of the shit, but you can't take the shit out of the girl."

There is a brief moment when no one quite knows how to respond. When the woman begins to laugh, the Brown Shirts and Colonel Thorason are quick to follow.

As the laughter dies, the woman's smile hardens. She turns to Colonel Thorason and says, "No need to double this girl's work time."

Hope lets out a small sigh.

131

Then the woman adds, "Let Dr. Gallingham have her instead."

With that, she does an abrupt about-face and exits the barracks, the *click click* of her heels echoing in the tar-paper shack long after she is gone.

21.

WE TRAVELED THE ENTIRE night without stopping. Along the trail, faded signs from long ago warned travelers of the perils of hiking.

"Mountains don't care," one read, describing the dangers of avalanches. As if the post-Omega world wasn't bad enough already.

Streaks of pink painted the eastern sky. By the time my horse pulled up, the others had already dismounted, stopped at a fork in the trail.

"What's going on?" I asked.

"Cat wants to take this smaller trail," Flush confided, a hint of panic in his voice. "But we don't know where it goes."

"We don't know where the other goes either," Cat said.

133

"Yeah, but at least it's a real path."

"Do you want to make it as easy as possible for the Brown Shirts to track us down? Is that it?" Anger welled up in Cat's chest as he spoke. "We need to get off the main trail and get out of sight. Now!"

No one dared utter a word. What could we say? Cat had more experience than all of us put together.

As the guys stumbled for their horses, we heard a sharp yapping sound. Cat drew his horse around.

"What was that?" he asked.

No one answered. Cat hurled himself down from his mare and strode through the group until he came to Four Fingers.

"Turn around," Cat snapped.

"Why?" Four Fingers muttered.

"Turn around, I said."

Four did as he was commanded. Cat reached for the opening of his backpack and released the drawstring.

A dog's head popped out and Cat recoiled. The dog panted, smiling brightly, its brown fur creased by a wide grin. One ear flopped upward, one down.

"What's this?" Cat asked.

"A dog."

"I know that. What's it doing here?" Cat grabbed the younger LT's shoulder and pushed him back around so he could face him.

Four Fingers faltered. "It's a puppy. . . . We found it

last week. . . . It was starving to death . . . so we took it in."

"And you thought you could just bring the dog along? What happens when it starts barking and we're trying to hide?"

"But I couldn't just . . . leave it back at camp. . . . The Brown Shirts'd kill it."

"Who says we won't?"

June Bug placed a hand on Cat's shoulder. "It's all right. We can manage."

Cat flung off June Bug's hand. "You all don't get it, do you?" His piercing stare traveled to each of us. "If those soldiers catch us, we're dead. You saw what Westbrook did to me. And even if we do manage to escape, we still have to figure out some way to eat. There's barely enough food to last us a couple of days."

Cat's gaze returned to Four Fingers. "If that thing makes a sound when we don't want it to—even a peep— it's gone. Are we clear?"

Everyone nodded. Cat mounted his horse and spurred it into action. A part of me wanted to help Four Fingers, to say something comforting. But I didn't. Chalk it up to the K2 Effect. Safer just to keep my distance.

"Bet you can't guess how I got my name," K2 said to me that day.

It was four years earlier—the day I first met him.

135

I was eating by myself, my face buried in a book, and this hulking LT was suddenly sitting next to me. "Huh?" I said.

"I said, bet you can't guess how I got my name."

"You're right, 'cause I don't even know who you are." I'd seen him around camp, of course—how could you miss someone who stood a good half foot taller than the rest of us?—but I'd never had reason to talk to him.

"I'm K2. And you're Book."

"How'd you know—"

"So how do you think I got my name?"

My eyes did a sweep of him—of his massive frame and his smallish head.

"K2's the second highest mountain in the world," I said. "After Mount Everest, of course. Way over on the other side of the world. It's also called Savage Mountain because back in pre-Omega days so many people died trying to climb it."

"You still didn't answer my question; how'd I get my name?"

I sighed. "Because you're big?"

"Not just big. *Jumbo-honkin'* big!"

"Fine. *Jumbo-honkin'* big."

His face lit up into a broad smile and he slapped me on the back—so hard I nearly coughed up my spleen. But there was something about this K2 that was enormously likable; he was like a jovial giant. And if he wanted to be my friend, well, what was wrong with that? It was high time I broke out of my cocoon.

He suddenly jumped up and called out to two LTs at a far table. "I win! I told you the guy was smart."

I looked up from my book. "You win? At what?"

"I bet those losers over there you'd know the reason behind my name."

My face twisted. "That's why you spoke to me? To win a bet?"

"Yeah!"

And here I thought he'd sat down out of kindness. Turns out it was just so he could collect on a dumb wager. I felt foolish. Downright stupid. "I'm glad I could help you win your bet," I muttered.

"Don't mention it."

"Glad I'm nothing more than a game to you."

"Hey, you don't have to get your panties in a twist. It was just a harmless little bet. Besides, it's a compliment. You're a brainiac."

"Well, next time, have your fun at someone else's expense."

I got up and left. I didn't talk to K2 for a whole other year.

We rode on. When I happened to swipe a glance in Four Fingers's direction, I noticed he looked shaky. An encounter with Cat could do that to a guy. Against my better judgment, I spurred my horse forward until we were riding side by side.

"What's his name?" I asked.

"Huh?"

"Your dog. What's his name?"

The backpack shifted and the dog's head poked out of the narrow opening.

"Argos," Four Fingers said proudly. "That was—"

"The dog of Odysseus."

A smile spread across his face. "You've read *The Odyssey*, too?"

"Sure. Argos waited twenty years for Odysseus to come home . . ."

". . . and then he died. It was really sad." Four Fingers hesitated a moment before asking, "You think Cat'll let me keep him?"

"Who? Argos?" The dog's tongue was lolling out of his mouth. I didn't know much about dogs, but he seemed some mix of beagle and Labrador. Maybe even coyote. The flap of one ear remained continuously up, as though he was eavesdropping. "As long as you keep him quiet, I don't see why not."

Four Fingers beamed. Probably the first time in forever.

"So where're we going?" he asked.

"East."

"What's east?"

"Another territory."

"And things'll be different there?"

"They'd better be."

Cat suddenly motioned for us to be quiet. There was a sound—a faint drone, like bees buzzing. It grew steadily louder.

"What's that?" Four Fingers asked.

Red was searching the sky through a canopy of pine boughs. "A plane, maybe," he said, but there were precious few of those. What was the point of leaving a toxic, smoldering city if your only choice was to fly to *another* toxic, smoldering city?

We dismounted and ran toward a jutting boulder.

Far below us was a canyon, gouged into the mountain. On the other side was a ridge, nearly a mirror to our own . . .

. . . with a line of Humvees snaking up the mountainside. From the tops of the vehicles were soldiers in gunners' turrets, swiveling .50 caliber machine guns.

"Oh shit," Flush said.

"What do you think, Twitch?" June Bug asked.

The strange thing about Twitch was that when he was able to control his blinking, he had notoriously good eyesight. He was like a hawk that way. A tall, gangly hawk with a nervous tic.

"Eleven vehicles."

"How many in each?"

139

Twitch's eyes roamed from one Humvee to the next. "Three, maybe four. But that second to last is a troop carrier. There could be ten in there."

June Bug did the math.

"Anywhere from thirty to fifty then. Give or take."

Forty-some soldiers against the eight of us. Hardly a fair fight.

"Too bad someone didn't get the keys to the Humvees," Dozer said, as though Cat was at fault for not crippling every vehicle in Camp Liberty.

"But we're okay," Flush said. "I mean, even if they did spot us, they couldn't get those vehicles up here, right?"

The long silence that followed was hardly reassuring.

"Maybe their *vehicles* can't get up here," Cat said, "but the Brown Shirts can."

The thought settled over us. A regiment of soldiers tearing up the hill, firing as they came. What would we do? Pelt them with rocks? Fling a few arrows in their direction?

A high-pitched whine accompanied six dirt bikes as they began tearing up the trail. The column of Humvees ground to a halt and out of the lead vehicle stepped Colonel Westbrook in full military camo, a hulking pistol strapped to his waist.

A biker pulled up alongside and removed his helmet and goggles. It was Sergeant Dekker, sunlight glistening off his oily hair. He and the colonel pored over a map on the hood of Westbrook's vehicle.

"Looks like they can't find us," Flush said, a little too hopefully.

"Not yet," Cat said, "but the dirt bikes are probably examining every trail and gully, looking for a way for the vehicles to make it up here."

Our prospects just got worse.

"So what do we do?" Twitch asked. A nervous tic jerked his eye open and closed.

Cat gave a shrug as if the answer was obvious. "We get the hell out of this territory."

He began crawling back to the clearing.

I dared a final look. Colonel Westbrook had a pair of binoculars pressed to his face, and it seemed as though he was staring right at me. I was nearly certain I could see his coal-black eyes through the binocs' thick lenses.

I didn't waste a minute getting back to my horse.

Later that morning, we heard the sound of faraway engines. Generators. We dismounted, tied up our horses, then crawled forward on our bellies. When we reached the edge of the ridge, a wide valley spread out before us. There was a barn, a large vegetable garden, a grove of birch trees . . .

. . . and a camp.

The girls' camp. *Hope's camp.* While it surprised me,

it also made a kind of sense: of course there was a trail connecting the two camps. "Let's go talk to 'em," Flush said.

"How do you suggest we do that?" Dozer asked. "Or maybe you didn't notice that little fence down there."

"We can talk through it."

"Right. And the goons in those guard towers are just gonna let us stroll right up to it. Maybe they'll even throw us some food while they're at it."

"We've gotta make contact somehow. . . ."

"Why? That one chick already told Book Worm where we had to go. What else do we need from 'em?"

He was partially right; she had already given me directions, but maybe that was why I thought we owed it to her—to all of them—to let them know our plans.

"I'm going to go down there," I said.

"Gonna talk to your *girlfriend*?" Dozer mocked.

"I'm going to leave them a note."

"A note. Awww."

"Just to let 'em know where we're headed, that's all."

"Fine. Your funeral."

"I don't think I have a choice."

"Sure you have a choice. Don't do it!" Then he added, "Well, don't expect us to come."

"I'm only telling you what I'm going to do. Nothing more."

I looked to Cat.

142

He sighed. "Fine," he said. "But we're not waiting for you. Catch up on your own."

"I need a couple of guys to go with me."

"You get one."

"I need a couple."

"You get one."

It was obvious there was no changing his mind.

So it was set: that night, under the cover of darkness, Four Fingers and I were going to sneak past the guard towers and the Brown Shirts and their semiautomatic weapons . . . and back into that barn. All because of a girl named Hope.

22.

HOPE LIES ON THE floor, absently fingering her father's locket. The kerosene lanterns have been switched off and the only illumination is a rectangle of moonlight.

She thinks about Book. She hasn't told anyone about his visit, in part because—outside of Faith—she doesn't trust anyone. But also because she doesn't want to share him. It was *her* he visited. And although it's probably crazy to think this way, she allows herself a moment of flattery. That maybe he picked her out of everyone.

And the way he looked at her and touched her hand. It was like he recognized something in her—just as she did in him. Almost like they'd known each other in some past life. Were friends perhaps. Maybe even lovers.

The thought sends a rush of blood to her cheeks, and even as she wonders who he is and where he came from, she traces his name in the dark, the tip of her index finger pressing against the night as though it were his skin, imagining his touch.

Book, she writes. *Book Book Book.*

She gives her head a shake and lets her hand fall.

Who am I kidding? He's either back in his own camp or on his way to the Brown Forest or killed by soldiers. In any case, I'll never see him again. And even if I did, so what? I'm just a bald inmate wearing a prison uniform that reeks of manure. Why would he want anything to do with me?

The thought of it—of where she is and what she looks like now—forms a small lump in the back of her throat.

Live today, tears tomorrow, her mind reminds her, but her heart won't listen. A lone drop of moisture escapes her eye and trickles down her cheek. She gives it an angry swipe.

Stop it! she tells herself, but the tears keep coming, especially when she remembers the compassion in Book's voice, the deep eyes filled with intensity, the firm, reassuring touch of his outstretched hand. And even though she wants to luxuriate in that memory, she won't let herself. It's too painful. Not if she'll never see him again.

She rolls to her side and tries to rock herself to sleep.

The tears have finally stopped when rattling chains jolt her awake. The front doors swing open and four Brown Shirts come marching in—thugs in Republic uniforms interrupting everyone's sleep.

They head straight for Hope and Faith, grab them beneath their arms, and yank them to their feet. Hope kicks and screams every second of the way. Faith is limper than a rag doll, her heels scraping the pine floor as the Brown Shirts drag the two girls from one end of the barracks to the other. The door is locked behind them.

The sights and smells of the infirmary are the same as before: peeling paint, bar-covered windows, the sickly aroma of mold and burning hair. From somewhere down the hall, Hope hears the crunch of a saw tearing through bone followed by a girl's muted screams. Faith hears it, too. Her taut limbs strain against the straps.

"Normally, we like to give Participants time off between visits to the infirmary," Dr. Gallingham says. He busies himself at a small desk. "To clear the blood-stream, as it were, so the experiment is pure."

"Why are we here then?" Hope asks defiantly.

The doctor looks up from his paperwork. "Sometimes behavior dictates otherwise." He dabs his eye.

Hope wrestles with the leather bindings. No give whatsoever.

"Who was that woman?" she asks.

Dr. Gallingham's eyes peer at her under heavy lids. "You honestly don't know?" He gives his head a mournful shake. "It's disturbing how uneducated the youth of today are." Hope realizes he has no intention of answering her question.

"You won't get away with it, you know," she says.

"Won't get away with what?"

"Whatever it is you intend to do to us."

A phlegmy laugh erupts from the back of the doctor's throat. He pushes himself up from the chair and waddles over until his jowly face is peering down at Hope.

"You're so much like your father, you know. Stubborn. Vain. Headstrong."

The blood in Hope's veins runs cold. It's the second time Gallingham has spoken of her father.

"Oh, don't tell me he hasn't mentioned me. I'd be so hurt."

Hope makes no attempt to hide her hatred. "You never knew our father."

"Didn't I?" He reaches over to the rust-spotted tray, picks up a syringe, and holds it to the light. "There was a time when we worked together very closely, he and I."

"That's not true," Hope bursts out. "How dare you even say such a thing!"

"I *dare* because it's true. Why do you think we've been after you all these years?"

Hope's mind scrambles as she tries to remember what her father said about his past. Whenever she and Faith asked, he told them he was a scientist and left it at that. "That was a different time," he'd say. "It's the future I'm interested in now."

Yesterday was yesterday, today is today.

"Oh yes, he did good work, your father. In fact, much of what I do here is based on what I learned from him."

"You lie! He never did these kinds of things to people!"

Dr. Gallingham goes on as though she hasn't spoken.

"He was quite skilled. I've never seen anyone manipulate a scalpel so effectively. Of course, then something happened and he just . . . disappeared." Gallingham pretends as though he can't remember, before slapping his forehead. "I know: his wife gave birth. To *twins*. That's when he went into hiding. What an odd coincidence." He smirks at his own cleverness.

Hope is stunned. She's never heard this before.

"He really didn't tell you about his past?" Gallingham asks. "The famed Butcher of the West? Curious. What some men hide from their children. Tsk-tsk."

Hope is so startled she barely notices when the needle pierces her skin.

"Time to serve the Republic," the doctor announces cheerfully. He goes to Faith and injects her as well. "Sweet dreams," he says, and shuffles out the door.

•   •   •

It's worse than before. Whatever strain of illness they've been given, it leads to the most intense aches and fever Hope has ever experienced. For days she's in a cold sweat, bubbling perspiration. Her body radiates pain. Her throat is so constricted she can barely swallow the most meager sips of water.

Worse still are the nightmares. In one, Hope, Faith, and their father are tearing through thick underbrush when they come to a wide chasm. Far below them lies a river. The only passage across is a flimsy bridge made of frayed ropes. It sways in the wind. Their father goes first. When he reaches the other side, he motions for the girls.

Faith follows, her body rigid with fear.

"Come on!" her father yells. "You can do it."

But the skies turn dark and a gust of wind turns the bridge on its side. Faith topples to the rope floor, the lower half of her body sliding off.

"Help!" she screams. "Save me!"

Hope looks across the chasm for her father, but he's no longer in sight.

"Help!" Faith screams again.

It's up to Hope. She crawls forward, stretches out her hand to grab Faith's wrist, then leans backward and begins to lift. But the wind is strong and the bridge is swaying. Rain is pouring down. Hope's grip is slipping.

"Don't let go," Faith cries.

"I won't," Hope answers, but the more she holds on to Faith, the more she's being dragged off herself. Suddenly, her father is back again, as if he's been there all along. "Let her go, Hope!" he screams. "Let her go!"

"I can't!"

"Let her go!"

And Hope does, she lets Faith go, and Faith plummets through the airy expanse of the gorge, falling forever, her eyes firmly locked on Hope until she disappears into the river with a crushing splash.

Hope wakes with a start. Perspiration soaks her body. *It's just a dream,* she tells herself. *A drug-induced nightmare.*

There was something else, too. On the far side of the chasm, standing alone in the pouring rain, was the Less Than: Book.

His clothes were soaking wet and he looked at her with a pleading expression, hand outstretched. When he opened his mouth to speak, she couldn't hear him through the wind and lashing rain. But she could read his lips.

Come join me, he said. *We'll run away from here.*

And more than anything in the world, Hope wants to.

23.

SITTING UNDER THE UMBRELLA of an enormous pine tree, I stared into the dark, serenaded by a thousand frogs. The steady snores of Four Fingers and Argos filled the night.

Although the possibility of seeing Hope again had buoyed my spirits, there was no mistaking the feeling behind her final words to me: *Don't come back. Not if you want to live.* The message couldn't have been clearer.

I pushed myself up from the ground and left my two sleeping companions. I needed to do this on my own. If someone was going to put their life at risk making contact with Hope, it had to be me.

I *wanted* it to be me.

The night was dark, and as I circled the camp I hid in the black shade of thick trees. The silhouette of a guard tower was etched against the night sky. In front of it stood the barn, where I had first spoken with Hope. I eased forward and slipped into it.

There were animals, of course—goats, cows, some chickens—but no people. Still, I tiptoed across the straw-covered floor and checked every nook and corner. Just to be safe.

I clambered up the ladder, the mingling aroma of hay and dung reminding me of my first visit there. Although I half hoped, half prayed I'd see Hope in the loft, of course she wasn't there. Not in the middle of the night. There were just stacks and stacks of hay bales.

I fished the note from my pocket and reread it for the umpteenth time.

Headed to Brown Forest. See you there?
Book

As I searched for the best place to hide it, a piercing scream sliced the night. It was a girl's scream—terror filled—and it raised the hairs on my arms.

Was I crazy to think the scream might have been Hope?

It came again, even more panic-stricken than before, and it was an unbearable eternity before the night

152

swallowed the last echo of sound.

My hands fumbled for the note . . . and I had a change of heart.

I would stay until the morning. I wanted to see Hope for myself. To make sure she was okay. I'd spend the night, talk with her when she came to the barn, and then sneak away when the guards weren't looking.

If it didn't work out, fine, I'd still leave the slip of paper with its few scrawled words. But if I *did* see her, well, what could be better than that?

Making my way to the far corner where I'd originally hid, I carved a makeshift bed in the narrow space. I lay down and tried to sleep, but it was no use. Not as long as Hope was on one side of the fence and I was on the other.

24.

ONCE AGAIN, DR. GALLINGHAM administers a full dose of medicine to Hope and half a dose to Faith. Even when Faith's fever eventually breaks and her pain ebbs, her ribs press against her skin and her stare is vacant. For Hope, it's like looking at a total stranger.

They're released from the infirmary and the two girls hurry back to Barracks B. Settling in for sleep, Hope clutches the tiny gold locket in her hands. Even in the dark she can feel her parents' stares. She squeezes her eyes shut and prays for dreamless sleep.

Her prayers aren't answered.

The fingers that clamp across Hope's mouth smell of dirt. Her eyes snap open and she struggles for breath. Her hands go up to her assailant's wrist, but stop when she feels the knife blade kissing her neck.

"I wouldn't if I were you," comes the voice.

Hope lies still. Red-haired Athena is crouched over her, stifling Hope's mouth with one hand, holding a knife in the other. Behind her stand four other girls, their silhouettes edged by moonlight.

"Don't make a sound," Athena whispers. "Okay?"

Hope nods. Fear races through her body.

"Get up."

Hope casts her thin blanket aside and stands. Her eyes land on a sleeping Faith. Athena seems to read her mind.

"Just you."

Hope nods in relief. Whatever kind of punishment they have in mind, it's better if they leave Faith out of it. How much more can her sister take?

Athena leads Hope to the back of the barracks. They reach the latrine, but instead of entering, Athena motions to the door on the other side of the hall—one that leads to a closet housing a hot water heater.

"In there," Athena instructs.

To Hope's surprise, there is light in the small closet— coming from the floor. Warm candlelight emanates from behind the rusted water heater. Hope turns sideways until her entire body is in the tiny chamber. That's when she sees a narrow, gaping hole.

"Keep going," Athena says.

155

Hope casts a glance into the burial chamber. *So this is where they imprison girls who don't play along*, she thinks. *Fine. I survived those years in a cave; I can survive this.*

She grips a ladder's rungs and descends into the hole. She lets go once her feet make contact with the hard-packed earth . . .

. . . and can't believe her eyes.

It isn't a dungeon at all, but a long, narrow tunnel, ablaze with candlelight. It's no more than three feet wide, slightly more in height, and the sagging beams that support the archways are broomsticks and branches, even furniture. A table leg here, a desktop there. It's entirely primitive and horribly claustrophobic . . . but it's a tunnel. Right beneath Barracks B.

Athena and the other girls are crouched alongside her.

"Well?" Athena asks.

"It's a tunnel," Hope manages. It would be too much to say the girls smile, but they come as close to it as possible. "This is what you've been keeping a secret?"

"That's right."

"So why . . ."

"We had to know we could trust you." Athena casts a glance at her sister. "Apparently, that's no longer an issue."

Helen blushes.

156

Suddenly, things click in Hope's brain. "So that day behind the barn, Helen wasn't looking through the dirt, she was *depositing* it."

"That's the tricky part. We dig up all this dirt and have to get rid of it without the Brown Shirts noticing. Sometimes in the gardens, sometimes on the infield . . ."

"And sometimes behind the barn," Hope finishes.

Athena nods.

"That's why I couldn't tell you what I was doing," Helen blurts out.

"I understand," Hope says, trying to ease the frail girl's pain. Then she turns back to Athena. "How long've you been working on it?"

"Nearly a year. Scylla here's in charge of the engineering."

Scylla is the silent, muscular stub of a girl who'd pinned Hope's arms behind her back. She nods, her grim expression intact.

"When do you dig?"

"At night," Athena says. "Three-hour shifts."

Hope begins piecing it all together, the metallic sounds she's been hearing. "And the lookouts by the latrine . . ."

"Are to let the diggers know if any Brown Shirts make a sudden appearance."

"How long before it's finished?"

Athena looks to Scylla, who makes a series of hand

157

gestures. Athena translates. "We've dug about a hundred yards, but to be safe, we need to do about twenty more. So maybe another month or two."

Hope thinks of her latest bout with whatever disease she was injected with. She isn't convinced Faith can last another two months—maybe not even two weeks.

"Who knows about this?"

"Just the Sisters of Barracks B. No one else."

"The *Sisters*?"

"That's what we call ourselves. Because that's what we are. Sisters." She gives a glance to the others. They return her look with affection.

"You don't trust anyone else?" Hope asks.

"Not enough to put the entire operation at risk."

Hope remembers the girl in the infirmary, the one with the eye patch. She had it wrong when she said that Barracks B didn't trust each other. They trust each other just fine; it's the rest of Camp Freedom they aren't so sure about.

"So why'd you bring me down here?" Hope asks.

Athena gives the other Sisters a long, hard look. "Because we want to know something." She hesitates. "Are you in?"

Hope studies their faces. "Are you asking me to help you dig your tunnel?"

"That's right."

"After the way you've treated me and my sister?"

158

"Yes."

"After beating me within an inch of my life?"

"Yup."

"How soon can I start?"

Athena actually smiles.

25.

I WOKE WITH A start, my sleep interrupted by a sudden pounding. Lurching to a sitting position, I needed a moment to get my bearings. Hayloft. Camp Freedom. Early morning.

The pounding I'd heard was rain slamming against the barn roof. A spring storm. My heart rate slowed to something resembling normal.

Peeking through the barn's slats, I saw that Camp Freedom was still pretty much asleep. If I hurried, I could forage for food down below. There had to be some carrots or old apples or something I could steal from the livestock.

I shimmied down the ladder and began poking through the animal stalls, examining anything that looked remotely edible. My pockets were nearly full when I heard voices. Male voices. From inside the barn. I pressed myself behind a large cow and prayed for invisibility. I could've kicked myself for not staying hidden in the safety of the hay bales.

". . . resolution to the question of the Less Thans," one of the voices said.

"Who says we need one?" the other responded.

"The Eagle's Nest."

"The chancellor?"

"Who else?"

There was an urgency to the conversation that grabbed my attention—that made me want to hear their words more clearly.

The stall planks were old and rotting and it was easy enough to find a knothole to peek through. There stood two men, facing the barn entrance, their backs to me. One was heavyset and wore a black suit. He dabbed a soiled hanky at the corners of his eyes. The other wore a soldier's uniform and, judging by the stripes on his sleeve, was a colonel. Possibly the camp overseer— Camp Freedom's version of Colonel Westbrook. In his hand, hanging limply by his side, was what appeared to be a letter.

"When did you get this?" the heavyset man asked.

"Just today."

"And you mean to follow it?"

"What choice do we have?"

The rain started coming down harder—in sheets—pounding the tin roof and making it impossible to hear. I realized if I wanted to hear more, I'd have to get closer. A wildly stupid idea.

I inched forward.

I whipped around the planking and eased into the next stall. And then the one after that. With each move I half expected to spy a guard with a semiautomatic.

". . . letter saying what I think it's saying?" the heavy man asked, dabbing his eye.

"No trace."

"Of what?"

"Everything. And everyone."

"But my research—Dr. Samadi's research . . ."

"Still needs to be completed."

The heavy man sighed. "And the girls?"

"Same as the Less Thans. Eliminated. Up to us, of course, as to how, but the important thing is we're thorough."

"Leave no trace?"

"Leave no trace."

The rain let up as quickly as it began, leaving in its wake gurgling gutters and dripping eaves.

"We can talk more about this in my office," the overseer said, and their footsteps splashed through the mud as they exited the barn.

For the longest time I remained pressed against the stall, my knees wobbly. A million questions raced through my mind. Who was this chancellor they were talking about? Why were they looking for a "resolution to the question of the Less Thans"?

And worst of all: did "eliminated" really mean what I thought it meant?

I edged my way to the barn door and stared at the camp. Just past the barbed wire fence glinting with rain, scores of female prisoners shuffled through the mud. They had absolutely no idea what was in store for them.

And I was the only one who did. Leaving a note was no longer enough. Hope had to know about this conversation. I had to tell her in person.

What I was thinking was crazy—downright suicidal. I was going to break into a prison camp. Not *out of*, but *into*.

Had I suddenly lost my mind?

26.

HOPE FEELS A HAND on her shoulder, and in the drowsiness of dreams she imagines it's the hand of Book. He has come to wake her, to jostle her from sleep, to join her even. Her body quivers at the thought.

But when she opens her eyes, it's Scylla she sees. Grim Scylla. Gesturing that it's time for her shift. Hope nods gruffly and sits up.

On the cot next to her, Faith sleeps soundly. Hope doesn't bother to wake her. Maybe it's the shock at how thin her sister has gotten—her arms aren't much thicker than twigs and her eyes have sunken into her face.

In any case, *Let her sleep*, Hope thinks, tucking the blanket beneath Faith's chin.

She tiptoes through the maze of sleeping girls, her

footsteps drowned out by pounding rain.

"All quiet?" Hope asks Helen, who stands watch.

Helen doesn't say a word; she just gives a tight-lipped smile and drops her eyes. Scylla, too, seems in a bigger hurry than usual.

What's going on? Hope wonders. She can't understand it.

She steps into the closet and descends into the tunnel. The rumble of the thunderstorm is replaced with the clinking of digging. Other sounds too. The *whoosh* of arrows rushing down the length of the tunnel. The Sisters have constructed a number of primitive crossbows and practice when they can. They're not half bad.

But when Hope steps onto the tunnel floor, everything comes to a dead stop.

"What's happening?" she asks.

Red-haired Athena steps forward, her face rigid. "This. This is what's happening," she says, her eyes motioning behind her.

There sits the Less Than named Book, his hands tied behind his back.

Hope's heart gives a lurch. On the one hand, she's happy to see him—she hasn't stopped thinking about him since the day they met. Her dream was proof of that. But at the same time, she can't figure it out. Why is he here? Why is he *tied up*?

"We found him snooping behind the mess hall,"

Athena says. "Said he needed to speak to you."

Hope feels the blood rushing up her neck. Athena goes on.

"Thank God we're the ones who found him and not the Brown Shirts." Athena's eyes narrow. "You know him?"

"I met him once, yeah."

"And you talked to him?"

"That's right."

"Where?"

"In the barn."

"And you didn't tell us?"

Hope tries to give a casual shrug, realizing her fellow Sisters are eyeing her with outright suspicion. Here she's finally worked her way into their good graces and now Book has made a mess of it.

"What's to tell?" Hope says. "He wanted to know how to get out of the territory and I told him."

Athena runs her hand impatiently through her hair. "And you didn't think that was worth sharing?"

"You weren't speaking to me, remember?"

"But later? When we showed you the tunnel?"

"Guess I forgot to mention it."

"Yeah, I guess you did."

Athena stares at Hope. Hope stares back. Finally, the red-haired leader turns to Book. "How'd you get in?"

"There's a small opening," he says. "In the fence. I

noticed it the first time I was here."

"Why'd you come back?"

"I was going to leave a note for Hope."

"A note, huh?"

"Check my pocket if you don't believe me."

Athena nods to Scylla and the muscular girl fishes a slip of paper out of his front pocket. She hands it to Athena, who reads it aloud.

"'Headed to Brown Forest. See you there? Book.'"

All eyes turn to Hope. She tries to will away the flush creeping up her face.

"So you and Hope are pretty chummy," Athena says. Book doesn't respond. "Are you alone?"

"There're eight of us. We escaped from Camp Liberty."

The tunnel goes suddenly silent. All they can hear is the steady *drip drip* of water from the ceiling.

"Where are they now?"

"On their way to the next territory. I'm going to catch up with them."

Athena waves the note in his face. "And this? Why didn't you just leave it in the barn?"

"I was going to. . . ."

"But?"

"I overheard something—a conversation. I needed to tell Hope."

"Okay—here she is. Tell her."

"Alone."

167

Athena's jaw goes rigid. "You tell it to everyone or you tell it to no one."

Book gives an appealing look to Hope, but Hope just looks away. If he's hoping she'll stand up for him, she can't do it. Not under these circumstances. Not with her Sisters already thinking she's some kind of traitor.

Book begins to speak, telling them everything he heard. By the time he finishes, the Sisters' mouths are open, their eyes wide. Hope, in particular, feels like she's seen a ghost. The mention of her father has drained the blood right down to her feet.

"Did Colonel Thorason say when this *elimination* would begin?" Athena asks.

Book shakes his head. "But I got the feeling it'll be soon."

"So what do we do?" the one named Diana asks.

Athena hesitates only briefly. "Same thing as before," she answers. "Finish this tunnel and get the hell out of here."

"And him?"

"He's going to help us dig." She removes a knife, cuts through the cords that bind his hands, and yanks him to his feet. Then she turns to Hope. "He's your responsibility. Don't let him out of your sight."

"Come on," Hope says, crawling on hands and knees down the tunnel. Book follows. Dirt and water rain down from the ceiling. By the time they reach the far end, their backs and necks are covered with brown muck.

Still, that doesn't come close to the swirling mess inside her head. *Book's come back*. He wanted to talk to her. Ever since they first met and spoke—and *touched*—she's been praying a day like this could happen.

So why isn't she happy?

In part because he's put them in danger—*all of them*—and now her fellow Sisters regard her with a deeper suspicion than before. There's something else, too. Something she can't quite figure out.

She picks up two rusty butter knives and hands one to him.

"Here," she says, not meeting his eyes.

She adjusts the lantern and begins to dig, the dull edge of her knife biting into the wall. It's as much rock as it is dirt, and it takes a dozen sharp jabs to release anything of substance. Pebbles tumble to the ground.

She stops abruptly and turns to him.

"What're you doing here?" she snaps.

Book's expression is one of surprise. "I told you: I came to leave you that note. And then to tell you about the conversation."

"Who says we need to be told anything?"

"I thought it was important."

"You could've gotten caught."

169

"I didn't."

"But you *could've*. And then we would've had Brown Shirts crawling all over this place and they'd find this tunnel and all this work would've been for nothing and there'd be no way we could get out."

"Okay. I'm sorry."

"It's a little late."

Hope returns to her digging. A thin sheen of sweat paints her arms. Neither of them speaks.

It's Book who breaks the silence. "Stubborn much?"

Hope stops and wheels around. "What?"

"I tried to do you a favor. Breaking into your camp was a dangerous thing and I didn't have to do it, but I thought you'd want to know what I heard."

"You don't have to act like you're a hero or something."

"I'm not. I'm just saying I was trying to help you out."

"Maybe I don't need your help."

"You're right, maybe you don't. I just didn't think you'd bite my head off." He jabs his knife into the wall.

Hope digs harder than before. Rocks and pebbles arc through the air. She's damned if she is going to apologize. What did she do wrong? Why should she have to say she's sorry? *He's* the one who put them in danger.

This is not how she envisioned their reunion. Not at all. But what did she expect? Book lifting her in the air and twirling her like some fairy-tale princess? She gives her head an angry shake at the thought of it.

"Why are you so mad at me?" Book asks.

"Who says I'm mad?"

"You seem mad."

"I'm not mad." She stabs the knife into the dirt.

They work in silence.

"Tell me again about Dr. Samadi," she says at last.

"The heavyset man—"

"That was Dr. Gallingham."

"—asked about his research."

"Okay."

"And then he mentioned Dr. Samadi, like their research was one and the same."

"And then?"

"The colonel said it needed to be completed. That was the only time the doctor's name was mentioned."

Hope is quiet. What she can't understand—or doesn't *want* to understand—is why her father would have worked with Dr. Gallingham. Could he really have been the so-called Butcher of the West? It makes no sense.

She chips at the dirt wall. For the first time she's aware that just inches away is Book. She can sense the heat rising from his body, smell the same masculine scents as before.

She wonders about him: what his history is, who his parents were. She knows absolutely nothing—other than he's a Less Than and wants to escape to the next territory. All she knows for sure is the few words they've exchanged . . . and how he first looked at her.

His arm accidentally brushes hers and it sends an involuntary shiver down her spine. She forces herself to inch away. She's still angry at him—although at this particular moment she can't remember why.

She is midstrike when the earth shifts. Dirt funnels from the ceiling. Everyone up and down the tunnel stops what they're doing, placing their hands against the walls as if that will keep them from caving in.

When the last of the dirt has sifted to the ground, everyone breathes a sigh of relief. The tunnel is a short-term deal at best, constructed to get them from inside the camp out. Once they're on the other side of the fence, it can collapse for all Hope cares. But only after they've all escaped.

"That happen often?" Book asks.

"When it rains," Hope says.

Everyone returns to work. The *clink* and *ting* of tools echoes off the narrow walls.

Once more, Book's arm brushes Hope and this time she doesn't edge away. She lets it linger there.

She is just about to ask Book about Camp Liberty when the earth shifts again. This time the sound accompanying it is thunderous. Primal. Overwhelming. Screeching and ripping as the earth separates from itself.

The walls vibrate and sway and Hope is bounced to

172

the ground like a rubber ball. One moment there's a ceiling and the next it's cascading to the floor, sending an enormous gust of stale wind racing down the tunnel, extinguishing the lanterns. Book falls on top of Hope as the world collapses around them—two bodies pinned beneath debris and dirt.

They wait for the earth to settle.

When they finally raise their heads, the tunnel is cloaked in the blackest black either has ever experienced. There's not a hint of light. Not a whisper of sound. The earth has caved in all around them.

27.

"YOU OKAY?" I ASKED, when the last trickle of dirt sifted from the ceiling.

"I think so," Hope answered. Her voice was as shaky as mine.

"Sorry I jumped on top of you. . . ."

"That's okay. . . ."

"I was just trying to—"

"I'm glad you did."

Our breathing was heavy and fast and a little panicky.

"Give me your hand," I said. Our two hands flailed in the dark until they stumbled into each other. Our fingers intertwined, like outstretched vines, and we gripped each other hard, a kind of reminder we were both alive.

"Can you move?" I asked.

"I think so."

"Here."

I helped her to her hands and knees and we sat there for a moment, in the dark, breathing the other's exhalations.

"Well," she said.

Suddenly self-conscious, we pulled our hands apart and brushed away the dirt from our clothes. Like getting clean was a first priority.

"Let's get out of here," I said. Even though it was pitch-black, I could sense her nod.

We crawled back toward the entrance, picking our way over piles of debris and mounds of dirt. In the far distance, we heard screams. I wondered why they weren't louder. Why they were so muted.

I extended a hand, sensing where there was air and where there was wall. At first it worked, guiding us down the tunnel, but then my fingers led me astray. A side wall was to our right and another was to our left . . .

. . . and another was right in front of us. I didn't get it. And then it hit me.

"What?" Hope asked.

"This."

The cave-in had created a barrier at the very midpoint of the tunnel. We could go no farther. Both our hands began slapping the mound of dirt, searching for a hole, a space—some small passageway.

But there was no passageway. And the screams were muted because they were coming from the other side.

"Hey!" Hope cried at the top of her lungs, the voice bouncing back at us. "Can anyone hear me?"

"Is anyone there?" I yelled.

Echo. Then silence.

"Hey!" she hollered again, more desperately this time.

Still no response.

We were trapped in the far end of the tunnel—just Hope and me—and the blackness surrounding us was utter and complete. I tried to will away the panic. *Breathe*, I told myself. *Don't make things worse. Just breathe.*

I could feel my heart thumping against my chest. I wondered how thick the cave-in was. Five feet? Twenty? The answer could very well be the difference between life and death. But then again, the other Sisters were probably digging from the other side at that very moment. Right?

Right?

Hope began clawing at the mound. But this wasn't fine soil; it was rock and thick clay and small boulders. Earth itself.

"It was insane to think we could do this," she

mumbled under her breath. "Cave-ins and Brown Shirts and not enough time."

"It's okay," I said.

"No, it's not okay. It was stupid. *Stupid stupid stupid.*"

"We'll get out of here."

"No we won't. He told us to separate but I didn't want to and then he died and everything changed. . . ."

I didn't know what she was talking about but I let her go on.

". . . and then Faith left and by the time I caught up with her the Brown Shirts surrounded us and brought us here and started doing their experiments."

Although I couldn't make sense of her words, I heard her breath catch. A moment later the tears began.

"Poor Faith," she said. "She can't make it on her own."

Something about her tone made me reach for her. I found her in the dark and tried to put my arms around her, but she pushed me away.

"She needs me," she said, thrashing at the mound of earth.

Again I tried to hug her, to hold her; again she threw my arms away.

"It's so unfair!" she cried. "I want to live!"

"It's okay," I said.

"*I want to live!*"

She was ripping at the cave-in, throwing herself into

177

it like a person possessed, like a desperate dog digging at a hole. Then, slowly, she began singing aloud—some hymn I didn't recognize.

> *"Come, Thou Fount of every blessing,*
> *Tune my heart to sing Thy grace."*

I hugged her from behind and this time she didn't resist. My arms wrapped around her and my chest pressed against her back and I didn't let her push me away.

"We're okay," I whispered, my lips brushing her ear. "We're going to be okay."

"But Faith . . ."

"Shh," I said.

"And Mom. And Dad."

"Shh, Hope. Shhhhhhhh."

"What'll she do?"

"Shhhhhhhhhhh."

Her body grew limp until it melted into mine and I was supporting all her weight. It was so still I could hear the beating of my heart, and then hers. I couldn't tell whose beating was whose, or if they'd locked into each other's rhythm. Holding her there, I remembered that first time we met. The way the sunlight outlined the back of her head and neck. Her probing stare.

The look of pain in her eyes.

"We're going to be okay," I whispered, but even as I said it, the air was growing stale, sour, suffocating.

She sang more of her hymn. "'Streams of mercy . . . never ceasing.'"

She was gulping breath like a fish out of water, and I felt the full weight of her sink into me. I lowered her—*us*—to the ground, until we were huddled there, spooning in the dirt, my body pressed into her as if we'd been soldered together, lying on the damp earth.

"'Call for songs . . . of loudest praise.'"

A moment later she blacked out.

She lay there minutes or hours; I don't know. I never let her go. I dozed some, too—my face touching hers. Her breath was slow and steady and I could feel her chest beneath my forearms, rising and falling.

She woke with a start and struggled to sit up.

"What? Where am—"

"It's okay," I said. "Shh."

"Where are—"

"We're in the tunnel. It's okay."

Her body shifted away from me and even in the dark I could imagine first her panic, then her face registering the reality of our situation. Not just being stuck in this blackened tunnel but the fact I'd been holding her, my hands resting on her belly. Two bodies clutched against each other.

"Guess I passed out," she said apologetically.

"For a bit."

"Was I snoring?"

"Nope."

"Promise?"

"Promise. You drooled some, but you didn't snore."

"What?!"

"Just a little bit. Down your chin."

"No . . ."

"And onto my arm."

"I didn't."

"And my chest."

"I did not."

"You're right. You didn't."

She slapped me hard on the shoulder, and neither of us spoke. Maybe I'm wrong, but I could swear she was smiling. It was too dark to know for sure.

I heard her open her mouth, but she hesitated before speaking. "Thanks for . . ." She didn't finish the sentence. She didn't need to.

"Don't mention it," I said.

More silence. We were serenaded by a steady *drip* of water.

"Is anyone digging?" she asked.

"Not that I can hear."

"Do you think they've given up?"

"I don't know. You know them better than I do."

180

She didn't respond. "I'm so thirsty," she finally said.

I was too. It wasn't just the lack of water, but all the dirt in the air. Every breath tasted of grit and sand.

I placed a hand on the ceiling, slapping at the dirt.

"What're you doing?" she asked.

"Feeling for dampness. If I can locate that drip . . ."

My fingers flayed against the walls and ceiling until they fell on a root as thick as a rope. I gave it a tug and the dripping increased. I yanked again and even more water came down: a steady trickle off a ceiling panel. It was like I'd found a faucet.

"Here," I said.

In pure darkness, I reached for Hope and brought her forward, positioning her face beneath the mini-waterfall. She drank and drank, and when she'd had enough, her fingers gripped my arm.

"Your turn," she said.

I leaned forward and the water splashed against my nose and chin and eventually I got my mouth under it. It was gritty and bitter and thick with sludge . . . but water never tasted better. I drank until my stomach bulged.

"So what do we do?" Hope asked.

I shrugged. "Keep digging."

"Is there enough air?"

"I'm more worried about the drool."

She slapped me again, and this time I was the one

181

who smiled, but her question was real. And I honestly didn't know the answer.

I found our knives. "Put out your hand," I said.

She did, and I placed the tool in her palm. Even though we were cold and shaking and covered in dirt, I still felt a spark of something between us as our fingers touched. Skin against skin. I wondered if Hope felt it too. We pulled our hands away and began chipping at the earth.

We dug and dug, stopping only to catch our breath or get a drink of water. Although I had the urge to talk to her, to find out all about her, it felt suddenly strange. Awkward, even. Like my holding her had created an odd kind of tension between us.

We worked in silence.

Still, whenever our arms accidentally rubbed against each other, I felt a tingling shock. If our lives hadn't been at stake, I could've stayed there for eternity: alone with Hope, in the dark, as we worked as one.

She suddenly stopped.

"What's this?" she asked.

"What's what?"

"The floor."

I didn't know what she was talking about so I went to pat the ground. It wasn't the sound of hard-packed earth; it was splashing. It was all mud and slime . . . and a good two inches of water.

"What's going on?" I said aloud.

But I knew the answer as soon as I asked the question. A steady stream of rainwater was flowing into the tunnel. It was no longer a single drip but a dozen drips. A *hundred*.

And it wasn't the lack of oxygen that was going to kill us; it was drowning.

We attacked the mound with a sudden urgency, striking it with the dull knives and flinging the dirt behind us. Blisters on my palm erupted until the knife handle was slick with blood. Our breathing was fast and heavy.

In no time the water reached our waists, turning our world into a pit of mud. My muscles began to tighten, cramp, spasm. I wondered if Hope was feeling the same. Was it my imagination or were we slowing down? Giving up? I needed to do something to revive us.

"Tell me about yourself," I said.

"Huh?"

"Tell me about yourself. I want to hear everything."

"Now?"

"Of course now. What else are we doing?" There was more to it, of course. If this was it for us—our final living moments—I wanted to know who she was, who would go with me to the grave. And I had to distract us. "Like where'd you learn to sing?"

"My mom. She taught us hymns."

"And your dad?"

"A scientist. He did the hunting, chopped the wood, that kind of thing."

"Favorite memory?"

"Huh?"

"What was your favorite memory?"

"Are you sure you really—"

"Just tell me."

We continued to fling thick shards of earth away from the cave-in. The more focus I put on Hope, the less I thought about my bloody hands and the rising water and the stifling air.

"Autumn evenings," she said, panting, her sentences choppy from exertion. "Sitting around the fire. My mom playing piano. Dad telling stories. Faith playing with her dolls." She stopped talking.

"What?" I asked. She didn't respond. "What is it?" I asked again.

"Then the soldiers came," she whispered.

Her tone changed, and it was suddenly dark, sinister, joyless.

And she began digging harder. It was like whatever shift happened in her head caused her to find some extra reserve of strength. She thrust at the earthen mound with a newfound energy. As if the dirt itself was memory and her knife some magic force that would make it go away.

The water was chest level now, nearly to our necks.

184

It was all we could do to keep digging. *To keep breathing.* We both inched up toward the ceiling—to the last pockets of air.

Our breaths were rapid and shallow, in unison.

"Tell me about the soldiers," I said.

Her digging increased. Once more she was attacking the cave-in with a kind of ferociousness: slicing, slapping, tearing at the dirt and mud, ripping away large rocks.

And was that a shard of light poking through the top of the mound?

"Tell me about the soldiers," I said, more forcefully than before. The water was rising and our faces were angled upward and if we didn't do this now—at this very moment—there would be no second chance.

Hope clawed at the barrier with a sudden intensity, like some out-of-control beast, even as she shouted *"No"* over and over.

Suddenly there was a thrashing on the water's surface. Four hands, haloed by light, emerged from a narrow opening at the very top of the cave-in mound.

"Come on!" a voice cried out.

We blinked, adjusting to the sudden illumination, and for the longest time we just stared at the outstretched fingers, trying to make sense of them.

"Grab our hands!" the voice cried again.

Dumbly, as if commanded by some otherworldly

presence, we raised our arms and grabbed the hands, fingers interlocking, only to be pulled forward by Scylla and Athena, yanked through to the other side of the tunnel—a side with flickering candlelight, where the water was only a foot or so deep.

"Let's get out of here!" Athena shouted, and we all rushed to the tunnel ladder as water began pouring in behind us.

28.

"YOU WANT TO DO *what*?" Faith asks.

"Switch jobs," Hope says. "Just for tonight."

"Why would you want to do that?"

The answer's simple. By taking her sister's place on the cleaning crew, Hope can get access to Thorason's office in the Administration Building. But the less Faith knows about all this, the better.

"Is it because of him?" Faith asks. She points to Book, who stands alone in the corner.

Hope's eyes dart in his direction. Since they escaped the cave-in they've yet to really speak to each other. The things they said—the way they touched—felt natural. Felt *right*. But now, in the light of day, she's not so sure. The only thing they've agreed on is the need to find out what Gallingham and Thorason were talking about. And Hope has to know one last thing: how her father fits into all of this.

"I hurt my shoulder in the cave-in," Hope lies. "I need a break from the barn."

"But I can't take over for you there," Faith says.

"You don't have to. I got Scylla to cover."

"So why are you—"

"I thought you could use a night off."

Hope can tell Faith likes the idea. She's growing weaker by the day, dark circles paint the undersides of her eyes, and even though Hope is smuggling much of her own food to her sister, it seems to be doing little good.

"What if the guards realize you're not me?" Faith asks.

"They're not going to. I'll walk like you, talk like you, I'll even wear Mom's pink shawl. They'll never know the difference. And look."

She rolls up her sleeve. Their tattoos are only one number off—738 for Faith, 739 for Hope—and Hope has taken a bit of coal and altered her 9 to an 8.

"Are you sure?" Faith asks.

"Positive. And wouldn't you rather rest than work?"

So that night Hope joins the three other cleaning girls trudging across the parade ground.

The Admin Building is short and squat and made

of cinder block, and there is nothing about its frumpy appearance that suggests it houses the offices of the camp leaders. But it's where Hope is convinced she'll find out what Thorason is up to . . . and her father's connection to Dr. Gallingham.

Two guards stand waiting at the entrance. The first Sister in line is a girl named Iris with spiky black hair. She tugs up her sleeve and flashes her tattoo. The lummox of a guard—no older than nineteen who reeks of BO—glances at the number and makes a checkmark on his clipboard. Iris passes. The second girl steps forward; the guard glances, checks, and nods. Hope's heart is pounding as she moves up in line. To hide her trembling fingers, she clutches the sleeve's edge with a tight fist.

The guard takes in her number, staring at it longer than he did the others. Hope's heart rises in her throat, and when the guard's gaze drifts up to her face, she drops her eyes. A moment later she hears the pencil scratch of a checkmark and she passes by, cold sweat bathing the back of her neck. The guards shut the door behind them. No turning back now.

Iris goes to the supply closet and brings out cleaning supplies. Hope pretends to accept the materials with weary resignation.

But the fact is, Hope has never been inside this building before. So while she tries to give the impression she's done this a thousand times, her eyes probe the narrow hallways, attempting to figure out which one is Colonel Thorason's office.

A kick to her shin sends an excruciating pain up her leg.

"Pay attention," a guard snaps. He is tall with a jutting chin—the same guard who tattooed her number on her arm.

Hope realizes Iris is holding out a bucket, waiting for Hope to take it. Red-faced, Hope grabs the bucket and moves to the side.

Concentrate, she tells herself. *Pay attention*.

The girls begin marching off to their stations, but when Hope turns to go, a voice stops her.

"Not so fast," Jutting Chin says. He strolls closer, boots clicking on linoleum. "Aren't you forgetting something?"

Hope's mind scrambles.

"You planning on using water or don't you believe in it?"

The guard laughs and Lummox joins in.

"Right," Hope mutters under her breath and shuffles back to the supply closet, placing the bucket under the spigot.

"Not the sharpest knife in the drawer," Jutting Chin says, guffawing.

"All foam, no beer," Lummox replies. Both guards

190

are having a laugh fest.

Hope says nothing. She turns off the faucet and carries the sloshing bucket. She can't get away fast enough.

From what she's been told, Thorason's office is down this first hallway. Once she gets away from these two goons she can slip inside.

"One more thing," the guard calls out. "The overseer's office is off-limits tonight. Don't bother to clean it."

Hope's heart sinks. She has managed to gain entry into the camp headquarters only to be told there's no access to the very place she wants to see.

She tries to hide her despair, even as she passes a nameplate on a door that identifies the overseer's office. She doesn't stop until she reaches the end of the hallway, where she makes a show of mopping. The guards are still in sight, but they've ceased to watch her. A game of cards has stolen their attention.

She leans the mop against the corner and flicks out a dust rag. Stepping into the open office bordering Thorason's—someone named Major Hart—she lights a lantern, aware of the rectangle of light that lands in the hallway.

Returning to the bucket in the hallway, she noisily dips the rag in the water, wrings it out, and reenters Major Hart's office.

After her fourth visit to the bucket, she approaches

Colonel Thorason's office instead, placing her sweaty palm on the brass doorknob. To her relief, it's not locked. She quickly steps inside, pressing the door shut behind her.

Hope waits for her eyes to adjust to the gloom. A shaft of moonlight creeps past the window's blinds, tinting the floor a blackish blue. She goes to the window and slides it open. Book pops his head up from outside.

"Good?" he asks.

"Hurry," she says.

He slides into the room and she pulls the blinds shut. It's just the two of them in the dark room. Hope remembers the tunnel—how Book held her. Even as her body tingles with the memory, she tries to shake it away. Now is not the time.

On a far table stands a half-melted candle in a pewter candlestick. A box of matches rests nearby. Book picks out a match and prepares to strike it. Hope stops him at the last moment.

"Wait," she whispers, and points to the door.

Its bottom edge is a good inch above the floor. If they light the candle, yellow light will seep beneath the crack: a dead giveaway someone's inside.

"So what do we do?" he asks.

She shrugs, pulling the shawl tight around her shoulders.

And there lies the answer.

She lays the shawl on the floor and rolls it up tight as though sculpting a snake from clay. Trembling fingers jam the coil beneath the door, and she lights the candle, its flickering glow scattering moonlight.

Thank you, Faith. Thank you, Mom.

They start with the desk. There are dozens of files in the drawers, but just purchase orders, budget plans, and government-issued books. *Building a Strong Republic. What You Can Do For Your Territory. Action Steps to a Better Tomorrow.*

"Anything?" he asks.

"Not even close."

She retrieves the candle and makes her way to a file cabinet, her fingers skipping atop a thick nest of folders. All old correspondence, but nothing explaining the conversation . . . nothing about her father.

When Book joins her, they move to the next drawer. If someone comes in now, there is no disguising the fact that they're up to something. A lit candle. An open file cabinet. A shawl stuffed under the door. Not to mention the fact that there's a Less Than in Camp Freedom. They'd be as good as dead.

Hope's hands push the bottom drawer closed and she sits leaning against the cabinet, legs splayed, consumed by frustration.

"There's nothing here," she says.

Book sits across from her. "Maybe we already know enough."

Hope grunts but says nothing. She has yet to tell Book about her father's possible involvement. And why should she? Even if her father did collaborate with Dr. Gallingham in some distant past, she has no reason to believe he ever worked here in Camp Freedom. So why would there be a file on him? And why should she tell Book?

She pushes herself up from the floor and goes to the desk, collapsing in the chair. Her hands cradle her chin. Who was she kidding? What did she really expect to find?

"What do you want to do?" Book asks. "Keep looking?"

Hope gives her head a shake. "There's no point. There's no *time*." Her eyes dart up to his. "You better get going. I'll meet you back at the barracks."

When Book makes a move to the window, she rises from the chair. As she does, the sweat from her elbows lifts the leather blotter a fraction of an inch.

Just enough to reveal a corner of a piece of paper.

"Wait," Hope says. She lifts the blotter and pries the paper free. It's a letter, folded in three. As though picking up a wounded butterfly, her fingers pinch one corner and unfold it. Book rushes to her side and looks over Hope's shoulder. Their gaze is drawn to the signature at the bottom.

Their eyes race across the words.

. . . no choice but to perform extreme and necessary measures . . . ensure the safety of our territory . . . finish the research begun by Dr. Uzair Samadi.

Hope has stopped breathing. Her one hand holds the letter; the other covers her mouth as though stifling a silent scream. It can't be true. It *can't* be. Her father really was involved with all of this? But how? And *why*?

"What?" Book asks.

"Nothing," Hope lies. "I mean, I just can't believe what it's saying."

A still bigger surprise is in the letter's final paragraph. Sentences they have to read multiple times to make sure they're reading them correctly. Words that take their breath away . . . and convince them they can't stay at Camp Freedom a moment longer.

A nervous, clammy heat rises from Hope's body and her heart beats so loudly she hears the thudding in her temples. Which is why she doesn't hear the footsteps in the hallway, just outside the door.

29.

"HOPE," I SAID, AND pointed to the door.

She heard them, too: the heavy tread of footsteps.

"Brown Shirts," she said, more to herself than me. Then she whispered fiercely, "Go."

"No. I'm staying here with—"

"If they find you, they'll kill you. They can't hurt me." The footsteps became louder. "Hurry!"

There was no talking her out of it. "So where do we meet?" I asked.

Something passed across her face—something I couldn't read. "We don't."

I reached out a hand but she wouldn't take it.

"*Go,*" she said again.

Everything was happening too fast. The footsteps

were nearly to the door and Hope wouldn't take my hand. I didn't want to leave but I had no choice, so I launched myself through the open window, landing hard on the ground outside. Even as I pushed myself to a standing position and started to run, I saw how much distance I had to cover. The opening in the fence was a good fifty yards away. Not close, but I could make it if I hurried.

As I ran, I thought of the expression on Hope's face. What did she mean when she said *We don't*?

The searchlights flicked on with a bass-like *whoompf*. A moment later a siren blared. Gunshots peppered the ground but I was through the fence before they got me. I tore back to the barn. Four Fingers and Argos were there, waiting.

"What's going on?" he said.

"Long story. Come on, quick!"

The three of us took off for the cover of the trees. Behind us we heard the scraping groan of the metal gate. Then the growl of soldiers' vehicles.

The ground was covered in soggy leaves and twice I fell. It didn't help that we were running up a hill in pitch black. On pure mud. It was like one of those dreams where a killer's coming and you're stuck in slow motion. He's getting closer and closer and there's absolutely nothing you can do about it.

We heard a Humvee emerge from the trees and threw

ourselves to the ground, our breath ballooning in front of us. But while Argos and I were able to tuck ourselves behind a boulder, Four Fingers wasn't so lucky. Two jostling beams of light landed right on him.

The Humvee skidded to a stop and out jumped two soldiers. One of the Brown Shirts took the butt of his rifle and smashed it against Four's cheek. Blood and teeth rainbowed through the air, and Four crumpled to the ground.

I fired off a pebble from my slingshot. The projectile missiled through the air, hitting the heavier of the two soldiers just below the eye. He cried out and dropped to the ground, hands covering his face.

The other Brown Shirt, a wiry guy with a severe military crew cut, swung his rifle in my direction and let loose a volley of bullets. They ricocheted off granite. I cowered and pulled Argos into me behind the boulder.

I was loading up my slingshot again when Crew Cut yanked Four to his feet. Blood squirted through a gash on the side of his face. He seemed woozy and limp. The Brown Shirt lifted his rifle and placed the barrel against Four's temple.

"You come out now," he shouted, "or your friend here gets it."

I stared through the Y of my weapon. I could still fire. I could release the elastic and hope my rock would down the Brown Shirt before he had a chance to pull the trigger. I could give it a try.

But one look at Four's cringing face told me how improbable that was.

I lowered my slingshot, pushed myself to a standing position, and began marching to my surrender. I refused to be the cause of another LT's death.

As I eased my way down the slippery hill, another thought hit me: barring some miracle, Hope was completely on her own. There was no way I'd be coming back now.

30.

IT'S TOO LATE WHEN Hope sees the round figure of Dr. Gallingham filling the doorway. Guttering candlelight flickers on his piggish face. She fumbles with the letter, sliding it back beneath the blotter.

"It's always nice to see the girls taking initiative and cleaning rooms that don't need cleaning," Dr. Gallingham says in a snide voice. He wipes his eyes, moisture racing up his handkerchief. He takes in the open window, the swinging blinds.

"I don't suppose someone was here with you?"

Hope doesn't respond. Fear slackens her muscles.

"Okay. Then maybe you'll tell me what you were looking at."

Again, she doesn't respond. She's half afraid she's

200

going to empty her bladder right there in Colonel Thorason's chair.

Dr. Gallingham sighs and waddles forward. His sausage fingers pry beneath the blotter for the letter and he examines its contents.

"Ah, this," he says, as much to himself as Hope.

He returns the letter to its hiding place, studying Hope with rheumy eyes.

"Which aspect of this interests you?" he asks. "The part about your father? Or the final paragraph?"

Hope doesn't speak.

"Or do you think there's something you can do about it?"

When Hope remains silent, Dr. Gallingham lets out a long breath and rests a plump hand on Hope's shoulder. She stiffens.

"Not talking, huh? Well, I'm afraid there's nothing to be done about that letter. Our work here is finished. Or nearly so."

Heavy footsteps sound in the hall, stopping only when Jutting Chin and Lummox swing themselves into the room, M16s held alert.

"No need for all that," Dr. Gallingham says in a soothing tone, motioning for the Brown Shirts to lower their weapons.

"We told her not to come in here," Lummox pants, badly out of breath.

"I'm sure you did. But this one, well, she's rather simple." He winks a watery eye in their direction.

"That don't excuse her from disobeying an order."

"Agreed, and I'll see to it she's reprimanded."

"No disrespect, Doc, but we're under strict orders to report all infractions directly to the colonel."

For Hope, the silence that follows is nearly unbearable.

"Take a look around," Dr. Gallingham says. "Does anything look disturbed?"

The two guards sweep the room with their eyes. "No," Lummox concedes.

"Well then?"

Hope can't believe it. Dr. Gallingham has lied on her behalf. Has saved her from certain punishment.

"We still gotta report it."

"It's up to you, of course," Gallingham says, "but as we know, the girl is somewhat simple. It's possible she didn't understand your orders. In which case, you're more at fault than she."

Lummox and Jutting Chin look as though someone just threw a dead fish at their feet.

"But we didn't—"

"Exactly. You didn't do your job."

By now the guards have lowered their weapons. "Come along," Dr. Gallingham says to Hope. "Time you finished your chores and returned to barracks."

Hope picks up her shawl and shuffles out the door. She returns to her mopping, swiping the floor with wild, frenetic strokes, hands shaking violently. She can't decide which is worse: being sent to Colonel Thorason, or knowing she owes a debt of gratitude to Dr. Gallingham.

31.

"KEEP THOSE HANDS WHERE I can see 'em!" the Brown Shirt shouted. He lowered the M16 from Four's temple and aimed it at me. Even in the headlights' weak glare I could see the tension from his muscled arms spilling into the weapon. He needed little incentive to pull the trigger.

"Who are you and where're you from?"

We didn't answer. Crew Cut's face grew red, and a vein throbbed on his neck, thick and purple as an earthworm.

"I asked you a question!"

He swung the butt of his rifle into Four Fingers's stomach, and Four fell with a splat to his knees, eyes wide.

204

Crew Cut stuck his face within inches of mine. "Well?"

I felt my body go slack, knees buckling.

"We're from Camp Liberty," I managed. Four Fingers looked at me in surprise, but I didn't care. I couldn't bear to see him get hurt anymore.

"What're you doin' here?"

"We escaped."

"And made it all this way?"

I nodded. Crew Cut let out a long whistle. "Looks like we just caught us some Less Thans," he said to the other guard.

His friend forced a smile. A purple welt bulged beneath his eye where my rock had struck him.

Crew Cut leveled his gaze at me. "How many of you escaped?"

"Just us two," I said, too fast.

Crew Cut narrowed his eyes. "Just you two, huh?" He inched closer. "You should know I don't cotton to liars."

"I'm not lying. It's just us two. Do you see any others?"

"Just 'cause I don't see 'em don't mean they ain't there."

"Trust me. It's just us."

Crew Cut nodded, satisfied. He turned away. Then he pivoted back around and jammed the rifle barrel into my gut. I felt it poking against my ribs.

"I said I don't cotton to liars," he hissed, spittle splashing my face. "Seems to me we got us a report sayin' somethin' like eight Less Thans escaped from Liberty."

"I don't know anything about that," I said, trying to hide the quiver in my voice.

"'Cause it's just you and your pal and this little dog of yours."

"That's right."

Crew Cut motioned to the heavyset soldier, who walked over to Argos.

"And what if I told you we'd kill your pooch here if I thought you was lying."

Heavy Brown Shirt pointed his rifle at Argos's head and my own head began to swim. I couldn't let Argos die, but I couldn't tell them about the other Less Thans either. Crew Cut's eyes drilled into me. The heavy soldier edged his finger on the trigger, just waiting for the command. All color drained from Four's face.

"All right," I said. "I lied."

A noxious smile spread across Crew Cut's face. "You oughtn't to've done that," he said, his breath smelling like a bag of rotten onions. "As I said—"

"I know. You don't cotton to liars."

If this was in fact my last moment on earth, I didn't want to have to spend it listening to a lecture from the likes of him.

His smile collapsed and he whipped his weapon

around. The butt of it caught me in the chin with a shuddering crack and sent me sprawling. A moment later, I felt the cold circle of the M16's barrel imprinting itself against my temple, and I squeezed my eyes shut. I had no desire to watch the bullet travel the short distance from his rifle to my brain.

I only heard what happened next: the *whoosh* of air, the thud of slicing flesh, the gurgle of blood.

I opened my eyes to see an arrow protruding through Crew Cut's neck. The nock and fletching were all that remained by his Adam's apple; the point and shaft extended out the back. He dropped to his knees and fell face forward in the mud.

His friend raised his rifle, but too late. Before he had a chance to fire, an arrow caught him in the chest, taking him to the ground. He was dead within seconds.

I swung my head around and there was Cat, helping Four Fingers to his feet.

"Figured you Janes might need some help," he said. "You good to run?"

We nodded dumbly.

"Good. 'Cause we'd better move."

We heard wheels spinning in mud; another Humvee was struggling to make it up the hill. As we took off back up the mountain, I had a sinking realization. We were safe—Cat had saved us—but every step from Camp Freedom was a step away from Hope.

32.

HOPE ADDS EXTRA HOURS to her tunnel shift and encourages others to do the same. She doesn't mention the letter or its final paragraph to anyone. No point scaring them.

There's the other part also. The stuff about her father. To realize he's not the man she thought he was is enough to make her sick to her stomach.

And then there's Book. She hasn't seen him since he leaped out Thorason's window. Did he make it out of camp? More than a few times she catches herself with her hand on her stomach, imagining it as Book's, remembering how he held her in the darkness of the cave-in, his arms wrapped tightly around her.

She has just finished a five-hour shift and slid beneath

her threadbare blanket on the floor when she hears a frail, thin voice.

"Do we stand a chance?"

Hope rolls over and stares up at her sister. Each day her body seems to cave in on itself a little bit more, like a piece of fruit rotting on the vine.

"Of course," Hope answers. "The water's going down and we can dig again. In another couple of months—"

Faith shakes her head. "Not the tunnel. *Us.*"

"That's what I'm saying. Once this tunnel's done, we're outta here."

"But can we make it until then?"

Hope doesn't know. She's usually the one who asks the hard questions, not Faith. As their mother once said, Faith is the sister who studies the scab; Hope is the one who picks at it.

"We've made it this long. We can easily make it another couple of months."

"But the girls are saying the colonel's up to something."

"They don't know what they're talking about."

"But do you?"

Faith's words are like a cold wind.

"*Do* you?" Faith asks again. Her eyes, which have been vacant for so long, peer into Hope's face with a sudden clarity.

"Yes," she says quietly.

209

That seems enough for Faith. She doesn't press for details. "So do we stand a chance?" she asks again.

"As long as we have each other, we *always* stand a chance. H and FT."

"H and FT," Faith repeats weakly. Then she shuts her eyes.

Suddenly Hope isn't tired. Is she being truthful? she wonders. Do they stand even a remote chance of finishing the tunnel in time?

Her thoughts are interrupted by the sound of the rattling chain as it shivers through the handles of the front door. Four Brown Shirts march in. The Sisters wake with a start, clutching blankets to their chests.

Two Brown Shirts stop at the foot of Hope's bed; two at Faith's. A moment later Hope hears heavy, thudding footsteps. She's not surprised when Dr. Gallingham comes into view.

"Yes, these are the day's Participants," he says, his voice syrupy with self-congratulation. "Hope and Faith." His focus darts from one to the other. "Or is it Faith and Hope? In any case, the greatest of these is Love."

He giggles at his cleverness.

The guards yank the twins to their feet, drag them outside, and lock the door behind them.

Hope stares at the water-stained ceiling, the bars on the window. They can call it an infirmary if they like, but it's really a prison. A prison within a prison.

Dr. Gallingham drops a metal clipboard onto the desk with a clatter. Faith lets out a scream.

"It's okay," Hope whispers, but her sister's eyes are wide with terror. Her bony arms strain against the leather manacles.

"Now, now," Dr. Gallingham says in his most reassuring voice. "There's nothing to be afraid of. Today is all about cleanliness."

Hope wants to believe him. Wants that desperately. But she doesn't for a second. The scabbing needle pricks on the underside of her arm are testament to what he's capable of. Weeks' worth of injections and chemical experiments.

"You owe me, you know," he says. He leans over Hope until the moisture from his eyes nearly drips on her face. "If it hadn't been for me, the guards would've taken you straight to Colonel Thorason. And in honor of my graciousness, I thought you could return the favor and help *me* out. For example, you could tell me who was in the office with you. And don't pretend you were alone; I saw the open window, and we have a report of two downed guards that night."

He leans in close until his rank breath splashes her face. "Well?"

Hope doesn't look away. She can play chicken with the best of them.

"So let me get this straight: you'd rather be the subject of another experiment than tell me what's going on?"

Faith makes a strangled noise from the other bed. Hope knows what she's trying to say. *Tell him. Tell him so we can go free.*

But Hope refuses to speak.

Gallingham goes on. "And then there's the matter of your father. You still haven't shared where he is."

"I told you. He died."

"So you say, but for some reason I don't believe you." Gallingham stands up straight as two female technicians stride in, pushing a metal cart. "Field trip," he says brightly. "Make sure you have a buddy. Unless you've had a change of heart and decide to open up."

Hope turns her head away.

"Fine," he says. "But you may regret that decision."

The techs push the two sisters into the hall, gurney wheels squealing. They're rolled into a room with no beds, no examination tables, no silver trays with syringes. Instead, the centerpiece is an enormous rust-splotched metal tank—a drinking trough for livestock. It seems wildly out of place in a hospital. A garden hose coils over one edge and vomits water into the tank.

A sudden bang makes both girls jump. Hope swivels her head and sees three Brown Shirts dumping trays of ice cubes into the metal tank. The chunks clatter against the sides.

"H and FT," Hope whispers to her sister.

Faith doesn't appear to be listening. She is pressed into the mattress, eyes squeezed shut, nostrils flared.

Dr. Gallingham pulls a thermometer from the trough and examines it.

"Make it colder," he commands. The three soldiers oblige by dumping in still more trays of ice.

Gallingham returns his attention to the twins. "You might get a trifle chilly during this experiment." He smiles, his thin lips vanishing into his jowly face. "Of course, we can avoid all this unpleasantness if you'd just tell me what I want to know."

Hope grits her teeth and says nothing.

"Fine," the doctor says. "Then we'll begin."

The female technicians strip Hope and Faith down to their underwear and then dress them again—as Brown Shirts. The wool uniforms are scratchy and ill-fitting, but more puzzling to Hope is why. Why go to the trouble to dress them as soldiers at all?

Dr. Gallingham supplies the answer. "You're providing a great service, you know—allowing us to see which rewarming methods are more effective than others. So for that, the Republic thanks you." He gives a mock bow and goes on.

"Our generals predict more and more of our battles will be fought in the mountains, so we need to know how much cold our good soldiers can endure."

"Ready," one of the techs proclaims.

"Temperature?"

"Forty degrees."

"Splendid."

Hope feels suddenly nauseous. It isn't the fear of icy water—although that's certainly part of it—but something else, too. Shame. For not doing a better job of taking care of her sister. If she hadn't been snooping around in the Admin Building, they wouldn't be in this fix. All she has to do is tell Gallingham about Book and it will put an end to it. She and Faith will live. No icy experiment. No freezing water.

"What makes you think we'll stay in your little pond?" she asks.

A lipless smirk oozes across Gallingham's face, and he nods at the three Brown Shirts as they begin attaching a series of heavy objects to Hope's and Faith's lower legs. Ankle weights. Hope kicks and squirms and tries to make their task as difficult as possible; Faith lies there lifeless, her face pale with dread.

While the Brown Shirts finish strapping on the weights, the female techs attach a series of electrodes. Once plugged into the machines, the girls' vitals appear on an electronic screen. Both hearts are racing.

The three Brown Shirts lift Hope from the bed and plop her into the icy water. The sudden cold sucks the breath right from her; she feels like she's being squeezed by an enormous vise. The weights drag her feet to the bottom of the vat, where they make a muffled clank. Even though she tries to give a kick, a numbing paralysis sets in. Her wrists, too, are immobilized—strapped to the top edge of the tank.

A moment later Faith is dropped in the opposite end and Hope sees her sister clenching her jaw so hard she's bitten her tongue. A thin rivulet of blood sneaks past her lower lip and dribbles down her chin.

"And just to document our little experiment today . . ." Gallingham picks up a camera from the desk, aims it at the girls, and clicks. A flash strobes the air.

"Now what?" Hope asks through chattering teeth.

"Very simple," the doctor answers. "We wait."

The cold is excruciating—like a million wasp stings all at once. Hope's legs are two unwieldy pieces of steel. Even if the Brown Shirts took away the ankle weights, she'd be powerless to move her legs even a little. There's no feeling there whatsoever. Her body shivers violently.

"You should be happy," Dr. Gallingham says smugly, jotting notes on his clipboard. "Shivering means your body is doing its best to generate heat. If you weren't shivering, you'd be dead." He says this as though it were a consolation.

"Eighty-eight point two," a female tech calls out, and Hope realizes the woman is talking about her body temperature. It's plummeted over ten degrees.

Breathing becomes difficult. Her teeth are chattering and she's afraid they're going to break off. Faith is faring even worse. Her face has paled beyond recognition; her lips are the color of blueberries.

"Eighty-three point zero."

Faith's and Hope's bodies shake so much they're creating a whirlpool in the icy tank. Hope fears she'll break a rib from shivering.

"Last chance," Gallingham explains. "Tell me who was in the office and I'll pull you out of the tank myself."

Hope thinks of Book. Thinks of how he covered her when the cave-in happened, how he soothed her when she freaked out. She looks at Dr. Gallingham . . . and doesn't respond.

Time grinds to a halt. Whenever she dares a peek at the clock, it's always no later than the last time she looked. She begins to have difficulties distinguishing between the hour hand and the second hand, as if she's suddenly forgotten how to tell time.

"Eighty-two point three."

They're no longer wasp stings; they're knife thrusts. Jabbing blades of cold steel. Her trembling body is one huge open wound, radiating pain. Oddly enough, Hope feels beads of sweat popping on her forehead. It's as though her body has given up telling her she's cold; now it's suggesting she's hot.

Across the tank, Faith struggles to stay conscious,

216

eyes rolling back in her head. Hope tries to speak, tries to whisper *H & FT* but can't. Her teeth are chattering so much she's incapable of forming sentences. It's Faith, her sister, Faith, and yet the more Hope looks at her, the more she sees her mother lying lifeless on the porch, her black hair fanning out around her.

"Eighty-one point six."

The words startle Hope. Who is this woman in the white lab coat calling out numbers? Are those numbers on her forearm? Or are they *all* numbers? Is everything and everyone a number?

"Seventy-nine point seven."

Hope's eyes grow heavy; the world becomes blurry and dim. Her body explodes in heat. It's as though she's on fire, flames dancing from her arms.

"Seventy-nine point three."

All she has to do is say one word—"Book"—and they'll be freed. That's it. One word means the difference between life and death. But her mind grows suddenly cloudy. What does the word mean anyway? And is there a cost in saying it? She seems to think there is, but she can't remember what.

"Seventy-eight point six."

Everything is turning black. Darkness taking over. She's lost control of her muscles. Her thoughts as well.

"Time," Hope hears a male voice say. The nasal voice is both familiar and not. Even as she stares through squeezed eyes at the round-faced man—the heavy jowls, the watery eyes—she can't recall if she's met him.

Hope's body is yanked from the watery prison and thrust onto the gurney. Her soldier's uniform clings to her like skin, water dripping onto the linoleum floor. She sees but has no sensation of warmth as the uniform is ripped open and hot water bottles are pressed into her armpits, her crotch, the space behind her knees.

Her head rolls to one side as she sees the other girl— *what is her name?*—being ripped from the water and dumped on a gurney next to her. In her case, a single, thin blanket is tossed carelessly on her shivering frame. Hope doesn't know her, but she feels a pang of pity for her. There's no way that poor girl will make it. No way in the world.

A moment later Hope blacks out.

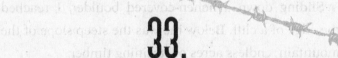

33.

SHE CAME BACK. THE woman from my dreams. The one with long black hair.

"There you will go," she said.

Though bullets whizzed overhead and thick, gunpowdery smoke made a haze of the world around us, there was something oddly pleasing about her voice. And ever since the dream of her reading to me, I felt a strange sense of trust in her. I couldn't explain it.

"There you will go," she said again, her hair framing reddish-brown skin. "My beloved, in whom I am well pleased."

And then she was gone.

The sun woke me, jabbing me in the eyes with rays of amber. The others were still fast asleep. Cat had led

Four Fingers, Argos, and me back to the rest of the Less Thans and we'd been lying low in the mountains, making sure the Brown Shirts couldn't find us.

I got up and edged away from camp. The terrain was rocky and difficult: enormous boulders tossed by erupting volcanoes however many millions of years ago. More than once I had to get on hands and knees to scramble over the largest of them. In no time I'd worked up a sweat.

Sliding down a lichen-covered boulder, I reached the edge of a cliff. Below me was the steep slope of the mountain, endless acres of straining timber.

The sight reminded me of K2.

After the incident in the mess hall, he and I went a whole year without speaking. I was shoveling after a January blizzard when he offered to lend a hand.

"I can manage," I replied.

"I didn't say you couldn't. I'm just asking if you'd like some help."

As if to prove otherwise, I sank the shovel into a chest-high drift. My arms quivered under the strain. K2 nudged me to the side and grabbed the shovel from me. He made it look a whole lot easier.

"So is this another bet?" I asked, still breathing heavy.

"What? Can't a guy lend a hand without you getting all suspicious?"

"I just want to make sure. . . ."

"Relax. No bet this time."

I admired how far he was able to toss the snow. The guy was not just big, he was—how had he said it?—*jumbo-honkin'* big.

"I do have an ulterior motive," he admitted, clearing a path in the snow.

Here we go, I thought. *What is it this time?*

"I got a bargain for you."

"A bargain?" I asked.

"That's right: a bargain. I've seen you around camp. You don't hang out much with the other guys."

"I read," I said defensively.

"Exactly, you read, but you don't do much with anyone else. So here's what I'm proposing." He stopped working for a moment and leaned on the shovel. "I've seen you on the ball field and you're actually better than you think. You'd probably be a decent athlete if you ever gave it a shot, even with your limp."

I didn't know whether to be offended or not. "Go on."

"I mean, not as good as me or Cannon, but you know . . . ."

"Go on," I said again.

"So all you need is someone to get you on their team. I'd be willing to do that."

I couldn't believe it. Someone promising to pick me? I wondered what the catch was. "And in exchange . . . ?"

"You help me get smarter." He explained, "I can read

and all, but just okay, and I don't really know *what* to read. But if I help you on the field, I thought you could maybe help me with some books. I mean, I don't want to get all *Shakespearean* or nothin', but what do you say?"

I didn't trust it. There was something about the bargain that was too good to be true. I swung my head around, looking for his friends laughing behind some corner.

"No bet?" I asked.

"No bet."

"Real bargain?"

"Yeah."

I hesitated. "Okay," I finally said.

His face erupted in a smile, and he shook my hand, engulfing it like an ocean swallowing a tiny boat. And so began a most unlikely partnership that turned into an even more unlikely friendship . . . until its untimely end.

"What're you doing?"

I nearly jumped out of my skin. If I hadn't been holding on to a branch, I might have gone tumbling down the mountain.

It was Cat, his words shaking me from my memory. He was standing right behind me.

"How'd you know I was here?" I asked.

"Followed you."

I didn't know if I should be grateful or irritated. Was

I so helpless I couldn't even go off on my own?

"You didn't answer my question," he said. "What're you doing?"

"Just getting away for a few minutes."

"I can see that, smartass. *Why* are you getting away?"

What could I say? That I had a dream and some old woman was trying to tell me something?

"We need to rethink what we're doing," I said. "Maybe we should change things up."

"And . . . ?"

"And maybe instead of going forward, we go back. Just temporarily."

Cat's eyes narrowed. "What're you saying?"

My gaze lowered; I could barely look him in the eye. "I want to go back to that girls' camp."

"I thought you just tried that."

"This time I want to rescue them."

"You wanna do *what*?"

"I want to rescue them."

He just stared at me. Then he sighed noisily. "You remember how that ended last time, right?"

"Of course."

"You and Four Fingers and your little dog were a trigger pull from being worm food."

"I remember."

"If I hadn't gotten there when I did, there'd be no more Book."

223

"I know."

"And you still want to do this? For the sake of some girls you never met?"

"I met them." *One in particular,* I didn't bother to add.

Cat scoffed.

"I know it's crazy and it's probably the wrong thing to do," I said, "but maybe that's exactly why it's the *right* thing to do. Besides, if we join up with them, it'll increase our numbers. Give us a better chance."

There was far more to it than that—but I wasn't about to admit that to Cat.

"It's not numbers we need to worry about," Cat said, "it's speed. The sooner we get to the next territory, the better."

"You really think we can do this with just the eight of us?"

Cat didn't respond right away and I could see him processing what I'd said. He rubbed his jaw and peered at the far horizon. We were like two explorers standing on an ocean's edge, imagining faraway continents.

"We can't afford to stop," he finally said. "We gotta keep going."

"I understand that. Then I'll go back with Four Fingers. We'll get the girls and catch up."

"Not this time. No one goes with you."

"I need Four."

"No one goes with you."

224

"But I need—"

"No one goes with you."

Why was I always losing this argument to Cat? "Okay," I sighed, realizing it wouldn't be easy to pull this off on my own . . . but the words from the dream kept echoing in my head. *There you will go.* For whatever reason, the old woman's message led me back to Hope.

I could still sense the curve of her back against my chest, the press of her skin, how our bodies fit into each other like two pieces of a puzzle. But what I thought about most were her eyes—those enormous brown pools. There was something below the surface I couldn't make out. Something impenetrable and dark. Something heartbreaking.

I returned to camp and began packing my things. It was a risk going back for those girls, I knew that, but I also knew I had to do it. I had promised. And if I died in the process, well, at least I'd be doing something that mattered.

Something for someone else. And maybe that would rid me of K2's ghosts—and the demons that had haunted me since the day of his death would finally fade away.

There you will go.

34.

"Fifty-three minutes," Dr. Gallingham says in a voice beaming with pride.

Hope opens her eyes. The water-stained ceiling of the infirmary looks down at her. So the vat of ice-cold water wasn't a nightmare. It really happened.

"You were in a tank of forty-one-degree water for fifty-three minutes," he goes on to explain. "And using only external rewarming methods, we were able to raise your core temperature to something resembling normal. That's good news for our soldiers fighting in the north."

"And Faith?"

"Hmm?"

"My sister?"

"Oh, she didn't make it," the doctor says, as casually as though describing the day's weather. "We tried passive rewarming for her and it simply wasn't enough. She died on the spot." He pats Hope on the leg. "I knew you'd be willing to help out the Republic. Your father would be proud."

He shuffles out of the room. Now Hope can see the other bed . . . and a lifeless Faith lying atop the sheets. Her skin has already purpled and a death stare carves two holes into the ceiling.

"Faith," Hope says, not letting herself believe her eyes. "Faith!" she calls again, hoping to wake her, hoping this is just some parlor trick that gives the *appearance* of death.

But it's no trick, and when Hope realizes it, she is overcome with grief, with *guilt*—for not taking better care of her sister. She thrusts and squirms against the leather manacles, shouting "No!" at the very top of her lungs until her throat is raw and hoarse.

And then she begins to sob, the kind that rips at her stomach and convulses her shoulders. Hot tears stain her cheeks, and for once, Hope doesn't try to stop them. *Let 'em come,* she thinks. *If they can wash away the pain, let 'em come.*

She's alone. Not just in the room, but in the world. Dead are her mother and father and now her sister too. And Book is far, far away. She is utterly, entirely alone.

227

When there are no tears left to shed, her eyes catch sight of something else. Next to Faith's lifeless body, lying in a small, untidy heap, is her pink shawl. Never to cover her sister's frail shoulders.

The tears begin again.

Two days later Hope is discharged from the infirmary. When she returns to the barracks, several Sisters pat her on the shoulder and Scylla grabs her by the arms and stares into her eyes. There's something in her expression that tells Hope this is why Scylla doesn't speak. At some point, she lost her sister, too. Just as they've all lost sisters. As Hope casts a wild gaze around the room, she realizes Athena and Helen are the only set of twins remaining.

Hope stumbles to her spot on the floor, flinging the ratty blanket over her shivering body. She no longer cares about the chancellor's letter and Thorason's intentions and the "question of the Less Thans." Her father's involvement means nothing to her. Warmth is what she craves now. And sleep.

And Faith.

She abandons the tunnel. *What's the point?* Maybe they can finish it, and maybe they can even escape—but why? Will that make their lives any safer? Is a life on the run really better than all this? She did that for ten years and where did it get her?

She goes through the motions. Breakfast, roll call, daily chores. She's reassigned from cleaning stables to gardening in the fields. It's thought she needs more "supervision."

Late one morning her group is assembled in the roll call yard and handed hoes and spades. As four Brown Shirts lead them outside the camp, the girls sling the tools over their shoulders like soldiers on parade. Past the barbed wire they trudge, stopping only when they reach the fields.

Hope works with a kind of dull precision. As she chops at the offending weeds, thoughts swirl in her head like falling leaves. Maybe if she and Book hadn't gone nosing around in the Admin Building, Dr. Gallingham wouldn't have subjected Faith and her to the water tank. Maybe her sister would still be alive. Maybe Hope wouldn't feel like she does—devoid of any feeling whatsoever. Numb. No sharper than the dull edge of her hoe that bites into the ground.

At one point, Hope hears a strangled scream. A girl's voice, coming from the infirmary. The Sisters hesitate, look up briefly, then return to their labors. They've grown accustomed to such sounds. It saddens Hope. They're getting used to things they have no business getting used to.

This isn't a life they're leading, she realizes, it's a life sentence.

At the same time, something feels different. Something she can't define. It's almost like they're being watched. Not just by the guards—she's used to that—but when she lifts her head and casts a sweeping gaze across the landscape, all she sees are guard towers and fences topped with coils of concertina wire and the jagged silhouette of Skeleton Ridge.

Hell on earth.

35.

I WATCHED HER . . . AND I knew.

The night before, I'd scampered down the mountain until I reached the ridge above Camp Freedom, where I observed Hope at work in the fields. Once, she gave a glance right in my direction. If I didn't know better, I would've said she could sense me.

That's when it hit me, what we had in common. Pain. Something about those liquid brown eyes and the expression on her face told me she knew pain. That was the quality the two of us shared—and why I had to save her.

So how do I get to her? I wondered. After all, those guards weren't going anywhere.

I watched as the day went on. I kept thinking about

231

that book I'd read at camp—one of those left in my trunk. *The Art of War.* There'd been something in there about diversions. *All warfare is deception,* it had said. The thought stayed with me.

The idea came in the middle of the night.

I circled around the camp until I reached the barn, sneaking inside before the morning arrival of guards or inmates. I found a goat—a kid—and placed a strip of duct tape around his white muzzle. Then I carried him off into the woods until I came to a small mound of boulders.

"Sorry about this," I said, and the goat looked at me with a fearful expression. "You'll be free soon enough."

I pinned one of his legs beneath the rocks so it looked like he'd escaped and gotten stuck. Then I ripped off the tape and ran as fast as I could to the side of the field. As I hurried away, I heard the goat's bleating, insistent and high-pitched.

I crawled to a hiding place at the edge of the field and waited. It began to pour.

Finally, the gate groaned open and the female prisoners marched out, two dozen of them, surrounded by the same four guards as before. They all wore dark green ponchos because of the rain.

The guards took their stations and the prisoners began chopping away at the muddy, brown canals. Hope was smack-dab in the middle. Figured.

Three of the guards drew together to share a cigarette, and that's when they heard the goat. They lowered their M16s and swung them toward the woods. When they realized it was animal and not human, they relaxed, slinging their rifles back over their shoulders. The three Brown Shirts gestured to the fourth that they would go investigate.

Once they disappeared into the woods, I launched a pebble from my slingshot. It landed near Hope's foot. She seemed not to notice. I swore silently and loaded up again. This time the rock bounced off her left boot. Her head snapped up. The other inmates were oblivious.

The guard's back was turned to me, so I rose to a standing position.

Hope's eyes went round. Just as quickly she regained her composure and speared her hoe into the sopping earth. I lowered myself back down and waited. The girls worked. The rain fell. The guard watched.

Hope made a motion to the guard: bathroom break. The guard nodded brusquely, watching as the girl marched into the woods. I flattened myself behind the ridge, face digging into mud.

I heard rather than saw Hope making her way toward me. When the trees hid her from the Brown Shirt, she stopped and stared at me.

"What're you doing here?" she hissed.

"What do you think? I came back to rescue you."

233

She snorted with derision. "Who says we need rescuing?"

Her words caught me off guard. So did her attitude. I thought she'd be relieved to see me. Grateful, even. Didn't she know the sacrifice I'd made to return? Instead, she seemed downright hostile.

"But I thought that was the plan," I said. "Build a tunnel. Escape to the next territory."

"Maybe that *was* the plan—not anymore. What's the point?"

I didn't know what to say. How to react. I wondered what happened to the old Hope—and who this imposter was.

"What's going on?" I asked. "You seem . . . different."

Her expression changed quicker than the flick of a switch. The anger melted away and her eyes welled with moisture: big, fat tears that spilled over her bottom lids and trailed down her cheeks. When she began to speak, the words were unintelligible.

"I can't understand you," I said, leaning in.

Again, her mouth moved, but her words were swallowed by tears.

"I'm sorry," I said. "I still can't quite . . ."

"Experiments," she murmured, swiping at a tear with muddy fingertips.

"Go on."

She gulped for air. "I had a sister."

"I know," I said. "Faith." I was still trying to understand. What did this have to do with anything? Was her sister missing? Did she want me to look for her?

Hope turned away and covered her mouth. I thought she was about to cough, but then I realized: she was sobbing. Her shoulders jerked up and down in a kind of pantomime. Somewhere along the way she had learned to cry silently.

I reached out a hand and touched her shoulder. "I'm sorry . . ." I didn't know what else to say.

She turned and her eyes met mine—I couldn't help but recoil. It was a look of hopelessness, of a kind of sorrow I'd never seen or experienced. I was about to speak when I noticed the guard squinting in our direction. Hope noticed, too.

"You really want to help?" Hope asked. "Then leave me alone. . . . Don't ever come back here again."

Before I could respond, she picked up her hoe and walked back to the field.

235

36.

HOPE WORKS IN A kind of trance the rest of that day.

A chill air raises goose bumps on her arms, and her feet radiate pain from standing so long. Despite that—despite all of it—she thinks about Book.

She questions her decision to send him away. But she's afraid of getting hurt. Afraid to put her faith in a total *stranger*, only to have him break that trust . . . and her heart. No, it's better this way, she tells herself. It's better.

She doesn't really know if she believes it or not.

They've just settled into bed when two Brown Shirts undo the lock, blue moonlight catching them in silhouette. *Who have they come for now?* Hope wonders. It's what they all wonder.

When the Brown Shirts know every eye is on them, they throw something to the floor. It lands with a skidding thud. The guards turn and exit, chaining the door shut.

Hope sits up and looks. What she sees takes her breath away.

It isn't something that was tossed to the floor, but some*one*. Helen. Frail, little Helen. She is shivering uncontrollably, and Hope's first thought is that they dunked her in the tank of freezing water. But a closer inspection reveals a series of burn marks up and down her arm, her neck, the side of her face. Helen isn't shaking from cold; it's from shock.

"Give me a hand!" Hope calls out. They take Helen to her bed, covering her with blankets, grabbing extras from their own beds to warm her up.

"You're okay," Hope says, placing a soothing hand atop Helen's forehead. "Everything's okay." But even as she says it her eyes catch sight of Athena's bed. Empty. A single strand of red hair coiled atop her pillow.

Gallingham took both twins after morning roll call . . . and only one returned. Hope realizes there are no more sets of twins in Barracks B.

Helen isn't the first girl to lose her sister, of course. Nor the first to be tortured. Dr. Gallingham's experiments have become more barbaric in recent weeks. There's no longer a pretense at science; it's pure sadism.

He wants to see just how much pain the human body can endure.

White light breaks through the window and splashes the wall. Not guard towers' searchlights—something else entirely.

Hope slides forward and peers above the windowsill. The front gates shriek open and a small convoy of military vehicles streams in, thick tires crunching gravel. As Hope watches them circle the infield, she notices the .50 caliber machine guns mounted in the Humvees' turrets.

Her throat goes dry as she pieces it together. The letter. Thorason's words. *Eliminate. Leave no trace.* The Brown Shirts mean to finish them off—sooner rather than later. Their days are numbered . . . unless they do something right away.

Hope turns to Diana. "How long till the tunnel's done?"

Diana's surprised. "The water's still high—"

"I know."

". . . and filling up again—"

"So how long?"

"I don't know. Five, six weeks."

Hope takes this in. "How about five or six *hours*?"

Diana nearly chokes. "That's not possible," she stammers. "There's too much water. And if we dig up too fast we're liable to cause another cave-in and you know what that's like."

Hope does know. But it doesn't lessen her determination. "We leave tonight," she says, looking at the other Sisters.

They can't believe what they're hearing. "But the gear's not gathered," they say. "We only have a portion of the food."

Hope goes on as if they hadn't spoken. "Could we reach the surface tonight?" she asks Scylla. "If we dig straight up?"

Scylla answers with a vague shrug.

"Could we?" Hope asks again.

Scylla casts a glance at Diana, then looks back at Hope. She nods yes.

Hope sighs gratefully. "Then let's do it."

At first, no one moves. They're paralyzed—not only by this sudden change of plans but by this sudden change in Hope. It's like she's a different person. A new leader, stepping in for a departed one.

They're about to head to the tunnel when a frail, quavering voice calls out from beneath the blankets.

"Why, Hope?" It's Helen. Her first words since returning.

Hope walks to Helen's cot and sits by her side, eyeing the burn marks that spot her body. "Because we can't wait a minute longer," she says.

They divide into groups. Some chip away at the damp ceiling. Others form a bucket brigade, passing water up from the tunnel. Still, the water continues to rise, the black surface glinting yellow from candlelight. For every bucket they empty, two buckets seem to dribble in.

But whenever Hope doubts—whenever she thinks the task is too big—she remembers Faith. And Athena. And the weapons the Brown Shirts just drove in. This tunnel is the Sisters' only chance of salvation.

Something else as well. Unless they manage to escape, she'll never see Book again. Never curl her body into his and share her innermost thoughts. Never find out *his* favorite memory.

She's suddenly convinced only Book can release those haunting demons that dance around her head. Only he can help her get past her guilt of losing Faith. *Oh, Faith, my sister, Faith, I tried to take care of you but it wasn't enough.*

It matters that she sees Book again. She hopes it's not too late.

Scylla's knife slices up through grass, and dirt rains down on her. She takes a quick peek at the stars, scurries back down, and eases into the water.

Hope pats Scylla on the back and scales the wall of earth herself. Her head pokes through the narrow opening like some forest rodent. The nearest trees are still ten yards away; the barbed wire fence is twenty yards behind them. Not ideal, but not terrible either.

Hope descends and faces the girls of Barracks B, their heads bobbing above the surface of the water.

"Okay," she says. They know what to do.

One by one, the Sisters hoist themselves to the top of the opening, look around, and then scuttle to the woods. It takes far longer than Hope would like, but so far the searchlight hasn't caught a Sister midrun.

Finally, it's down to Hope. All the others have gone. She's ready to make a run for it when she realizes: There's no Helen. She's not here.

Where is she? Hope wonders. *Is it possible she's still back in the barracks?*

The Sisters wait impatiently in the woods, pointing toward the east. The sky is beginning to gray. Hope motions that she won't be long and pops back down the hole.

The water is at the ceiling now. It is cold and black and swirling. The only way to reach the other end is to swim. Assuming Hope can hold her breath that long.

She bobs once, twice, inhales deeply, and plunges beneath the surface.

It takes her longer than expected and halfway there her lungs begin to tighten—like a giant fist squeezing her abdomen. When she finally reaches the other end, she's never been so grateful for breath. Even though the air is stale and musty, she gulps it greedily.

241

A lone candle sputters by the ladder, allowing her to see the moisture eating away the sides. Great jags of earth separate themselves and splash into the water. There's precious little time to find Helen and get out of there.

Hope pulls herself up into the closet and tiptoes to the barracks, water pooling beneath her feet. There's a vague shape on a far bunk. Helen. Sitting hunched over, face buried in her hands. Hope hurries to her side.

"What's going on?" Hope asks. "Why're you still here?"

Helen hiccups through her tears. "You came back," she says, not answering Hope's question. Her fingers absently tap the burn marks on her arm.

"Of course. We're family. I'm your Sister." The words just come out. Not a denial of Faith, but rather an acknowledgment. Hope needs Helen just as much as Helen needs Hope.

A fresh batch of tears makes their way down Helen's cheeks. Through the front window, Hope sees an orange glow. Sunrise.

"But we need to get going if we're going to swim out of here in time," Hope says. She attempts to pull Helen to her feet; Helen resists.

"I can't," the frail girl says.

"Of course you can. What's stopping you?"

"I don't know how to swim."

242

Hope can't hide her surprise.

Helen's chin begins to tremble all over again. "Does that mean I can't go?"

"Of course not," Hope says. "It doesn't mean that at all." Even as she speaks, her mind scrambles. How can Helen possibly make it from one end of the tunnel to the other without swimming?

"I have just the thing for you," Hope says. She reaches in her dress pocket and fishes out a small object: the gold locket on the tarnished chain. She undoes the clasp and slips it around Helen's neck. "A good luck charm."

Helen's expression is doubtful. "And this'll work?"

"It's kept me alive all these years. Come on, I have a plan." As Hope eases Helen to her feet and they make their way to the back of the barracks, Hope wonders if she's really up for this.

They're about to step into the back closet when Hope takes a final glance at the barracks. She sees a small mound atop a cot. Faith's shawl. Hope doesn't let herself look at it for long. She swivels back around and she and Helen lower themselves into the tunnel.

The water has continued to rise, extinguishing the last candle and putting them in darkness. Hope feels Helen's hand stiffen in hers.

"It's okay," Hope says. "We don't need light to swim."

The surface of the water is black and impenetrable, and Hope suddenly realizes the tunnel isn't wide enough to allow the two of them to swim side by side. She needs a new plan.

A large *kerplunk* sounds behind them.

"What was that?" Helen asks, afraid.

"Just dirt," Hope says. The tunnel is collapsing in on itself. Support beams bend with the strain. No time to waste.

"Here's what we're going to do," Hope says, looking Helen in the eyes. "I'm going first, you're going to grab my ankle, and I'll pull us along."

"But what if I let go? What if I lose you?" Hysteria rises in Helen's throat.

"You're not going to lose me, because I'm not going to move that leg," Hope reassures her. "And if we do get separated, I'll just turn around and come get you."

"That's not possible! I don't think—"

Hope leans forward until their foreheads are touching. "Hope and Helen together. All right?"

"All right," Helen murmurs, chin quivering.

Another shard of earth collapses into the water. Time is running out. Hope gets horizontal in the water and lifts her right foot above the surface. "Now grab hold."

Helen lets go of the rungs and flings herself forward—paddling like a panicked dog. Her tiny hands encircle Hope's ankle.

"Ready?" Hope asks, and counts aloud, "One . . . two . . . three!"

244

They each take a big gulp of air and plunge beneath the black surface.

Silence. Muffled, murky silence.

Hope puts everything she has into that first stroke . . . and realizes how difficult this is going to be. It was hard enough the first time, swimming from one end of the tunnel to the other without taking a breath—but this time she's pulling Helen.

Live today, tears tomorrow.

She flings her arms forward and snaps them back. Her left foot kicks at the water, fluttering in inky blackness. She finds a rhythm and it begins to happen. They're moving through the narrow tunnel. Slowly. Slowly.

But just when Hope thinks it's working, her legs cramp and her lungs begin to tighten—a twisting, clenching pain that seems to engulf her entire body. Her head aches. Stars dance in her periphery.

The end has gotta be here, she tells herself.

But it isn't.

She starts tugging at support beams. It's slower than swimming, but it's still forward movement. All she can ask for at the moment.

The pain spreads from chest to head. Muscles become slack. Her legs grow heavy as if ankle weights are dragging them down. Like the weights in the freezing tank.

Oh, Faith. I didn't leave you. I came back for you, even though it meant our capture.

Hope grows dizzy. The water seems to be wringing every last ounce of air from her lungs. She's no longer aware if she and Helen are moving or not. She honestly doesn't know.

Nightmare images flash through her mind. Dr. Gallingham and his piggish smile. The blond woman with her ruthless expression. The bullies from Barracks D, the ones who taunted Helen, now taunting her.

Give up yet? they ask. *You'll never make it. You never should've come back in the first place. Not for Faith. Not for Helen.*

Hope wants to scream, but when she opens her mouth there is only water there.

Without her knowing, she comes to a dead drift, her body floating lifelessly to the surface, arms outstretched, her spine and the back of her head bumping against the tunnel ceiling.

And then she sees her father.

There he is now, returning from a hunt, skinned carcasses hanging from his belt. And her mom spying him out the window and ordering the girls to get washed up and they squeal with excitement as they go running off. And after dinner, Hope hanging on her dad's every word and wanting the evening to last forever, never wanting him to leave again, who cares if they have meat or

246

not, and then the soldiers come and shoot Mom and blood—blood more purple than red—spilling from her forehead like a turned-over bottle and her lifeless eyes staring into the porch. Their father finding them in the log and hustling them away and living off the land until infection—caused by a stupid little nail—brings her father down and he utters words Hope can't forget—*You have a choice to make*—and why? *Why did she and Faith have to end up here in Camp Freedom?* And there's Book and their eyes are locked and their hands are touching and it's just the two of them, surrounded by warm barn smells and a shaft of pure sunlight. And standing in her way is Dr. Gallingham with an enormous syringe in his hand, and she pushes him away, but of course there is no pushing him away, and the more she realizes that the more she senses his pudgy, sausage fingers coming at her, grabbing her, groping her face, her hair, her wrists.

"No!" she screams. "You can't have me! I won't go back! I won't!"

And the voice answers back, "But I want you to."

"I won't!"

"But I'm here to save you."

"You're not here to save me. You're here to kill me."

"No! Look at me. Look at *me*!"

Forcing Hope to open her eyes and see what's in front of her. There in the gloom, water to his chin, is

247

Book—Book the Less Than—arms outstretched, reaching for her, grabbing her, pulling her and Helen from the flooded tunnel as they catch their breath.

"What happened?" Hope asks at last.

"Book saved us," Helen says breathlessly. "He appeared out of nowhere and saved us."

Hope eyes the locket around Helen's neck and nods. Then she turns to Book, and when she speaks, her voice is soft, muffled, disbelieving. "You came back."

"I said I would," Book answers her.

Their eyes lock, and without a second thought, Hope leans forward and presses her lips against his. The kiss is hasty and clumsy and awkward and brief . . . and still it takes all her willpower to pull away. She is once more out of breath.

"Well," she says.

"Well," he says back.

There is more she could say—*wants* to say—but not with Helen there. As she studies Book's face and notices the color in his cheeks, she suffers a jolt of panic. How is she able to see so clearly?

Her head tilts back, catching an oval of warming sky. Dawn, appearing in the tunnel opening.

"Come on," she says. "We better hurry."

One at a time, the three go dashing across the final ten yards to the woods. The Sisters smother them with hugs and do all they can to warm them. A couple girls rush back with pine boughs and cover the exit hole.

They look at each other—twenty Sisters and one Less Than who have somehow managed to escape from Barracks B and Camp Freedom and the nightmare of the infirmary.

But Hope knows they're far from safe.

"Let's get out of here," she says.

As they scurry through the woods, the morning sun begins to chase away the night.

Live today, tears tomorrow.

37.

WE MADE OUR WAY up Skeleton Ridge, twenty Sisters and I, following what I hoped was the Less Thans' trail. The trail was steep, and we had to stop often while some of the Sisters caught their breath. The little one—Helen—was as frail as any person I'd ever met.

As for Hope, it seemed that each time I looked at her, she looked away. And I did the same. Like we wanted to talk to each other but didn't know what to say . . . or how to say it. Like that kiss had made us suddenly self-conscious.

One of the things that also made it hard for me to talk to her was the way she looked at me. She didn't look *at* me; she looked *through* me. As if she could see my innermost thoughts. It was no wonder I kept averting my gaze.

Of course, the fact was neither of us really knew the other's intention. All we knew for sure was that we wanted to get out of the territory. And maybe that was enough for now.

In addition to Hope, there was Scylla—a short sparkplug of a girl with a permanently grim expression who never opened her mouth. And Diana, who was willowy in stature and bright in demeanor. Also Helen—the small, frail girl with strawberry-blond hair who seemed always on the verge of flinching.

There were others too, of course, but those three were the ones who seemed closest to Hope . . . and so they were the ones I paid most attention to.

But what they all had in common was what I'd first noticed in the camp: something in their eyes. It was different from the desperation of the Less Thans—even the ones in the bunker. It was like some unfathomable sorrow—a grief as deep and dark as a bottomless well. I couldn't begin to understand it.

By the time we caught up with the others, the Less Thans were well up the mountainside. We spied them just as the sun was beginning to set. They sat huddled under a tarp on the edge of a mountain stream.

"What are *they* doing here?" Dozer asked. As usual, there was nothing friendly in his tone.

"They're coming with us," I said.

Dozer shook his head and spat. "First Four Fingers, now these girls?"

There was no point responding, so I bit my tongue. Argos was really the only one who seemed happy to see us, and he circled the Sisters, trying to determine if they were friend or foe.

Hasty introductions were made, and I couldn't help but notice how Hope's eyes widened when she met Cat. Their handshake, too, lingered longer than the others. Like they knew each other or something.

"Why isn't there a fire?" I asked.

"Ask him," Dozer said, referring to Cat.

"Too risky," he said. "Can't let the Brown Shirts know our position."

As we went to bed that night—Sisters huddled under one tarp, Less Thans huddled under another— my eyes kept landing on Hope. Despite the haunted expression, despite the ragged clothes and the scarf that barely covered her shaved head, I thought I'd never seen anyone more beautiful in all my life. And I swear I could actually feel the touch of her skin, her soft body beneath my hand, the brush of her lips against mine.

But who was I kidding? Once she found out my secrets, she wouldn't want anything to do with me.

We woke to steady rain. After eating our small allotment of nuts and raisins, we headed up the mountain, trailing the stream. We took turns walking and riding horses. All of us were soaked to the bone and our bodies shivered uncontrollably.

But when we stopped that night, we still didn't dare build a fire. Too risky. So we huddled beneath our separate tarps. The only sounds were the familiar ones: aspen trees dripping rain; nickering of horses; muted pounding of river.

At the end of three days, my teeth were chattering, my fingers were pruned from wet and cold, and bloodstains painted my jeans from where the saddle chafed. As miserable as I was, it was the hint of freedom that kept me going—the idea that if we survived all this and made it into the next territory, we wouldn't be Less Thans anymore.

It was nearing dusk when we rounded a bend and spied the river's source: a lake, stretching a good mile in all directions, with water gushing over a spillway at the end nearest us. A steep mountain stood at its northern border, scarred by a landslide of boulders. There was no way we could get our horses over that kind of terrain.

Perched on the lake's edge was a little log cabin, bordered by two outbuildings: a faded red barn on the near side and a dilapidated shed on the far. A tendril of

253

smoke ribboned from the cabin's stone chimney.

On the other side of a grove of aspens was a large, fenced-in garden and an empty corral. Closer at hand was a newer garden, a shovel leaning idly against the trunk of a tree. All in all, the ranch looked like something from a picture book. An oasis in this godforsaken landscape.

Except this oasis included an old man standing on the porch—with a shotgun in his hands. A shotgun aimed directly at us.

What little hair the man had was white and unkempt, pointing in a hundred different directions. He was unshaven, his shirttails untucked, and there was a wild look in his eye.

"Just passing through, are you?" he asked, his mouth partly hidden behind the stock of his 12-gauge.

"That's right," June Bug said, dismounting. He was only five feet tall and looked downright dwarfish standing next to his horse. Still, despite his small stature, we trusted him to speak for us.

"Ain't nothing in this direction. Best turn around."

"We were hoping to cross the river."

"Be my guest." The man shot a snide look toward the raging spillway.

A couple of us shivered in our saddles. The thought of another night in the open rain was more than we could stomach.

"Maybe we could rest here for the night. Sleep in your barn. Eat some food if you could spare us some. Then we'll be on our way tomorrow."

"I ain't got but food for one. And that's me." The old man worked his jaw restlessly from side to side. White spittle formed at the corners of his mouth.

Although he denied the existence of others, I wasn't convinced. I wondered if there were other guns trained on us that very moment. A glance at Hope and some of the other Sisters told me they were thinking the same thing.

"Fine. Then just let us stay the night. We won't be in your way, and we'll catch our own dinner." June Bug gestured to the lake. A series of circles marked where fish were rising for insects in the waning light.

The man shook his head more vigorously than before. "Nope. No staying in my barn, and no fishing in my lake."

Hope took a step forward. "I doubt it's your lake, Mister," she said.

"If I say it's my lake, it's my lake. Now git!"

"We don't mean you any harm. We just want to eat and get dry."

The man took a closer look at the crew of us, eyes sweeping past the Sisters and settling on the guys. "Why should I trust a bunch of Less Thans?" he shouted, saliva now spewing from his mouth. "If it weren't for

255

you all, maybe those bombs wouldn't've gone off and we wouldn't be in the position we're in today."

So there it was: exactly the kind of thinking Cat said existed out there. We'd been sheltered from it in camp. No wonder those Hunters wanted to kill us; in their minds, we were the source of the world's problems.

"Look, Mister," June Bug said, "we didn't have anything to do with *the position we're in today*. All that happened long before we were born. If anyone's to blame, maybe it's you."

The man gave his head a vehement shake. "Don't you be puttin' that on me. I don't bother no one. We've just been mindin' our own business."

The word "we" prompted me to look around.

For the first time I noticed a neglected automobile off to one side. It was covered in a thick layer of dust and ash. Judging from the weeds and pine needles bunched around its tires, I guessed it hadn't been driven in years. Maybe decades.

"Now git!" the man went on. "I ain't fooling here." He brought the gun up.

"You don't mean that," Hope said.

"Try me." He cocked the shotgun. "Then see if I don't mean it or not."

No one said anything. We were desperate. Cold, half starved, weary to the point of collapse. The prospect of sleeping under a roof—even if it was the roof of an old

256

barn—seemed the height of luxury. And yet what could we do? He had a gun and, it seemed, every intention of firing it.

A pungent odor suddenly tickled my nose. Because I'd been the last to ride up, I was closest to the barn. The door was slightly cracked and I was able to peek in. I expected to spy some sickly farm animal lying in its own dung.

But it wasn't that at all.

"We'll finish it for you," I blurted out, surprising myself.

The other LTs and Sisters looked at me as if I was half crazy. The old man turned my way, and I could see down the long, dark barrel of his shotgun.

"Finish what?" he asked gruffly. A dare more than a question.

"The grave," I said. "We'll finish digging the grave."

38.

"I AIN'T ASKING YOU to do that," the old man murmurs.

"We know that," Book says. "But we'll finish it. It's the least we can do."

At first, Hope and the others have no idea what he's talking about. But there it is in the barn: a coffin, handmade of polished pine, resting atop two aged sawhorses. A kerosene lamp hangs on a post and drops a yellow glow on the coffin's top.

Now that Hope sees it, it's easy to piece together. A coffin. The smell of a corpse. A neglected shovel next to a half-dug hole. It isn't for gardening at all.

The old man shudders. "It may not be possible. Soil's awfully rocky here."

"I'm sure we can find a way to dig a hole," Book says.

"It's gotta be long enough."

"We know."

"And deep. No less than six feet."

"We've had experience with graves." Hope notices the assurance in Book's voice. Like he knows what he's talking about.

"I ain't got food enough to feed you. Don't be thinking just because you do this I can be all loaves and fishes."

"We're not expecting anything. We're just going to help you out, that's all." Book dismounts, grabs the shovel, and spears the tip into the ground. It clangs when it hits rock. He lifts it and casts its contents to the side. In no time he's working up a sweat. After a few minutes, Red takes the shovel from him and he begins digging.

Then Hope joins in. And Scylla. And soon, everyone is bent over on hands and knees, some with knives, others with bare hands, all scratching into the soil to deepen the hole. The *grave*.

The old man's 12-gauge lowers to his side, forgotten.

When the grave is finished, the twenty-eight stand back and admire their work. Sweating, chests heaving, hands covered in dirt—but they've done it.

"I'm much obliged," the old man murmurs.

Stars burst in the sky like popcorn. Little tufts of light against a coal-black backdrop. June Bug gives Book a nod and he takes a tentative step forward.

"What do you want us to do now?" he asks. The man's head snaps up, almost as though he'd forgotten they are there. "Shall we lower the coffin in the grave?"

He shifts his gaze until it settles on the pine box and gives a little nod. Hope and a group of others move to the barn and swing open the doors. When they get to the coffin, bathed in its cone of amber light, the smell is noticeably stronger. Rank, even.

They strain as they lift it from its trestles. Helen follows with the lantern. For the first time Hope can see the coffin's handiwork. Beveled edges, clean seams, the carved design of a rose—it looks more like fine furniture than something to be buried beneath six feet of rock and soil.

They reach the graveside, lower the coffin to the ground, and hesitate. Now that they have it out of the barn, how will they actually get it down into the bottom of the grave?

"Ropes," Twitch says. "Two sets." Hope has already figured out he's the engineer of the bunch.

Using ropes and aspen limbs they create makeshift pulleys and the four strongest—Dozer, Cat, Red, and Scylla—lower the coffin.

The old man rests his shotgun against the railing and shuffles to the graveside. He bows his head, mumbling something about shepherds and green pastures. When he finishes, his eyes glisten with moisture.

260

He picks up the shovel, thrusts its tip into the mound of freshly dug earth, and casts the contents into the yawning grave. He hands the shovel to Red and motions for him to continue. Soon all of them are scooping and kicking the dirt back into the hole.

When the ground is once again flat, the old man hobbles to the far side of the aspen grove and retrieves a wooden cross—two branches nailed together. He spears the cross into the earth and takes a step back.

"'Spect you'll be wanting someplace to stay," he says.

"If it's not too much trouble," Book answers.

"I don't run an inn."

"Any shelter would be worth it."

The old man considers it. "The barn'll do ya. You can spread the hay around."

He turns and starts to go.

"And food?" Book asks.

The old man stops. "There's smoked fish drying from the beams," he says. And then, grudgingly: "Help yourselves."

He shuffles the rest of the way to the cabin, grabbing the railing to hoist himself up the steps. Before he opens the door, June Bug calls out, "Thank you."

The old man hesitates. Hope thinks he is going to acknowledge the comment, maybe even thank them for digging the grave. Instead, he slips inside and shuts the door firmly behind him. The dead bolt clicks.

The Sisters and Less Thans stagger into the barn and see them: rows and rows of smoked fish—lake trout—hanging from the beams like icicles. Hope's mouth waters at the sight.

Twitch begins pulling them down and handing them off. They try not to eat more than their share, but it's impossible not to gobble the food ravenously.

Hope watches Book as he drifts away, finding a spot in a far corner to make his bed. As he's fluffing the hay into something vaguely resembling a mattress, he spies a rope dangling from a thick cedar beam. And a milking stool beneath it. The rope ends in a loop.

No, not a loop—a noose.

Another story easy to put together: an old man, unable to dig a grave for a loved one, was going to hang himself—and would have, if he hadn't been interrupted by twenty-eight young intruders.

Hope watches as Book steps up on the stool and untangles the rope until it's simply that: a coiled rope hanging from the ceiling. Hope notices the care he uses in untying the knot, how he quickly surveys the room to make sure no one sees him. But the two of them catch eyes—then quickly look away.

As her body collapses into her own crude bed, Hope wonders about Book's past . . . and the secrets that he carries.

39.

DUST MOTES DANCED IN sleepy diagonals. Since falling asleep however many hours earlier, I hadn't moved an inch; I was in exactly the same position as when I'd lain down. So was everyone else: Less Thans in one part of the barn, Sisters in another. My eyes found Hope and lingered there. Her breathing was steady and calm—soothing to watch.

From outside came a steady, muffled *ffft . . . ffft . . . ffft*. It was too quiet for a hammer. Not violent enough to be an ax.

I staggered to my feet, ripe barn smell scenting the morning air. When I edged outside I saw Flush and Twitch firing arrows into haystacks. Flush pulled back an arrow and sent it flying. It sailed wildly, landing in a bed of weeds. *Ffft*.

"Any chance the old guy has more food?" Flush asked.

I shrugged. "Got me. We ate most of his trout last night."

As if on cue, our gazes landed on the cabin. There was no hint of activity. No smoke from the chimney. After the coil of rope I'd found in the barn, I wondered if one of us should go knock on the door.

"I was thinking we could catch some fish before we leave," Twitch said, letting an arrow sail. It impaled itself into damp earth. *Ffft*. "Assuming we can."

We had never proven ourselves the most adept fishermen. Nor hunters. Nor the most adept at *anything*. Now I understood why: if the Brown Shirts trained us too well, we'd put up too much of a fight against the Hunters.

"You'd think we could catch *something*," Flush said, nocking an arrow. It wobbled drunkenly in the air before falling harmlessly to the ground.

"What's going on out here?" a voice demanded. It was the old man. He was alive. Awake. And angry. He came charging down the porch steps, moving at a far faster clip than the night before.

"What do you think you're doing?" he asked, ripping the bow from Flush's fingers.

I stumbled for words. "Just some target practice. So

264

we're able to get food. Maybe even bring you back a buck before we go."

"You expect me to believe that?"

"Yes, sir, because it's true."

"Not shooting like that, it's not."

"Huh?"

"I've been watching from the window and you all couldn't hit the ocean from the shore."

Our mouths were agape. What bothered the old guy wasn't the fact that we were shooting his arrows, but that we were doing it so poorly. He was the first adult we'd ever met who was bothered by our incompetence.

He drew an arrow from Twitch's quiver, nocked it, and pulled the string back until his thumb grazed his jaw. He inhaled and held his breath, as still as a statue. His face was so relaxed he looked decades younger.

When he released the string, the arrow zipped through air, landing in the very center of the target with a resounding *thwack*.

"That's how you use a bow and arrow," he said. "Not all twisting and yanking and prying and pulling and hoping it'll somehow hit *some*where near the target. You gotta hold the draw."

We all shared a look of astonishment. It was as if we were talking to a different man altogether. His temper was still intact, but there was suddenly a spring in his step that hadn't been there when we'd first met him.

"So will you teach us?" I ventured to ask.

The old man rubbed his jaw. "'Spect I'll have to, if you aim to actually kill something. You all haven't got the skills God gave a toad. But don't be expectin' no free meal. I barely got stores enough for me."

"We're not asking for more food," I said. "Last night's fish was enough."

Flush sent an elbow in my ribs, but I meant it. If the old man could teach us how to use a bow and arrow, we'd be in better shape than ever.

The old man's gaze drifted toward the barn. "I thought there were a couple dozen of you."

"The rest are still asleep."

"Well, wake 'em up. If I'm teaching you, I aim to do it a single time. No point repeating myself."

"Yes, sir," I said, and Twitch went loping off to get the others.

We stood there awkwardly, no one quite knowing what to say. Finally, I mustered up the courage and said, "My name's Book. What's yours?"

The old man studied me suspiciously. "Why do you want to know?"

"If you're going to be our teacher, it only seems right we know your name."

The man regarded the request a moment longer. "Frank," he said at last, as though he'd not had reason to say his name aloud for many years. He cleared his

266

throat and said it again. "It's Frank."

"Hello, Mr. Frank."

"Not *Mr.* Frank," he snapped. "Just Frank. Got it?"

"Yes, sir . . . Frank." I'd never called an adult by his first name before.

When the Sisters and other LTs arrived, he began teaching us the finer points of nocking arrows and releasing bowstrings. He raised his voice and wasn't afraid to yell. Taught Dozer how to compensate for his one bad arm, and Four Fingers for his lack of digits. Showed Helen how to use a smaller bow and Scylla a bigger one. Even Cat didn't escape Frank's badgering. Frank told him he was relying too much on strength and not enough on form. Craft. *Technique.*

"You've gotta think of it as an extension of yourself, not just a weapon. Do it your way and you'll be wildly successful some of the time. Do it mine and you'll be very successful *all* of the time."

Cat didn't seem to mind the advice one bit.

As for the rest of us, we could barely suppress our smiles. Although we didn't know it earlier, it was the kind of instruction we'd been craving all our lives.

There wasn't a moment in those next two days when we weren't busy. Archery, fishing, tracking prey—we did it all. Making weapons, too. Bows and arrows. Slingshots. Hope took a branch from an ash tree and whittled it

267

into a spear—with an ease that made me think she'd done it a hundred other times.

In the late afternoon of the third day, Frank invited us into his cabin. It was like entering another world. There was a tidy kitchen. A small dining room table with placemats. Even a couple of reclining chairs angled in front of a fireplace. There was something else as well: books. Thousands of them, jammed onto shelves and in towering piles.

"Take a breath," June Bug whispered to me.

Frank saw me ogling them. "You a reader?" he asked. I nodded dumbly. "Help yourself then. A book's no good unless it's being read. Just takin' up space otherwise."

In no time we were cooking up the fruits of our labors: rabbit pie, raccoon stew, fried squirrel. Added to that were mounds of potatoes, countless jars of green beans, and stewed tomatoes from Gloria's garden.

That was his wife's name: Gloria. That's who we'd buried several nights before.

When it came time to actually eat, we gobbled down what was easily the most delicious meal we'd ever had. As I was licking my fingers for the tenth or fifteenth time, a spring storm blew in, thunder rattling the walls, rain clawing at the windows. To be inside and sheltered—and now *full*—seemed the most luxurious feeling ever.

"So tell me," Frank said, sitting in a reclining chair

and scratching Argos's ears. "Who are you, anyway?"

We looked at each other.

"Just some teenagers," I answered, as casually as possible.

"Uh-huh. Who just happened to be riding horses that don't belong to them. Or didn't you think I'd notice the brands?"

I felt the stares of the others. My cheeks warmed.

"I'm listening," he said.

Something about the look on his face made me feel ashamed. Here he'd taught us all these things, made us dinner, invited us into his home, and I couldn't even give him a straight answer.

"We're on the run," I admitted. Dozer shot me a venomous look.

"I figured that. From where?"

"We're from Camp Freedom," Hope said.

"And we're from Camp Liberty," I added.

He nodded briskly. "Those the camps at the base of the mountain?"

"Yes, sir."

"And you escaped from there?"

"That's right," Hope said.

He nodded briskly and my stomach tightened as I waited for his response.

"Good for you," he said at last, giving his thigh a playful slap.

I wasn't sure I'd heard correctly.

"It's about time someone had sense enough to get away from them Brown Shirts, what with their *badges* and their *inverted triangles*." He let loose a laugh that was more cackle than anything else.

"But the other night you cursed us for being Less Thans," Twitch pointed out.

His gaze fell downward. "That was wrong of me. I'm sorry."

It occurred to me I'd never heard an adult apologize before.

"For years, the government's fed us all this nonsense and after a while it starts to seep in. I don't give a whit about a person's skin color or their radiation sores or whatever else the government's against. Guess I was thinkin' more about your parents than you." We looked at him blankly. "You know—them being terrorists and all."

"But we never knew our parents," I said.

He opened his mouth to say something and then let it close. "No, I guess you didn't," he said, like he was just piecing something together for the first time. "More lies from the Republic," he muttered.

"Have you ever run into them?" Hope asked. "The Brown Shirts?"

"Twenty years ago. Just after Omega. No desire to see 'em again."

"You don't trust them?"

"About as far as I can throw 'em." He went on to explain how he and his wife had been at the cabin the day the bombs fell—watching the first reports on TV, then switching to radio when the TV went out. "That's when we heard," he said.

"About what?"

"Our new country. The United States was no more, replaced with the *Republic of the True America*." He said this last with a touch of scorn. "The few politicians who survived started up a new government. Made everyone sign loyalty oaths. Got rid of the Constitution and replaced it with a Compact."

"What's that?" Helen asked.

"Like an agreement—a promise."

"A promise to do what?"

"Rebuild. Become better than ever. And the government said the only way to achieve that was through the purity of its citizens."

"What's that mean?" June Bug asked.

"Nothing good." Then he added, *"Beware the Less Thans* is what it means."

A chill ran up my spine.

"Why do they consider us Less Thans?" Flush asked.

He rubbed his whiskered chin before he spoke. "Because you're different—different body shapes, different belief systems, different skin color, you name

271

it—and people don't like different. They like what they recognize. And we all know there're two ways to feel good about yourself in this world. Either make yourself better . . . or put others down." He paused. "I did it, too."

I felt bad for him. Truth was, if it weren't for him we probably would've starved to death or frozen to death or who knows what.

He went on to say how, in the days following Omega, he and his wife tried to reach their kids and grandkids in Oklahoma.

"But there weren't nothin' to find. The cities were just smoldering craters, and the towns that did remain were run by gun-toting Crazies who had as much sense as a lynch mob. And then there were the Brown Shirts, instructed to shoot first and ask questions later. Just seemed safer to come back up here." Then, in a whisper: "Even if it meant not seeing our children again."

I didn't know about the Sisters, but we Less Thans had never known our families. He had a family but lost it to Omega. I wondered which was worse.

His rheumy eyes settled on Hope. "It's *your* camp I don't understand. Why were you all there?"

Hope hesitated before answering. "Because we were twins," she said. The other Sisters dropped their eyes.

"Yes, and?"

"You don't want to know."

272

Something about her tone gave me goose bumps, and it was like I suspected all along: they had experienced things the rest of us couldn't imagine.

"Was the whole country hit by bombs?" June Bug asked.

"All except Iowa," Frank said, nodding.

"Why not Iowa?"

"Nothing there worth bombing."

When he smiled, it occurred to us we were meant to smile too, even though we didn't really get the joke. Then he tousled Red's hair until it was standing straight up and that made us laugh out loud—a sound we'd nearly forgotten how to make. Argos got in on the act and barked and howled and that made us laugh harder still.

We were still laughing when Four Fingers came bursting through the door. He'd been assigned to the watch, and he bent over at the waist, trying to catch his breath.

"What is it, son?" Frank asked. "Seen a ghost?"

We were all set to laugh again when Four Fingers blurted out, "Brown Shirts! Coming this way."

The laughter died in our throats.

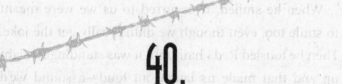

40.

"How many?" Frank asks.

"Six. On dirt bikes."

Hope tenses. She knows what the Brown Shirts—and Dr. Gallingham—are capable of.

Frank rises from his chair. "A few of you, take the horses and go hide in the boulder field. Now git!"

June Bug, Four Fingers, and Scylla dash out of the cabin. Argos trails after them. The rest begin putting away dishes so the soldiers won't suspect anything.

"Where should we hide?" Flush asks. He looks on the verge of throwing up.

"Under the barn. There's a space beneath the floorboards."

"And they won't find us?"

"Not unless they know to look there."

Everyone races to the barn. The drone of dirt bikes grows louder.

When the Sisters and Less Thans step inside the barn, Hope's heart sinks. Strewn about are clothes, packs, saddles—everything they own. And twenty-eight mattresses made of straw.

Frank isn't fazed. "Grab your stuff and bring it here." He drops to his knees and sweeps away a layer of straw. Then he begins prying up floorboards, revealing a small pit of dark earth beneath the floor.

They stuff everything down there—canteens, saddles, bows and arrows, slingshots—then they spread the hay around.

"Now climb in and I'll cover you up," Frank commands.

Nearly all of the twenty-five manage to fold their bodies into the small cavity, but there isn't room for Cat, Book, and Hope. They look at Frank, alarmed, but he just lays the wood planks back in place and hammers in some nails.

"Don't worry," he says to those beneath the floor. "We'll come git ya." Then he turns to the remaining three. "Come on."

He leads them out the rear of the barn to the back door of the cabin. Just as the screen door shuts behind them, Hope hears the first of the dirt bikes pulling up.

Frank drags a footstool to the middle of the kitchen, ventures onto the bottom step, and pushes up a ceiling tile. Stale, musty air comes tumbling down.

"Git up there and don't move," he says in a sharp whisper.

Hope goes first, then Book and Cat. They scramble into the attic, brushing away cobwebs and mouse turds. The panel slips back in place, throwing them in black.

There's a rapping on the door, followed a moment later by muffled voices. Frank's, of course. And a man who identifies himself as Colonel Westbrook.

There's a tiny hole in the attic floor, and with just slight maneuvering Hope can look down and see Frank and Westbrook sitting opposite each other like a couple of old friends having afternoon tea. Surrounding them are three Brown Shirts.

"No idea at all?" Westbrook asks, his voice dripping kindness.

"If I knew, I'd tell ya," Frank says. "I got nothin' to hide. What'd they do that was so terrible, anyway?"

"They ran away."

"You mean escaped."

"I mean *ran away*. We have no fences. We're a resettlement camp, trying to help boys adjust to the complexities of a life without parents. That's all."

"Then why'd they run away?"

Westbrook laughs good-naturedly. "You know kids. A rough day at school. Not getting along with friends. Who can say? The important thing is they need our help. You know as well as I they'll never survive in these mountains."

"And what if I were to say I don't believe it's no orphanage?"

The colonel's voice tightens. "Then you'd be wrong."

There's a long moment of silence. When Westbrook speaks again, the pleasantness is back in his voice. "I'm a military man. I do what the Eagle's Nest tells me. Do you think I want to head up an orphanage in the middle of nowhere? Don't you think I'd rather be on the front lines, fighting the terrorists that brought on Omega?"

"Just followin' orders, huh?"

"That's right."

"Doin' what Chancellor Maddox bids you do?"

"Something like that. And if it's for the good of the country as it tries to pick itself up from the ashes, I'm not the least bit apologetic about that." His voice grows thick with emotion. "I love these boys—I do—and I can understand their running away. But we're not talking about running out to the neighborhood grocery store. We're talking life and death here." His eyes get all teary and he asks, "You're certain you've seen no sign of them?"

Frank shakes his head. "Wish I could help you out."

"No strange sounds? No missing food? Nothing like that?"

"I think I'd know if I heard something."

"Yes, of course." Westbrook doesn't bother to hide his displeasure.

Hope realizes the colonel has been asking about the Less Thans, not the Sisters. He must not know they're traveling together. She wonders if that's a good thing or not.

Book is lying next to her, his arm pressed tightly against hers, his skin radiating warmth. Even in this moment of peril, with the enemy several feet below her, she feels a shudder of pleasure. Of possibility.

The screen door bangs and brings her back to the present. Another Brown Shirt has just come in.

"Nothing in the barn," the soldier says. At the sound of his voice, Book inhales sharply.

Hope looks at him, and Book mouths, "Sergeant Dekker." The name means nothing to her—but it obviously does to Book.

"It's just a big, empty barn," Dekker goes on to say. "However"—he pauses dramatically—"there are fresh horse droppings in the corral."

"Of course there are," Frank chimes in. "Horses poop. It's what they do."

"And where are these horses now?" Colonel Westbrook asks.

278

Frank shrugs. "Who can keep track? They come, they go. They're horses."

It seems like Westbrook wants to say something, but holds his tongue.

"One other thing, too," Dekker adds. He points out the window to the grave. "Should we dig it up?"

Frank shoots up from his chair like a rocket. "You lay one hand on that dirt and I'll see to it you get buried as well!"

Dekker goes for his sidearm, but Westbrook motions for him to leave it holstered.

"Now now," the colonel says, placing a hand atop Frank's shoulder. "No one's going to dig up a grave, if that's what it is."

"Of course that's what it is, you jackass. What else do you think it'd be?"

Hope can see the color rise on Westbrook's face. It's obvious he isn't used to being addressed this way. "And whose grave might it be?"

"My wife's. Buried her a few nights ago."

"I see. And you built the coffin?"

"If you don't believe me, I'd be happy to make one for your friend there."

Westbrook actually smiles. "That won't be necessary. I'm sure you're a man of many talents." Then he adds, "Let's just hope lying isn't one of them."

Frank doesn't respond. Hope can see his jaw is set,

his teeth clenched. It's the Frank they encountered when they rode up that first night.

"So you built this coffin by yourself?"

"I just said so, didn't I?"

"Where?"

"Where else? The barn."

"And carried your wife to it?"

"She weren't but skin and bones by the time she passed."

"Right, right." Westbrook paces around the room. "So I'm not clear on one thing. How'd you get the coffin to the grave?"

"I dragged it," he sputters, not nearly as convincing as before.

"By yourself?"

"That's right."

"All the way from the barn to that grove of aspens?"

"If you want, I'll demonstrate with your friend there. He's dead weight."

This time Westbrook allows Sergeant Dekker to unholster his weapon and point the barrel at Frank's forehead. "I'd be careful about getting on Sergeant Dekker's bad side," Westbrook says. "He happens to have a bit of a temper."

Frank doesn't flinch. Finally, Westbrook leads the Brown Shirts to the door.

"You keep an eye out for those boys," he says, then

steps outside, the screen door slamming behind him. A few moments later Hope hears the coughing ignitions of six dirt bikes, and the buzz of their engines receding in the distance.

Frank lowers himself in his chair. It's another fifteen minutes before he makes even the slightest move.

By the time they all reassemble in the cabin, Frank has a map spread out on the dining room table. With a shaking index finger he points to a snaking line of mountains due east—on the other side of the lake.

"There's a trail here I used to follow when I'd hunt elk. It's steep and rocky, but you should be able to hike it."

"Where's it lead?" June Bug wants to know.

"To a pass. Follow that along the ridge to the very end. There's a desert down below called the Flats. You'll want to avoid it for as long as you can. And keep your eyes open for wolves. They're different now."

"Different how?" Twitch asks.

"Just different."

Hope tries to swallow but can't.

"And once we get down the mountain?" June Bug asks. "What then?"

"Cross over the Flats and make your way to the Heartland."

"The Heartland?"

"The next territory."

281

A silence falls over the group. For many of them, it's the first time they've heard the name of their destination.

"You still haven't told us how we get there," Dozer demands. "You're pointing to a ridge, but how the heck're we supposed to get across the lake?"

"How else? Boats."

They make their way to the shed. The *boathouse*.

It isn't much bigger than an outhouse and it lists to one side, its black timbers old and rotting. They peer into the dark interior and there before them are the mingled shapes of wooden crates, rusted bicycles, old TVs . . . and two rowboats. Everything is piled atop everything else.

They clear the rowboats and drag them to the thin grass that borders the lake like a margin on a page. Even in the falling twilight Hope can see holes as big as fists in the rotting planks.

"If we plug those gaps, you could leave in the morning," Frank says.

Their eyes widen. "So soon?" June Bug asks.

"I have a feeling those goons'll be back in a day or two."

Hope thinks some of the Sisters—and Less Thans, too—are going to break down on the spot. It's crazy, but in a few short days this place has begun to feel like home. And now they have to leave.

"Why can't we fight 'em? There's twenty-nine of us and only six of them."

"They've got guns," Frank reminds them. "All we have is one twelve-gauge, a rifle, some crossbows, and bows and arrows."

"And slingshots," Flush adds.

Frank pats him on the back. "I don't think they'll be any match for M16s. Even though I'd rather have you twenty-eight on my side than hundreds of them."

Maybe he's just saying it, but Hope doesn't think so. She thinks he means it.

"So how do we plug the holes?" Dozer asks.

Twitch breaks the silence. "You're not planning on driving anywhere soon, are you, Frank?"

Frank looks at him, confused. "No, son."

Twitch smiles and takes off running.

They spend the rest of the evening sawing planks to replace the rotting ones. In a fire pit behind the barn, Twitch boils a steamy cauldron of black rubber, melted down from chunks of the Jeep Cherokee's tires. They slather the noxious goo onto the boats' hulls and let it harden.

Frank drags out a cardboard box full of old clothes, neatly folded and smelling of mothballs. His sons' things, he tells them. "They're yours if you want 'em."

They're thrilled, of course, and some of them even fit—hoodies and flannel shirts and wool socks. It's like

283

a Christmas they've never had, and Frank seems as pleased about it as them. Before they say good night, Hope finally asks him the question stirring within her: "So, what's the Eagle's Nest that Colonel Westbrook mentioned?"

"Near as I can tell, the headquarters of our chancellor."

"Who's that?"

Frank emits a low growl. "Chancellor Maddox. The head of our territory. Makes Westbrook look like the Pillsbury Doughboy."

Hope doesn't get the reference, but she understands the gist.

"Have you ever seen him?" she asks.

"*Her*. And only on TV, back before Omega. Former beauty queen turned Midwestern congresswoman." He doesn't bother to hide his disdain. "When Omega happened, she just plain took charge. It was her idea to scrap the Constitution. And she was the one who came up with loyalty oaths and the notion of Less Thans." He drums his fingers on his chin. "I have a feeling she's up to something, but what that is I have no idea."

Hope knows who he's talking about. The woman with the blond hair. The one who's taken such pleasure in humiliating her. She wrote the letter to Colonel Thorason demanding he "leave no trace." A shared look with Book tells her he's thinking the same thing.

"That's why you're wise to leave this territory," Frank says.

"You think the other territories are better?" Hope asks.

"They can't be any worse."

"And we can't convince you to come with us?"

A smile creases Frank's weathered face. "I'd just slow you down. No, it's better this way." Then he turns away, eyes damp with tears. "But I'm much obliged to you for asking."

When they crawl into their makeshift beds that night, muscles aching, Hope thinks of everything these few days have brought them: new skills, good food, preparations for the rest of their journey. And a friend in Frank.

Despite all the dangers, a new and better life seems close at hand.

41.

THE SHARP BUZZ OF engines startled us awake and we raced to the barn door. The jostling headlights of dirt bikes fell on the trees.

"Come on," Cat whispered, motioning us toward the rear exit.

The twenty-eight of us edged along the lake until we reached the boats, our breaths frosty in the dark.

"What about the rubber?" Twitch asked. "There's no way it's set."

"It's gotta be," Cat answered.

We lifted the two boats from their sawhorses and eased them into the water. Eight Sisters in one boat, eight in the second. As I held one of the boats steady, I noticed it had a name scrawled in faded white paint along the hull.

Gloria.

Frank's wife.

Feet slurping in mud, we pushed the two boats away from the shallows and into the lake. As the Sisters paddled silently, the boats drifted away. Every noise was magnified a hundred times, but the drone of engines drowned out all other sounds.

The boats reached the other side of the lake just as the six dirt bikes returned, spewing gravel. Colonel Westbrook marched up the steps to the cabin porch and pounded on the door. So much for returning in a day or two.

The boats were headed back now for the rest of us: Hope rowing one, Scylla the other.

I looked behind me and saw Frank in front of his cabin, lit by the glare of dirt bike headlamps. He wore a nightshirt, his pants' suspenders hanging limply by his sides, his white hair sticking out in odd angles. He and Colonel Westbrook were arguing.

The two boats returned and we stumbled on board as quickly and quietly as we could.

"You okay?" I asked Hope.

She nodded yes, but I could see her shirt was damp with sweat. Flush and June Bug took her place at the oars to give her a breather. They began easing us into the lake.

We weren't far when Hope gestured behind us, back toward the cabin. I turned just in time to see a Brown

Shirt run up to Colonel Westbrook, pointing toward the barn. Then my heart sank as I heard him shout the word "mattresses."

I watched as Colonel Westbrook unholstered his sidearm and fired twice at point-blank range. *Pop, pop.* Frank crumpled to the ground.

My hand went to my mouth and all of us froze, paddles suspended in air, our breaths shallow and gasping. Red—big, tough Red—emitted a strangled sob. Just loud enough for a couple of Brown Shirts to look our way.

The dirt bikes came to life, their lights bouncing off the side of Frank's cabin, not stopping until they reached the shore. Their dim beams pointed in our direction.

"Book," Red said.

"I see."

Although the soldiers were just now reaching the shore, I knew they couldn't chase us across the water. Ours were the only two boats in the boathouse.

"B-Book," Red said again.

His eyes led me to the bottom of the boat, where a foot of water sloshed from side to side. The rubber hadn't set. It had held for one trip across, but now the lake was pouring in.

We lifted our feet to avoid the icy wet, and Argos jumped up to a seat. The gunwales were nearly even with the lake itself; if we didn't act fast we would sink for sure.

I ripped off my hoodie. "Start stuffing!" I cried.

Once the others figured out what I was doing, they did the same: tearing off layers and jamming bunched-up clothing in the keel's gaping fissures.

"Hands!" I cried.

We cupped them together like ladles and began flinging water back into the lake. In no time my fingers were numb with cold. The water level lowered, but whenever we stopped to catch our breath, it rose again, just as fast. It didn't help that there were seven of us on board.

"Keep going!" I commanded, looking over at the other boat, hoping they could come to our rescue. Their situation was no better.

Suddenly there was another sound: deep, slapping splashes.

"B-b-bullets," Red whispered, and my stomach knotted. A glance back toward shore showed me the silhouettes of Westbrook, Dekker, and four Brown Shirts calmly firing at us as though we were ducks on a pond. Target practice.

"Come on, *Gloria*," I whispered, dipping the two numb stubs that were my hands into the water. "Get us across."

Flush and June Bug rowed harder than ever, and I didn't know if it was the bullets or what, but for the first time we were actually moving in something resembling a straight line, gliding atop the black surface of the lake.

"That's it, *Gloria*. Almost there."

A bullet whizzed past, followed this time not by a splash but by a sickening thud. The sound of a knife slicing into a too-ripe melon. June Bug slumped forward, his hands releasing the oar. It slipped through the oarlock and into the water.

"June Bug!" I cried. A dark stain was visible on his chest. When I yanked open the shirt to get a better look, a gaping hole was spitting blood like a garden hose. I ripped off my T-shirt and bunched it up, placing it on the bullet hole to stanch the flow of blood.

"Keep rowing!" I shouted to Flush, his eyes as wide as coins.

"But there's just one oar."

While he worked the lone paddle, the rest of us dipped our torsos over the sides and shooed the water backward with our arms. We were like some primordial beast, propelling ourselves awkwardly forward. The air sang with bullets.

"You're going to be all right," I kept repeating to June Bug. "You're going to be all right."

But whether I meant it or not, I couldn't honestly say, and the sight of the blood spurting from his chest prompted a nightmare of sights and sounds. *Squealing fingers on white tile. A knife's blade rimmed in red. Stomping of feet.* My face grew clammy and the horizon tilted wildly.

"B-Book!" It was Red, pointing back behind us.

An orange glow erupted on the shoreline like a rising sun. For an instant everyone stopped paddling, and all we could hear was our own heavy breathing and the gurgle of water slapping the sides of the *Gloria*.

"What is it?" Flush asked.

"The ranch," Hope answered flatly. "They're burning the ranch."

42.

THE FLAMES LICK THE black underbelly of night until it's impossible to tell where embers end and stars begin. The cabin is on fire. And the barn. All the books, the canned vegetables, the *home* where Frank and Gloria lived for twenty years.

The other boat's keel scrapes the shore and they stumble onto dry earth, where they huddle by the lake's edge. Some holy mixture of luck and sheer will have delivered them across the lake.

And *Gloria*.

Their boat comes to a stop on the rocky beach and the others stretch out their hands. When they see June Bug they freeze.

"Bad?" Twitch asks.

No one answers.

Scylla and Twitch gather branches and construct a triangular stretcher. They slip June Bug onto it, covering him with blankets. Helen gives him willow bark to chew to ease the pain. They're still tending to him when Cat orders them to sink the boats.

"Sink the boats?" Flush asks, incredulous.

"You heard me."

"But if things don't work out, we'll need 'em if we want to turn back." He doesn't need to say the words *wolves* or *Skull People* for the others to know exactly what he's thinking.

Cat levels his gaze at him. "There *is* no turning back." He looks at everyone else, daring someone to contradict him.

As crazy as it is, Hope understands Cat's logic. They're on the run; they've escaped from two separate camps and killed Brown Shirts in the process. There's no point even having the option to return.

So they do as he instructs: dropping handfuls of rocks into the two boats until both are resting on the bottom of the cove.

As Cat goes searching for the trail, Book and Hope empty out the backpacks and share a glance. It's a meager mishmash of objects: a tarp, fishing line, rope, binocs, first aid kit, and flint for starting fires. Although they managed to bring along most of their weapons, they're both thinking the same thing: the odds are stacked against them.

Cat returns. "Let's go," he says sharply.

"You found it?" Twitch asks.

He grunts.

"Where's it lead?"

"How the hell should I know? I didn't have time to go up it."

That's when they hear it: a voice, tinny and muffled and slowly gaining clarity as it sweeps across the lake.

". . . urge you to come back," the voice says, *Colonel Westbrook's voice*. It sounds as though it's being projected through a bullhorn. "We're concerned about your safety. And besides"—he pauses—"it'll be easy enough for us to build a bridge and cross the spillway."

The meaning is clear: Westbrook isn't done chasing them.

"Come on," says Red. "We'd better catch up with Cat before he climbs the mountain on his own."

A moment later they're trudging along the bumpy terrain in search of a trail they hope will take them far away, from Brown Shirts and Colonel Westbrook, far away from life as they currently know it.

PART THREE
PREY

For he today that sheds his blood with me
Shall be my brother. . . .
—WILLIAM SHAKESPEARE
from *Henry V*

43.

THE FIRST SNOWFLAKES FELL within the hour—big, wet flakes that made a soft thudding sound when they collided with our clothes. In no time our shoulders were topped with a thick layer of white. A spring snow.

The cold was bad, the footing was worse. More than a couple of us tumbled to the ground on slippery, snow-covered granite, scraping knees, burying hands in icy slush. I remembered the sign from before: *Mountains don't care.*

We reached the top of the ridge and followed the trail east. We marched in silence, our feet crunching through snow. The Sisters rarely spoke to the Less Thans, and the Less Thans rarely spoke to the Sisters. Despite those days at Frank's cabin, it was like there was still a divide between the groups. Even Hope and me.

Especially Hope and me.

Ever since that kiss in the tunnel, there'd been a certain self-consciousness between the two of us. Which was weird because—for reasons I couldn't put my finger on—I got the feeling she understood me in ways no one else did.

"What happened to you?" I asked, sidling up to her.

"What do you mean?"

"After you were caught in the office. What'd they do?" I remembered her behavior in the fields that day—like a zombie from one of Flush's comic books.

"Who says they did anything?" she said brusquely.

"I just figured. I mean . . ."

"They didn't do anything."

"Nothing? They must've—"

"I'm here, aren't I?" Her tone of voice made it clear she didn't want to talk about it. She picked up her pace, and I hurried to catch up. We walked in silence. She used her spear like a walking stick.

"What's his name?" she asked, when it was obvious I wasn't going anywhere.

"Who?"

She pointed to Cat; as usual, he was at the front of the line.

"Cat," I said. "Why?"

"I met him once."

298

I could feel my eyes going wide. "You met Cat?"

"He stayed with us. In our cave."

I suddenly remembered Cat telling me—the night we'd seen the massacre—how he'd been given shelter by a man and his two daughters. How they were on the run from soldiers.

"So that was you," I said blankly. I wondered what happened to her family. Remembered what she said in the field. *I had a sister.*

Hope gave a nod, and I felt a pang of—what?— jealousy at the thought of Cat meeting Hope before I had. For some reason, I wanted to be the one who saw her first.

She walked on ahead before I got a chance to say anything else.

The sun rose and the sky cleared—a blue so intense it hurt to look at it. Whether it was the warming weather or the fact we were one step closer to the Heartland, conversations began springing up.

"Seriously, Batman has a soul," Twitch said to Flush. "He lost his parents, so he's fueled by pain. That's what propels him forward."

"Superman lost his parents, too," Flush countered.

"He never really *knew* his parents. There's a difference."

Then they abruptly stopped talking, and I looked up. The trees had suddenly ended. All around were

299

mountain peaks, capped in the purest white. It's like we were on top of the world. A beauty that defied description.

"This is the saddle Frank talked about," Cat explained, pointing to the stretch of ridgeline that connected one range to the next. The trail looked dangerously narrow, with steep drop-offs on either side, but we were buoyed by the possibility of a new territory. A new life.

We made our way ahead, and soon we came upon a series of red pearls: tiny spheres like cranberries scattered atop the snow. Flush ran to pick one up. No sooner was it in his hand when it squished between his thumb and finger. What was once a perfect sphere was now a messy oval.

"Yuck," he said, wiping the red goo on his pants. "What is it?"

Twitch scooped up another of the red balls and examined it. "Blood," he said. "Coagulated blood."

"From what?"

When we looked farther up the trail, we noticed even more of the globules. Hundreds of them. *Thousands.*

We rounded the next bend and saw the source: a huge bull elk with half its stomach missing. The snow encircling the corpse was bright red, as though someone overturned a can of paint. A big, red target, with a dead elk in the bull's-eye. The snow was patted down. Footprints. Animal footprints.

Hope knelt by the dead beast and poked it with her knife.

"Wolves," she said, then stuck her index finger into the steaming entrails. "Still warm. This was recent."

"How many, do you think?" Flush asked, trying to maintain a steady voice.

"At least ten. Maybe more." When she stood up and surveyed the scene, we all became very aware of our surroundings: we were exposed on a naked saddle of land connecting one mountain peak with another. No place to hide. Not from soldiers. Not from wolves. A ripple of fear ran through us all.

"Come on," Cat said. "We need to find some trees."

I understood his thinking. A forest would provide wood and wood would provide fire and fire . . . would maybe keep the wolves away.

We marched without speaking. The angle of the sun deepened, lengthening our shadows until they were grotesque beings that didn't resemble us in the least. And still there was no sign of trees for as far as we could see. It was just white mountaintop followed by white mountaintop.

The pace quickened. The lower arc of sun dipped behind a far peak, painting the snow pink and salmon. But the beauty was lost on me. Panic was rising in my throat.

44.

THEY MARCH IN SILENCE.

Swirling thoughts dance around Hope's head. She regrets snapping at Book—she does—but she's in no mood to talk about Faith. Not now. Maybe not ever.

As for Book, she doesn't know what to make of him. Yes, he came back for her—even when she warned him not to. She'll never forget it. But as much as she's drawn to him, there's something there that concerns her. Something hidden.

And then there's Cat. There's no denying his rugged good looks, but he's as perplexing as the animal he's named for. She has even less idea what he's about. Still, she can't forget the night they shared their cave with him, how she and Faith stayed up into the wee hours just listening to him and their father talk. Even when they all finally went to bed, she still remembers the steady rise and fall of his chest as he fell asleep.

The procession stops and her thoughts are cut short. Stretched out before them is an enormous swirl of the deepest black. They can't make out what it is. When they step forward, the black shape suddenly lifts from the ground—like a scarf caught in a gust of wind.

Flies. Thousands of them. Perfuming the air with the stench of death. The Sisters and Less Thans cover their mouths and noses.

Before the flies settle back down, Hope sees what they're feasting on: elk. But this time it's not a single corpse—more like two dozen. Faces ripped off, stomachs gouged open, intestines dragged across the snow. The bodies are reduced to a heaping pile of steaming entrails.

And left uneaten. These wolves are killing purely for sport.

Helen takes one look and falls to her knees, heaving up what little food is in her stomach. Hope goes over to comfort her. At just that instant the top curve of the sun slips behind the mountains. Utter darkness won't be far behind.

"W-what should we do?" Red asks.

"Keep moving," Cat says, his meaning clear. *We need to get the hell out of here.*

They skirt the corpses, the flies barely budging as they pass. The world around them slowly blackens; only the distant, snowcapped mountains reflect the moon's paltry light. They are suddenly out of snow, and although that makes their walking easier, it doesn't tell them which way the wolves have gone. For all Hope knows, they could be right behind them.

The ridge narrows. They are on the thinnest part of the saddle; a fall down either side would be a certain death. Every so often a shoe sends a rock flying, and they can hear its clattering descent as it plummets thousands of feet to the dark abyss below.

They're forced to stop. It would be suicide to keep going. With no fire, they draw into a tight circle, Less Thans and Sisters together, using the few blankets and one another to create a vague semblance of warmth. Dozer takes first watch, and one by one everyone nods off. In Hope's case, it's never for very long. Her own shivering keeps jolting her awake.

On her fourth or fifth attempt at sleep she hears a dim but insistent scraping, followed by a low, throaty rumble. Her eyes snap open.

A million stars wink overhead, so bright it seems like she can touch them. She lifts her head and peeks at the others. They are sleeping soundly. No one is awake . . . not even Dozer. He has fallen asleep sitting up, head resting on forearms.

She locates the guttural sound: Argos, pressed flat against the ground, teeth bared, having a nightmare of some kind. She's about to breathe a sigh of relief when she realizes something isn't right. Her eyes search the pile of sleeping Sisters and LTs.

June Bug and his stretcher are gone.

Her gaze follows Argos's and lands on the stretcher, a good fifteen feet away. Surrounding it are a dozen pairs of small green circles.

Eyes.

Wolf eyes.

They have dragged the stretcher and the wounded June Bug away from the others.

Her breath catches. She wants to wake the others but fears that any sound will prompt the wolves to attack. But the longer she waits, the more difficult it will be to rescue June Bug.

Something pushes against her side and she nearly jumps. Her eyes lower. It's a slingshot, the base of its handle pressed into her ribs.

The hand holding it is Cat's.

She glances at him. In his lap is a bow and arrow.

Her hand eases over and takes the slingshot. Cat waits until her grip is firm before releasing it. The very bed she's been sleeping on is littered with rocks and stones. Ammo. She lowers her fingers and grasps a handful. Ready.

She has just loaded a pebble into the deer-hide pocket when she feels a whoosh of air past her ear. Cat has sent the first arrow flying. The wolf tugging at the stretcher yelps and falls backward, the arrow's shaft sticking from its flank.

"What's going on?" Book asks, wiping sleep from his eyes. And then he sees. In one blurry moment of tense anticipation, the two sides face off, waiting to see who will attack next.

Teeth bared, claws outstretched, the wolves lunge forward. Hope draws back the elastic and lets it fly. The rock hits the lead wolf—the alpha male—hard in the snout and he yelps in pain. When he realizes he's not seriously hurt, his eyes narrow, saliva dripping from his canine teeth. Even in scant moonlight, Hope can make out his every hair.

He squats on his back haunches and leaps forward, body soaring through air. He is nearly at her neck when an arrow strikes him in the face. It penetrates his right eye and exits the back of his head. The charging animal thuds to the earth.

Hope glances back at Cat. He's already loading the next arrow on the bowstring.

By now everyone is scrambling for weapons and ammunition. As Hope presses another rock into the slingshot's pocket, she sees a wolf clamp its snarling teeth around Red's ankle. She sends the rock flying, and it bounces off the animal's side. The wolf, which has a diamond-shaped splotch of white fur on its muzzle, continues to gnaw away at Red.

"Get it off!" Red cries, twisting and squirming under the wolf's hot clutch.

The Sisters and LTs pelt Diamond Wolf with everything they have. Rocks, pebbles, stones—all bite into the animal's thick fur. Even Argos fastens his teeth to the wolf's hind leg and clamps down. With a blood-dripping snarl, the wolf releases his grip on Red and snaps at Argos, taking a small chunk out of the dog's side. Argos cries and falls backward. Diamond Wolf finally retreats down the rocky slope.

"You all right?" Twitch asks.

"Give me a bow," Red answers, ignoring the blood oozing from his ankle. The Sisters are firing darts from crossbows and the LTs are zipping arrows. The growling wolves tumble to the ground with such wild shrieks that it raises the hair on Hope's arms. The wolves' numbers are suddenly reduced from two dozen to half that many. The rest have either fled or lie dead and bleeding.

"That's it!" Red yells. "Keep 'em coming!"

Hope and all the others are feeling confident—invincible, even—and she is smiling as she reaches for the next pebble. But as she tries to pull her hand away, she feels a strong yank on her wrist, tugging at her arm. The wolf is back.

She shakes her arm to fling it off, the way you would a fly, but its grip is far too strong. In one swift move he pushes her on her back and rips at her arm as though trying to snap it free. As though it were a chicken leg. The splotch of white becomes a smoky blur as its head twists from side to side.

The others begin pelting the wolf, but nothing fazes him, not even a dart from Diana, which catches him in a rear leg, its shaft jutting out from bone. No longer content with her wrist, he dives for her neck instead. She lifts her hands and tries to pummel him away, but the wolf is too strong and soon his mouth is pressed against the silky flesh of her neck. She feels his searing, sour breath, reeking of dead rodents.

Hope looks away, and her gaze falls on Book. The rocks from his slingshot have no effect on the wolf. But at his feet is Hope's spear. "Pick it up!" she screams, but he doesn't hear her. He continues to pelt the wolf with one rock after another.

As the wolf's jaws widen and he leans in to press his sharp canines into Hope's jugular, a spear soars through the air and impales the wolf right in the back, sending him sprawling to the rocky soil. When he drops his head to the ground, life leaves him, and his yellow-gold eyes remain fixed on the person who threw it. Hope turns to see.

Cat. He holds his warrior's pose, the spear having

just left his outstretched hand. It was her own spear—thrown by Cat—that saved her life.

Helen rushes to her side. "You okay, Hope?"

Hope nods dumbly and Helen helps her sit up. As she does, Hope suddenly realizes there is silence. The wolves are gone, either dead or vanished. Everyone is breathing heavily, lungs expanding, trying to draw oxygen from the thin air.

"I'm fine," she says, although her wrist is a squishy, gnarled combination of meat and muscle. She nearly faints just looking at it.

"Let's get you cleaned up," Helen says.

While she begins tending to Hope's wound with rags and water, Cat faces Dozer.

"What the hell, Dozer? You fell asleep on *watch*?"

Dozer puffs out his chest. "Don't blame me. I tried waking Book, but he wouldn't take over. I can't stay awake all friggin' night."

Everyone turns to Book. His eyes open wide in surprise. "What? You didn't try to wake me."

Dozer doesn't back down. "Sure I did. But you said you were too tired."

"What're you talking about?"

"Don't act all surprised, Book *Worm*. Unless you're saying I'm a liar."

"I wasn't saying that. . . ."

"Then what *are* you saying?"

309

No one knows who to believe, and the Sisters glance back and forth between them.

A startled yell interrupts everything.

"Where's June Bug?" Flush asks, his voice hysterical. He's on his feet, eyes probing the ground.

Sure enough, the stretcher is empty. No June Bug. They all stand, weapons raised, pointing them in every possible direction.

It's Twitch who spots him, his keen eyesight cutting through the dark.

"There!" The others follow his gaze down the slope. A good hundred yards away they see the pack dragging June Bug . . . or what's left of him. They nip and tear at his body, ripping bits of flesh as though breaking off chunks from a loaf of bread.

"Let's get him!" Flush shouts. He's taken his first steps down the steep ridge when Cat stops him.

"No."

Flush wheels around. "What do you mean, no?"

"It's a trap."

They look at Cat as if he's crazy.

"They set us up," he explains. "This whole thing. They knew they couldn't overpower us, but they got what they wanted: the weakest of the tribe."

Twitch scowls. "No way wolves are that smart."

"They are now," Cat says, and an icy chill runs down Hope's spine. "These wolves did exactly what they set

310

out to do, and they'll get more of us if we're not careful."

Hope's eyes return down the mountain to June Bug: a still, small dot on the barren slope. One of the wolves seems to sense her stare. He tears a large piece from June Bug's body, tosses it in the air, and catches it expertly with his sharp incisors. He swallows it almost instantly.

"We gotta bury him," Flush says weakly.

"We gotta get away," Cat says.

"We can't just let him be eaten by wolves."

As Flush takes a step, Cat draws back an arrow, the bowstring taut and quivering. "You walk away from here and you'll get this arrow in your back."

Flush turns. Even in faint moonlight, the fear on his face is unmistakable. "You wouldn't do it."

"Try me."

No one says a word. It's just Flush and Cat staring each other down, until Flush drops his gaze and returns to his pack, stuffing his belongings back inside.

Cat removes the arrow from the bow and puts it in his quiver. He walks over to a dead wolf, jams his foot against the corpse's muzzle, and pulls the arrow free. Entrails hang from the arrow's tip. He wipes the intestines on his pants leg, slips the arrow back into his quiver, then moves on to the next wolf.

Meanwhile, Four Fingers washes out Argos's wound, and Helen wraps Hope's wrist in strips of cloth.

As they make their way back along the trail, all are silent. It's impossible not to think of June Bug. For him to die in such a way is absolutely horrible. But Hope sees what others aren't willing to understand: if it hadn't been for Cat, there would have been even more injuries, more deaths. Cat came to her rescue. There's no question that he just saved her life.

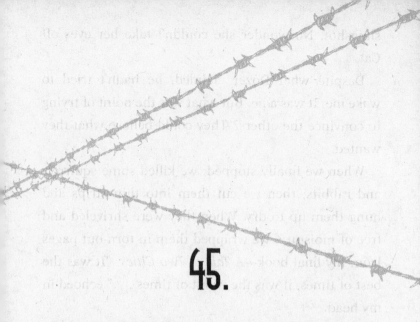

45.

THE DEATH OF JUNE Bug hit us hard. Among us Less Thans, he had always been something of a leader—precisely because he didn't act like one. Now that he was gone, I realized how much I'd miss him.

We marched eighteen hours straight, through the night and all the next day. Although I wanted to talk with Hope—wanted to see if she was okay—it seemed like she found reasons to steer clear of me. Maybe I was just paranoid, but if she was avoiding me, well, who could blame her?

All I had to do was pick up the spear—it was right there at my feet! Instead, I had been fighting my own demons, the ghoulish images dancing before my eyes. All I could do was fire a few harmless rocks with my slingshot. No wonder she couldn't take her eyes off Cat.

Despite what Dozer claimed, he hadn't tried to wake me. It was a lie. But what was the point of trying to convince the others? They could believe what they wanted.

When we finally stopped, we killed some squirrels and rabbits; then we cut them into thin strips and hung them up to dry. When they were shriveled and free of moisture, we wrapped them in torn-out pages from my final book—*A Tale of Two Cities*. "It was the best of times, it was the worst of times . . ." echoed in my head.

As we worked, I eased over to Hope. "I'm sorry about your wrist," I said.

She grunted something like "Thanks."

"You okay?"

"I'll live," she said.

"I guess my slingshot was no match for that wolf."

"No, I guess not."

We stuffed the dried meat in our packs.

"Thank God for Cat."

"I'll say," she agreed, a little too quickly. And then she found a reason to move away.

Whatever it was that I felt at that moment—jealousy? hurt?—I could barely acknowledge it. I wished it had been me who'd taken down that wolf—who'd had the sense to pick up Hope's spear and launch it through the wild beast.

Of course, even as I tried to convince myself of that, I knew better. I'd lost her, plain and simple. I might've spoken to her in the barn, might even have been the one who helped her escape the tunnel, but it was Cat who came through when the danger was greatest.

We stumbled down the mountain until we reached the edge of the Flats—a landscape more barren than anything I had ever seen. Pure, white, unblemished desert. Although there was a certain beauty to it, I knew from a glance it was as inhospitable a place as one could ever imagine. Endless miles of nothingness. A white floor under a blue sky. In the far distance, barely visible to the naked eye, was the jagged outline of *another* mountain range. We had had water up at the mountain. And shelter. Down here, all bets were off.

We rested in the mountain's shadow, knowing it was the last time we'd escape the sun for several days. Once we started out on the Flats, there'd be no shade. No trees.

No water.

"Why's it white?" Flush asked.

Unlike the desert back at Camp Liberty—brown sand dotted with small clumps of green—this was snowy white. A painter's canvas.

"It's not sand," Twitch answered. "It's alkali." He was rubbing a pinch of it between his fingers. "This was once a big lake. Then it dried up, leaving an enormous salt flat."

"Recently?"

"If you count a million years ago as recent, yeah."

We studied the terrain—a mosaic of cracked earth. Hard to imagine we'd be walking across a former lake bed.

The sky began to darken. Still we waited. Although we didn't think the Brown Shirts had followed us down the mountain, there was no point announcing our presence by emerging onto a barren desert. Better to wait for complete darkness.

Though the wolf attack had forced us to work together, there was still a wariness there, and little interaction between the groups. Less Thans vs. Sisters.

When the sky turned to velvet, Cat said, "Okay. Final sips."

Everyone removed canteens and measured out their small allotments. Then we shuffled forward. Our feet stirred up a noxious, low-hanging cloud of powdery dust, and we covered the bottom halves of our faces with bandannas.

If the dehydration didn't kill us, the nuclear fallout would.

I cast my gaze behind me. That's when I saw them.

Wolf eyes. Dozens of them. Gleaming like yellow jewels in the mountainside.

I wondered which was worse: wolves trailing us across the desert . . . or wolves stopping at its edge, wise enough to go no farther. As if they knew something we didn't.

46.

THE SUN IS BLAZING and unrelenting. Heat shoots up the soles of their boots as they drag themselves across the cracked tiles of the desert floor. Their skin darkens. Lips split and bleed.

They sleep briefly in the afternoon, resting in the meager shade of their hoodies, then walk into the evening and all during the night. For hours on end no one breathes a word.

In the morning, strips of lavender glow in the east, revealing vague silhouettes of mountains. They appear no closer than before. Hope's heart sinks. It's no longer a question of when they reach those distant foothills, but *if*.

Her feet drag across the white sand and any thoughts

of Cat and Book are pushed to the back corners of her mind. Survival is what she thinks about now. Putting one foot in front of the other. Ignoring the shooting pain in her arm where the wolf played tug-of-war with her wrist.

She hears a muffled sound and turns to see Twitch crumpling to the ground.

Book kneels by his friend's side. "You okay?" he asks.

Twitch doesn't answer. His eyes roll back.

Hope unscrews the top of her canteen and pours a tablespoon of warm water into the lid. "Here. Drink this."

She holds the lid to Twitch's lips and lets its contents slide down his throat. The water has to be nearly boiling, and yet it looks utterly refreshing.

"How much do we have left?" Book asks.

Everyone offers up canteens that are almost empty.

Helen's chin begins to quiver. "Are we going to be all right?"

For obvious reasons, no one answers her.

"So what do we do?" Red asks. His pale skin is burned to a crisp, his nose peeling like the skin of a snake.

"We keep going," Book says.

"With no water?"

"We can't stay here. We'll die for sure." There is no panic in his voice, just calm, grim determination.

"But my shoes have disintegrated," Flush says. Hope can see the blood oozing from his blisters.

"That's why we gotta keep moving. We need water."

"Ya think?" Dozer asks.

Twitch is sitting up, sipping another swallow of water, his back resting against Book's knee. For the first time, his eyes seem to focus.

"And them?" he mumbles, barely audible.

"The Sisters are with us now, Twitch," Book says. "We're all working together."

"Not them. *Them*." His gaze settles on the vast expanse.

Everyone turns to see what he is looking at. At first, they assume he's hallucinating. Then they see them: distant shapes. Wavy figures in the desert heat. Cat retrieves his binoculars.

"Wolves?" Flush asks.

"Brown Shirts?" Diana adds.

Cat shakes his head. "Hunters," he says.

"Hunters?" Hope asks. "Who are they?"

Cat's answer is short and to the point. "You'd better hope you don't find out."

The Less Thans help Twitch to his feet and resume marching. Hope and the Sisters hurry to catch up, suddenly aware there's a new enemy they know nothing about.

It's late afternoon when they stop next. Some of the Sisters and Less Thans seem incapable of walking in a straight line; others look on the verge of collapse. They're desperately in need of water. And food. And sleep.

Hope unzips her backpack and reaches for her last chunk of squirrel meat.

The moistness of the package surprises her. Despite the heat and dryness of the desert, the bundle is damp. Has her canteen leaked?

Cursing her luck, she unwraps the meat . . . and sees the reason for the wetness. The heat has baked the salted squirrel into something green and rotten, and now it's a playground for a thousand larvae. They squirm in and out of the putrefying meat, turning it a ghostly white.

"What is *that*?" Flush asks, horrified.

"Well, it ain't sugar," Diana says.

"Maggots," Twitch answers. He's still weak and speaks blankly, but there's no turning off his brain.

The others unwrap their own packages and discover the same. Some drop the squirming packages as if they're on fire.

"How'd those get here?" Dozer asks. "We didn't see 'em on the mountain."

"No, but we saw flies," Twitch says. "And flies lay eggs."

Hope stares at the rotten meat. Its stench is disgusting and it looks like a bowl of moving oatmeal. Flush wipes a string of vomit from his chin.

321

"So what do we do?" he asks.

"We eat," Twitch says, matter-of-factly.

He scoops up a handful of squirming squirrel meat and stuffs it in his mouth. One white worm dribbles down his chin. He pops it on his tongue as though it were a delicacy.

"You can do that?" Hope asks.

"They're better cooked," Twitch says, "but they're fine this way too."

"Won't they eat your stomach?"

Twitch shakes his head casually. "Stomach juices kill 'em before they have a chance. Assuming you haven't killed 'em already." As if to prove his point, he munches down on a particularly juicy maggot. They hear the squish in his mouth.

Helen and Scylla and all the Sisters look to Hope. She turns to Cat. When she sees him eating, she closes her eyes, dips her hand into the squirrel jerky, and stuffs the rancid food in her mouth. She swallows quickly. The putrid smell fills her senses, but there is a certain satisfaction in having *something* in her stomach, even if that something is white, squirming larvae.

Pretty soon everyone is forcing the rotten meat down their throats. All except Dozer. He takes one bite and makes a point of hurling his maggot-infested jerky onto the desert floor. White worms writhe in the harsh sunlight.

"I can't eat this crap," he says.

"Fine," Four Fingers says. He scoops the meat from the ground, gives it a good shake, then pops it in his mouth.

"I need *food*," Dozer says.

"We all do," Cat answers. "This is our only choice."

"It's not our *only* choice."

Something about his voice alarms Hope, and she sees where he is looking: Argos is panting off to one side.

"You can't be serious," Book says.

"Why not? He's just dead weight," Dozer says. "And if we don't eat something *real*, we'll never make it out of this hellhole."

"No one's eating Argos."

"So you want to kill us, is that it, Book *Worm*? We were doing just fine in the mountains. Then you bring us down here to starve and make us eat infected meat."

"It's not infected. . . ."

"It's got maggots! In *my* book, that's infected! And I'm not going to stand for it."

"You can stand for it or not," Cat says, finishing the last of his jerky and wiping his hands on his pants. "But that dog saved our lives up on the mountain because someone fell asleep on their watch."

"But I told you—"

"Yeah, I know what you told us."

Dozer looks away and grumbles. "Relax, I was just kidding about the damn dog."

They nap briefly before setting out, once again marching through the night. When the sun finally edges upward, they're given their first reward in days: a hazy silhouette of mountains. And before them, rippling like waves: rolling foothills, covered in green.

Grass.

When they stumble ahead they're faced with another surprise: a road. It's a two-lane blacktop, swept in sand, stretching from one horizon point to another. It's more potholes and gullies than anything resembling an actual highway, and years of heat have buckled the pavement. Still, it's a road, and roads lead to places. They follow it.

Soon, a distant object appears. At first Hope thinks it's a tree, but as they draw closer she sees that it catches the glinting reflection of the sun.

"An old gas station," Cat explains, holding the binocs to his eyes.

"Maybe there'll be food in there," Flush suggests.

"Maybe water," Diana adds.

Some of the Sisters and Less Thans take off in a slow trot, and Hope can see it clearly now: a decrepit structure covered in peeling paint and orange rust. A swaying sign, a rusted propane tank, the empty stalls of a car wash, strips of rubber flapping in the wind.

Flush is the first to reach it, and he yanks open the

glass door and disappears inside. Four Fingers and Diana follow.

The rest are just approaching when Flush comes bolting back out. He falls to his knees, spewing vomit. Four Fingers and Diana come running out and do the same. All three of them are dry heaving like sick dogs.

"What is it?" Cat asks, drawing an arrow.

Faces green, they jerk their thumbs behind them. Cat and Hope ready their weapons and edge their way past the puking LTs. The glass door, coated in a streaky layer of grime, groans as they pry it open. Inside is a counter, a propped-open cash register, and aisles and aisles of vacant shelves. On the counter, written with a finger in inch-thick dust, are the words WASH ME. Beneath it are two more words.

SAVE ME.

They spy an open door, made of stainless steel and approach it cautiously, drawing deep breaths before turning the corner. They stare into its dark interior.

There lies a woman—or what was once a woman— in the far corner on a wooden pallet. Her legs are splayed, her head cocked to one side as if pondering a complex question. But most disturbing is her skin; it has decomposed to something leathery and unnatural. A skeleton mummified in a thin layer of decay. Teeth bared. Sunken eye sockets.

Clutched in her bony hand is a small metallic object.

"Cell phone," Cat explains.

Hope wonders who the woman was calling. At that last moment of her life, who did she want to talk to? Husband? Mother? Son or daughter? Or maybe . . . sister? Hope's own aloneness has never been more obvious. Without Faith, she's on her own. She has no parents, no sister. Will she die like this, sprawled in a gas station freezer, all alone?

Hope averts her gaze and gives a glance to Cat. He's obviously the leader of the group, fearless, like herself. It's not just that he saved her from the wolves, it's more than that. It goes back to the very first time she saw him—when he stayed with them in the cave. Even then she recognized him as a kind of . . . protector.

As for the corpse, it does little to affect her. But then a large worm the size of a garden snake slithers out one eye in the woman's skull, and Hope's stomach heaves. She turns away.

"Who was she, do you think?" Hope manages, when she's caught her breath.

"An employee," Cat says. "Still has her name tag on." He takes a step closer. "Lois. Her name was Lois. Come on, let's see what we can salvage around here."

Hope is all too happy to have a reason to step outside.

They get lucky. The car wash has an enormous water tank with plenty of water left. All they have to do is figure out how to turn the valves back on, which Twitch and Scylla manage with ease.

Though the water is orangish-brown in color, tastes of metal, and smells of rust, they don't care. It's water. Four Fingers and Flush drink so much they puke it right back up. Then they just drink some more. They stay in that car wash the whole rest of the day.

They even take hot showers in the stalls. There's enough propane left to warm the water, and the nozzles tear away the layers of grit and dirt that have caked their bodies like plaster casts. Hope is able to clean out her wound. They dry off with paper towels, smelling of car wash shampoo.

It smells like heaven.

That night, Hope sleeps with a canteen tucked against her body. As she lies down, her eyes settle first on Cat, then drift to Book. The one rescued her from the wolves. The other seems to know her pain, just by looking in her eyes. When she eventually falls asleep, she dreams of both, imagining a place where she's no longer alone.

47.

I woke to the scent of burning sage, and saw Cat tending to a small fire. I stumbled over.

"A fire?" I asked.

"Breakfast."

My eyebrows arched. There was no food left.

"Lizards," he said. "The place is crawling with them."

He motioned to the side of the building. Sure enough, an army of green lizards clung to the wall, basking in the morning sun.

"Are they edible?"

"*Anything's* edible." He held out a branch, whittled to a fine point. At its tip was a charred lizard. "Have one."

I was starving, my mouth salivating from the smell alone. Any other time I would've accepted the offer in a heartbeat. But I wasn't in the mood. I couldn't handle the way Hope looked at him. It was hard to have an appetite when jealousy was tying my stomach in knots.

"Come on," he said. "You know you want it."

He was right—I desperately needed food. I took the burned lizard and ate it whole, letting the greasy meat slide down my throat. It was delicious.

"Thanks," I muttered.

Cat just shrugged.

"What's your deal?" I finally asked.

"What do you mean?"

"I mean even after all this time, I still don't know anything about you. None of us do. Like why'd you leave the Young Officers Camp?" A part of me wanted to get to the bottom of it, but a bigger part wanted to find some dirt—something to hold against him.

He gave his head a shake. "You don't want to know."

"Sure I do."

"No, you—"

"*I do.*"

He sighed loudly.

"They're so messed up over there," he said, talking more to himself than me. "They're convinced the only way to survive another Omega is to eliminate others. Dissidents, political activists . . . Less Thans."

"Why should you care? You said it yourself: we're not normal."

329

"Because they made us do some of the actual *eliminating*."

He gave his head a shake, as though trying to erase an image from his mind. Fat from the lizards dripped into the fire. *Sizzle. Pop.*

"That's why you got out of there?" I still wasn't sure I understood.

"And didn't stop until I reached the mountains. At first I liked it up there. I was able to catch enough food. I could stay up late, sleep in, fish when I wanted. . . ."

"But?"

"I couldn't stay forever. Didn't *want* to stay forever. So I burned off my marker, descended the mountain . . ."

". . . and came across the No Water," I finished.

"*Tried* to cross the No Water. Didn't quite make it." He shook his head, probably remembering how close he'd come to dying.

"Why Camp Liberty? Why not someplace else?"

"Because I knew someone there."

It suddenly dawned on me. "Your source."

"That's right."

"But you asked me to get you out of there."

"Because I didn't mean to be found like that. Didn't want to be discovered by Brown Shirts."

"So . . . who was it? Your source?" I ventured.

Cat let the silence lengthen to something odd and uncomfortable, and his eyes flickered. When he finally

330

looked back, he *really* looked at me.

"Major Karsten," he said at last. I felt the air leave my lungs.

"Major Karsten? But . . . how? Why?"

"Because he's not just my source. He's my father."

It was like movie night in the mess hall when the picture'd be all blurry and out of focus, and then, *presto*, one adjustment later, it was clear. All the details sharp. That's what happened when Cat told me about his dad. Everything suddenly turned crisp and clear.

"That day we found you in the No Water and Karsten checked your arm, he wasn't looking to read your marker, he was making sure it was burned off."

Cat nodded. "Otherwise, they would've been able to identify me for sure."

"And the slaughter up in the mountains. You'd seen one before."

"*Dozens*, actually. My dad used to take me. Officers teaching their sons to be men and all that *rah-rah* bullshit." He spat on the ground. "That's why I ran away. I wanted to get away from all that." He hesitated. "As it turns out, there's no avoiding it."

I suddenly remembered the roll call. "But when Karsten burned that tattoo on your arm, he seemed to be enjoying himself."

Cat shook his head. "Just a show. To fool Westbrook."

331

"But he was cursing you."

"That's what he wanted it to sound like."

"Why couldn't he just acknowledge you?"

"'Cause who knows how Westbrook would've reacted. An officer with a son who runs away from YO Camp? Not good. And the night we escaped—my dad made so much noise banging on that door to help us, to give us time to get away."

A picture began to take shape—a picture far different from one I'd ever imagined. "So the Brown Shirts really hope to wipe us out?"

"Anyone and everyone who doesn't look like them."

I was in shock. It didn't lessen my jealousy of Cat, but it gave me a fuller picture of who he was. There were still a million questions I was dying to ask, especially about his dad, but the aroma of grilled lizard had awakened the others. The conversation ended as abruptly as it'd begun.

Once the other Sisters and Less Thans saw what Cat was cooking, they went on a hunting rampage of their own, spearing and grilling as many lizards as possible. We devoured the blackened reptiles, bones and all. After a diet of grit and sand, they weren't half bad. The tails were like crunchy hash browns.

"What, no ketchup?" Flush asked.

"It's over there with the ice cream sundaes," Diana said.

Although it wasn't much, it marked the first time Less Thans and Sisters had really spoken to each other.

"How about some steaks?" Red asked.

"Right after we finish the lobsters," Helen said.

Ripples of laughter followed, and more jokes after that. Finally, when Twitch chimed in and said, "I think we've got company," we all assumed he was talking about the flies.

"You ain't kidding," Flush said, trying to shoo them away, as the rest of us laughed.

"That's not what I mean."

We looked up. In the far distance, coming straight across the desert itself, was a rising coil of smoke. Vehicles.

My heart rose in my throat.

"Smother the fire and head for that rise," Cat said, pointing to the far side of the road. "There's a gully there we can hide in."

The laughter was long gone, and everyone scrambled into action. We threw handfuls of sand onto the flames and retrieved our belongings. Racing across the black-top, we shot a look at the approaching vehicles. Not Humvees. Not dirt bikes.

Four-wheelers. Around a dozen of them.

Hunters.

Cat and I exchanged a look. In that brief glance was all that needed to be said.

We reached the gully at the same time, tumbling in the small ravine. Cat withdrew his binoculars and gave a look. His jaw tightened and he passed the binocs to me.

The four riders in front of the procession were painfully familiar; they were the very ones we'd seen in the mountain. Once more they were led by the man in blaze orange—the hunt master—who'd taken such pleasure in finishing off Cannon.

My mouth was so dry I could barely swallow.

I had to admit it was an impressive sight, especially for those of us who'd never seen the Hunters before. Twelve four-wheelers, all souped-up, tricked-out, armor-plated. Part prehistoric beast, part futuristic time machine. Locked and loaded, ready for battle.

They veered apart as they approached the gas station, arriving at the building from different angles. An impressive display of military precision. They lined up their four-wheelers at the gas pumps and switched off their engines.

"They don't know about us," Twitch whispered. "They're just here for gas."

It was true; they were jury-rigging the pumps, figuring out a way to siphon the fuel. Once they filled their tanks they'd be on their way. We'd caught a break and all of us knew it.

One of the Hunters went around to the side of the gas station, probably to take a leak. Something by his feet caught his attention and he bent down to pick it up. Even before he grabbed it I knew exactly what it was. Breakfast. Lizard-on-a-stick.

The Hunter motioned for the Man in Orange.

It wasn't long before the Hunters found the fire pit. They kicked at the sand, extending hands to feel the heat of the glowing embers. The more animated their voices grew, the more my stomach clenched.

"But they don't know which way we went," Flush said, as though his insistence would make it true. "Right?"

No one had the heart to answer him. All the Hunters had to do was cross the road to see twenty-some sets of footprints leading to the gully. A bunch of them began inserting magazines into their M4s. Even from a couple hundred yards away we could hear the cold, metallic clicks.

Cat slung a quiver of arrows over his shoulder and leveled his gaze at us. "Don't fire until you see them start to move," he whispered. "Then give 'em everything you've got."

He scrambled away, clutching his bow. I watched him leave, not knowing what he was planning, or if we'd ever see him again.

We spread out, stretching our line fifty yards from left to right. As the Hunters mounted their vehicles, I felt a tightening in my chest. The lead four-wheeler neared the road and Dozer yelled, "Fire!" We let loose a volley of arrows, darts, and stones. Although all fell off target, they were enough to get the Hunters' attention. They scrambled to find hiding places.

"More!" Red commanded. We loaded up as quickly as we could and fired again. We began to find our aim. An arrow struck a Hunter's leg. A Sister's dart grazed an arm. Maybe we could hold them after all.

"Take that!" Diana cried when one of her darts pinged against the pump a Hunter hid behind.

"Hunt *this*!" Flush screamed as he reached back and let loose the rubber sling. His rock shattered the gas station's front window. It spiderwebbed and left a gaping hole. Sisters and LTs alike let loose a full-throated yell.

Then the Hunters returned fire and the ground exploded. Bullets pockmarked the earth, spraying sand. We ducked into the gulley, shielding our bodies while the rounds went zinging overhead.

"Where the hell's Cat?" Dozer yelled.

He was nowhere in sight.

The Hunters were remounting their vehicles, shielded behind armor plating. We stood little chance of stopping them. Whatever Cat had planned, I knew it had to happen soon.

Then I caught sight of him. He had made his way

around their left flank, crawling low through the desert. An arrow was poised against his bowstring and it guided him forward. He raised and fired. The arrow caught a Hunter in the middle of the back and he crumpled to the ground. None of the other Hunters noticed.

Cat ran crouching to the Hunter's side, stripped the weapon from his hands, and scurried back to a low ditch.

A moment later we heard the revving of engines.

"They're coming!" Twitch shouted.

A rain of rocks and arrows bounced weakly off the vehicles' steel plating. The thought of running away suddenly made sense. Although I knew we couldn't outrun the Hunters, it seemed just as crazy to stay. Like we were serving ourselves up to be massacred.

That's when Cat rose to a kneeling position, the butt of the rifle pressed against his shoulder, eye peering through the scope. He was behind the Hunters now, out of their line of vision. He fired, smoke curling from the barrel. The bullet ricocheted off the back of the Man in Orange's ATV. He turned and pointed, and the Hunters swarmed in Cat's direction, guns blazing, muzzle flashes spitting orange.

"Cover!" Red yelled.

All of us pelted the Hunters with everything we had. The Hunters didn't seem to care. Their attention was suddenly on the lone Less Than who had the audacity to outflank them.

"He's gonna get himself killed," Flush said.

And it was true. There was no way out . . . and I regretted every jealous thought I'd had of him.

Bullets rained. The earth exploded at Cat's feet. Still, he knelt there, unfazed, sighting down the rifle barrel.

A bullet struck a rock and a fragment of stone bit into his shin. His leg buckled and he fell to the ground, the rifle nearly slipping from his hands. With a grimace he regained his balance. The injury only seemed to make him more determined.

"Come on, Cat," I found myself saying. "Get out of there."

Others were echoing me. "Get out of there, Cat. Run away!"

And then he did a curious thing. Right before he squeezed the trigger, he swung his weapon around, away from the Man in Orange, away from the other Hunters. It wasn't a person Cat was aiming at, but a *thing*.

The propane tank.

A blinding explosion swallowed up the world as we knew it. Cat was thrown off his feet and tossed backward some twenty yards. A wave of heat raced across the desert and shoved us on our backs, searing our bodies. By the time we reopened our eyes, an enormous orange-and-black fireball mushroomed upward into the sky.

Whoosh! The gas station, the car wash, the Hunters, and their ATVs were vaporized. All that remained was a yawning crater of scorched earth. The sand around it was inky and petrified. Shards of burning metal discharged a choking black smoke.

Everyone scrambled from the gully and ran for Cat. He lay sprawled on the desert sand, his hands still clutching the rifle. He wasn't moving. Hope was the first to reach him, and she knelt by his side and propped him up. Cat's clothes were singed. Wisps of smoke drifted from his shirt.

"Cat! Are you okay? Can you hear me?"

His eyelids butterflied open. "Did I get 'em?" he croaked. His face was charred.

"You blew 'em up to smithereens!" Flush shouted, and everyone began to cheer.

"What're you all so happy about?" Cat said. "Look at the mess we're in now."

We had no idea what he was talking about. Then he gestured to the still-ballooning cloud of black and red. It seemed to consume the very air itself, biting a hole in the pale blue sky. Even now, a full minute after the explosion, we could feel its scorching heat.

Although we'd managed to defeat the Hunters, we'd also just announced our exact location to the entire world.

"Look," Twitch said, pointing in the far distance.

Everyone turned. A lone four-wheeler scurried across

the Flats, trailing a plume of white. Apparently Cat hadn't killed *all* of them. Somehow one had managed to escape. And not just anyone: the Man in Orange. Flames lit the back of his jacket.

"Come on," Cat said bitterly. "Let's get the hell out of here."

He threw down the rifle with a look of disgust, and began to walk away. The rest of us scrambled to catch up.

48.

AS THEY HEAD EAST, everyone is talking nonstop about Cat's annihilation of the Hunters. Everyone except Hope. She races up to Book, staring him down. "What was that about?" she asks.

Book looks at her, startled. "What was *what* about?"

"Those Hunters. Why are they chasing us?"

"They're not chasing you. Just us."

"Um, in case you didn't notice, those bullets were aimed at all of us. Why?"

Book tells her the story, how sadistic "sportsmen" have paid for the right to hunt down Less Thans.

"And now that you've escaped and the Brown Shirts can't sell you off?" Hope asks.

Book shrugs. "Maybe the Brown Shirts are paying *them*."

"So how come no one told us? Don't you think it would've been nice for us to know there was a group of cold-blooded killers trying to finish us off? Or were you planning on keeping that little secret to yourselves?"

"We were going to tell you."

"Really? Like when Twitch spotted them in the Flats?"

"We just hadn't gotten around to it."

"Yeah, well, thanks for sharing. And thank God Cat came to the rescue—again."

Hope sees something change in Book's face. "No one forced you to come with us," he mutters.

"Then why'd you come back for me—for us?"

"Thought you needed rescuing."

"I told you in the fields: we didn't."

"Guess I missed that."

"Yeah, I guess you did."

They walk in silence.

"And twenty-eight was better than eight," Book says, finally.

Hope's eyes widen. "Oh, so that's it. It wasn't out of any affection for me or any interest in our well-being, it was because you wanted more numbers? Well, that's good to know."

"No, that's not what I—"

"Glad we could help you out." Her voice drips sarcasm, and she hurries ahead.

As she marches on, Book's words rattle around in her head. This is why she has no faith in the opposite sex. Her father is the only man she ever trusted . . . and now he's dead. She certainly never trusted the repulsive Dr. Gallingham or Colonel Thorason. Definitely none of the Brown Shirts back at Camp Freedom. And not Book either.

She comes to a sudden stop when she hears the dull, rhythmic sounds of metal. She knows these sounds.

With a series of quick gestures, she motions everyone into the underbrush, and they hide amid ferns and low-hanging branches. The sounds grow louder—*kuh-lunk, kuh-lunk*—coming straight for them. The others look to Hope for answers, but there's no time for an explanation. She holds her breath and ducks deeper into the foliage.

There are five of them, all middle-aged men, marching so close Hope can hear their labored breathing. They sport long, scraggly beards and look as though they haven't bathed in a year. Smell like it, too. Their rank, pungent odor drifts toward Hope from fifty feet away. While the Brown Shirts are outfitted with M16s and the Hunters with the newer M4s, the guns these men carry look like something from centuries past: more like muskets than actual rifles. Along with hubcap shields and rebar swords. They clank as they walk.

It's been a while since Hope has seen any, but it's

obvious who they are. Crazies. The ones who inhabit the towns, living in equal parts squalor, chaos, and radiation. Just laying eyes on them is enough to make her blood run cold.

Argos lets out a low growl. Book puts a hand over his mouth to muffle the sound, but it's too late. One of the Crazies stops in his tracks.

"You hear that?" he grunts.

"Hear what?" another Crazy asks.

"Sounded like an animal."

Hope grips her spear firmly. To one side, Cat lies facedown in a bed of weeds. He hasn't had time to draw an arrow, and his bow is clutched uselessly by his side. One move by him—or any of the Less Thans and Sisters—and the Crazies will spot them for sure. Hope holds her breath.

With squinty eyes, the Crazies peer into the underbrush. Their gazes dance across the moldy carpet of dead leaves and camouflaged bodies: the frozen forms of Book with his hand over the mouth of Argos, of Cat lying facedown, of Hope with her spear. Every sound—every breath—is magnified ten times.

A Crazy takes a step forward and Hope's grip tightens on her spear. Cat gives her the subtlest of shakes. *Don't do it,* his expression says.

Hope can feel the sweat mingling with the wooden shaft. She grips it tighter than ever.

Finally, one of the Crazies says, "Hell, Lem, it was probably just someone farting." As if to prove his point, he lets out a burst of flatulence.

Charming, Hope thinks.

The Crazy's buddies laugh, and they begin moving out, their metal gear clanking with each footstep.

Hope slowly exhales and shares a glance with Cat. They stay hidden long after the Crazies have passed. Even when they rise and resume marching, no one risks speaking, for fear their voices will carry. Hope notices her hands are shaking, her heart hammering in her chest.

One way or the other, she can't escape this territory soon enough.

The woods thin and they find themselves at a clearing. Stretching out before them is a wide valley, a hollow among hills. Prairie grass. A tiny stream. But what catches their eye is not the valley itself but what lies beyond it. Vast tracks of virgin forest.

No one needs to say its name. The Brown Forest. Acres and acres of dead evergreen trees—their needles as brown as the trunks themselves. Everything's the color of rust.

They all stand there, awestruck.

"How'd you know this was here?" Dozer asks. As usual, there is a hint of challenge in his voice.

"My father brought us," Hope says. "When we were young." *Us—her and Faith.*

"And he said the Heartland's on the other side?"

"Somewhere past it. He never said how far."

They stand there a moment, taking it in. It's hard to believe they're that close to freedom. After all this time.

"How do you think this happened?" Flush asks, referring to the trees.

"Poison," Twitch answers. "That's not just one type of tree. Those are pines, spruces, firs—all dead."

"So?"

"So whatever did this did it to everything."

"Nuclear fallout?"

"Or acid rain or poisoned groundwater. Take your pick."

It's easy to forget about bombs and radiation while they're traipsing around the countryside. All too convenient to pretend things aren't as bad as they actually are. But seeing the Brown Forest is another chilling reminder of reality.

"Is it dangerous?" Flush asks.

Twitch actually laughs. "After Hunters and Brown Shirts and wolves, what's a little poison in our systems?"

They leave the comfort of the woods and step into the clearing, wisps of fog hanging in the air. Cat orders everyone to spread out until they're a horizontal line moving through the meadow like the leading edge of a

346

storm. They're halfway across, the sun peeking through the rising mist, when they hear the sounds of engines. Four-wheelers.

Hunters.

"Oh crap," Flush whispers.

Cat's clenched jaw works back and forth. "Double time. No stopping until you get to the forest. We'll make preparations there." He takes off running, leading the way.

Everyone follows, fighting waist-high grass that pulls and tugs at their clothes. Sweat pours off Hope, running down her sides.

Cat is the first to reach the line of brown trees, and he throws himself to the ground and waits for the others. As they collapse on dead pine needles, a sense of relief surges through them. They made it. They're hidden now. Although the whining engines are louder than ever, there's still no sign of the enemy. It seems a cause for celebration.

Cat doesn't see it that way. "We gotta keep moving. They won't be far behind."

"Are you kidding?" Dozer says. "We just got here. I need to catch my breath."

"Let's be clear," Cat says, his voice steady. "Whoever's back there hasn't had any trouble tracking us. And I doubt they will now."

Everyone peers into the dead forest. A vehicle will

have little trouble navigating these woods.

"So what do you suggest?" Dozer asks.

"Keep going. Evade them until nightfall. Then make preparations."

Dozer looks like his head is going to implode. "That's the second time you've said that word! What're you saying?"

"I'm saying that sometimes the best offense is a strong defense."

A couple of the Sisters give him baffled looks, but Hope has an inkling of what he's getting at. They can't run forever; at some point they have to confront their pursuers. And better *they* choose where than their enemy.

Dozer offers one last challenge. "Any hints on how we defend ourselves?"

Cat shakes his head. "Not yet. But if we don't get away from here it won't matter. They'll slaughter us before we even get the chance."

There's no stopping to eat. Even peeing is on their own time. They do their business and then hurry to catch up. It's a grueling pace.

The sun sets behind them and they continue marching. Cat is determined to find the perfect ground to make their stand.

Possibly the final one.

At the top of a bouldered crest he calls a halt. Everyone collapses. Iris—the Sister with spiky hair—falls asleep before she even removes her pack. She looks like an overturned beetle.

The remaining LTs and Sisters huddle up. In pale starlight Hope can see Cat's blue eyes as he takes them in. They are focused, alert, serious. As sharp and bright as the North Star . . . and just as magnetic. It's like he always seems to know what to do and when to do it. A natural leader. Something she recognized the very first time she saw him—the night he stayed up talking with her father, telling him of his plans.

"Our only hope is if we fight back," he says. "Agreed?"

Everyone nods in reluctant agreement. Deep fatigue and gnawing hunger aren't enough; now they have work to do. But then again, what choice do they have?

As Cat begins to lay out the plan, Hope realizes how much they have to accomplish—and how little time they have to do it. She's still angry the Sisters got pulled into this mess without anyone telling them. This isn't the Sisters' battle. *Shouldn't* be their battle.

Still, there's no escaping it now. It's do-or-die time. One way or the other, this will be their final battle.

They work through the night: digging, gathering, building. By morning, their skin is oily with sweat. Exhaustion hangs over their shoulders like a heavy, rain-soaked cloak. The wound on Hope's arm throbs with pain, but she doesn't stop. When their preparations are complete, they go over the plan a final time. Cat turns to Iris and Diana.

"You're our eyes and ears," he tells them. "When you see any sign of the enemy, get back here as soon as possible. Otherwise, we're dead. Got it?"

They nod solemnly and take off in a dead run.

The sun is poking above the hills when Scylla gestures that she's put together breakfast. On top of all the heavy lifting, she's also managed to cook a bubbling stew of squirrel, mushrooms, and wild onions. To Hope, it seems nothing less than a feast. Even though she finds herself seated next to Book, they avoid looking at each other.

"We're too young to die," Flush says.

It comes out of nowhere, and yet Hope realizes it's the same thought everyone's having.

She suddenly feels Book's arm press against hers, the warm flesh of his skin. She doesn't move away. Maybe it's fatigue, maybe it's regret at what she said to him, maybe it's something else. The only thing she knows for sure is that all of her senses are heightened. There's something soothing about his touch, flesh against flesh, and for the first time she begins to understand why she's so drawn to him. It goes back to that first meeting in the barn, and the kindness in his eyes. There was warmth there. Comfort. *Safety.*

It occurs to her that Book is more of a protector than she realizes—maybe not against wolves, but against those forces that tug at her heart. Cat may know what actions to take, but Book knows *her.*

Her cheeks warm and she opens her mouth to speak to him . . . just as the two scouts rush back to camp. Book pulls away.

"They're on their way," Diana announces, her face red from running.

"How many?" Cat asks calmly.

"About two dozen."

"Brown Shirts or Hunters?"

"Hunters. All on four-wheelers."

Hope feels her throat go dry. In terms of numbers, it's a fair fight. But as far as weapons go, it's not even close.

"Grab some food," Cat tells the two Sisters. "Then head to your positions."

Iris and Diana fall to the ground and stuff themselves with stew. Cat turns to the others and meets their eyes.

"What're we waiting for?" he asks, tossing the rest of his breakfast to Argos. They pick up their weapons and begin heading to their stations. Hope shares a quick glance with Book and then races off. Neither says a final word.

49.

STILLNESS IS IN THE air. The only sounds are the breezes through the trees, dropping dead pine needles to the ground with a whisper.

And the beating of our hearts.

It's impossible not to think of all the deaths—Frank, June Bug, the two Brown Shirts, the Hunters at the gas station. At what point would it stop? When would we be allowed to live our lives without fear of being hunted?

We were spread out along the hillside, tucked behind boulders, buried in branches. Sweaty palms and curled fingers clutched weapons, waiting for the moment of attack.

We few, we happy few, we band of brothers.

Shakespeare, drifting through my mind like smoke.

I peek above a boulder, searching for Hope. I cared for her; that was the truth of it. She might've been angry or disappointed in me, or liked Cat a whole lot more, but the fact was she seemed to understand me in a way no one else did . . . and I thought I understood her. I recognized that haunted look in her eyes. I knew that kind of pain. And I wanted to be the one to comfort her, to hold her in the night when the demons wouldn't leave.

It was suddenly important that I find her—that I catch her eye, some glimpse of her in the dead and dying trees. But she was nowhere to be found.

I jumped when I heard the sound of engines. Their menacing growl made them sound like fifty or a hundred, and when I spied the Hunters, my breath caught. There they were on their armor-plated ATVs, and this time they wore Kevlar jackets. Black helmets with thick plastic shields safeguarded their faces. A herd of wild beasts, come to prey on twenty-seven innocent victims.

Twitch and Diana were halfway down the ridge. Even from my position at the top of the hill, I could only imagine how scared they must have been. They were completely exposed.

The four-wheelers got closer. Three hundred yards became two. Then one.

I could make out the Man in Orange. Unlike the others, he wore no Kevlar, just a blaze orange vest, as if he didn't fear our paltry ammunition. No helmet, either. Just a baseball cap.

One side of his face glistened pink with pus and blood, courtesy of the propane blast.

"Hold on," I whispered, as if Twitch and Diana could hear me. "Just hold on."

Twitch and Diana did. Finally, when they could wait no longer, when the Hunters were nearly on them, they rose and ran, tearing over the dead pine needles and racing back up the slope like two rocks skipping across a brown sea.

The Man in Orange gave a slight nod, and four of his comrades gunned their engines and took off in pursuit. They whipped through the forest, sliding effortlessly around the dead trees as though skiing an obstacle course. Twitch had trouble with the incline. Our time in the Flats had weakened him and it was all he could do to keep churning his gangly legs forward. Meanwhile, the four-wheelers grew closer and closer, the gap narrowing by the second.

"Come on!" Flush shouted, pleading for his friend.

Cat nocked an arrow. The Sisters readied crossbows.

The ATVs had nearly reached Twitch and Diana. The Hunter in front lifted a hand from the handlebar and removed an enormous knife from its sheath. Only ten yards separated its gleaming, serrated edge from Twitch's neck.

"Hurry!" I shouted, my words drowned out by the growling engines.

The knife-wielding Hunter had nearly caught up to Twitch, when, suddenly, Diana stopped and ducked. Then Twitch did the same. Before the Hunter could figure out what happened, his head snapped back and he was flung off his four-wheeler. He landed hard on the ground, his vehicle slamming into a tree. The next two riders were yanked off their vehicles as they ran into the fishing line we'd strung between trees. A fourth rider raised his hand to shield his face and his fingers were sliced off. Blood gushed forth.

We let loose a cheer. Cat, Red, Flush, and Dozer rose and pulled back arrows. Five Sisters aimed their crossbows. Even before the four Hunters had a chance to catch their breath, they were riddled with darts and arrows. Another cheer rose from our ranks.

Four down, twenty to go.

The Man in Orange scowled. The Hunters inched their way forward, cutting the braided line to pieces with their massive knives. The fishing line fell to the ground.

They began moving up the hill, firing their M4s. The bullets pinged off granite boulders and embedded in tree trunks. We stayed low, waiting for Cat to give us the signal. I shot him a pleading glance. Finally, when it seemed we could wait no longer, he let out a piercing whistle.

In groups of two, we rose and leaned on branches positioned beneath the boulders. The enormous stones budged, shifted, then began rolling down the hill, picking up speed.

The one I launched collided dead-on with a Hunter, bouncing over the metal plates of his vehicle and catching him square in the chest. He went tumbling to the ground, flattened and bloody. The boulder rolled off him and continued its descent, scattering ATVs.

We raced up the slope to the next sets of boulders. Four Fingers and I were lucky; we managed to throw ourselves behind cover without getting hit.

Others were not so lucky. To the far right I saw someone go sprawling—a Sister, by the looks of it. I couldn't tell who it was, but I prayed it wasn't Hope. The air was suddenly alive with lead and smoke.

When the bullets waned, Four Fingers and I repeated our actions and sent an unwieldy granite stone careening down the hill, scattering Hunters. Enough time for the Sisters to fire off a quick succession of darts. We raced to the next boulder and dove behind it. There was a fourth station to get to, but I wasn't convinced we'd make it.

Their bullets were coming fast, ricocheting off stone and splintering trees, making the air sing. We cowered behind rocks, ducking beneath the whizzing bullets. At this rate, we'd have no chance at pulling off the rest of our plan. We were stuck—helplessly pinned down. Unless we did something—soon—we'd be dead before we even got to the next phase of our attack.

Hope didn't wait for Cat's signal. She got up and took off, darting between trees so that none of the Hunters were able to get a clean shot. One of them gunned his four-wheeler, chasing after her.

My breath caught at the sight of her; she was still alive! But she was visibly panting, and the ATV had no problem closing the gap. He raised his weapon and tried to steady it. Hope zigzagged behind trees. The Hunter waited for just the right moment. The perfect shot.

Hope broke into a small clearing. It was madness, leaving the safety of the woods, but she tore straight up a small hill in the open ground. The Hunter revved his engine and followed. She was as good as dead. Nothing separated the Hunter from his prey.

"Come on, Hope! Come on!!" I yelled. "Get out of there!" Soon others were chanting as well.

"Hurry up, Hope!"

"He's right behind you!"

Then, without warning, Hope disappeared. Completely vanished. Here one moment, gone the next. A fraction of a second later, the Hunter's vehicle went airborne as though launched from a rocket pad. The four-wheeler sailed in one direction, the Hunter in the other. Both landed with ground-thumping thuds.

Hope popped up out of a tiny foxhole. On the downslope side was the ramp she and Scylla had created from rocks and logs, covered with pine needles. One moment the Hunter was gunning his ATV, ready to extinguish her life . . . and the next he was soaring through the air.

Now he writhed in pain, his left leg bent at a grotesque angle. Hope steadied a crossbow and fired a dart that pierced the Hunter's groin. No Kevlar there.

One less Hunter . . . and Hope was still alive. My heart hammered in relief.

We'd survived the first three phases of our plan—fishing line, boulder rolls, and ramps—and still more than half of the Hunters were uninjured. We were running out of options.

Cat gave a double whistle and we scrambled up the hill. Below us, Hunters moved forward like an advancing tidal wave, their engines rattling our teeth. We reached the crest of the hill and lowered ourselves into shallow foxholes. We were down to our final scheme. If this didn't work, we'd have to run.

I tried to swallow, but couldn't. We'd been in tough situations before, but nothing like this.

Dozer began freaking out. "I can't do this!" he shouted, tears streaming down his cheeks. "I can't take it anymore!"

Four Fingers and I tried to calm him. He shook us

off and kept screaming. "Lemme outta here! I wanna go home!"

Nothing we said or did could quiet him. Even when Four Fingers clamped his hand across Dozer's mouth, Dozer bit him, hard. Four Fingers let go and Dozer rose to his feet, walking toward the Hunters.

"I give up!" he cried, hands in the air. "Don't shoot! I surrender!"

Four Fingers took off in a mad run. He tackled Dozer to the ground just as the Hunters began firing. Somehow, Four Fingers was able to drag Dozer back without either of them getting shot. But Dozer put up one last challenge. He lifted Four Fingers up and threw him to the ground, smashing his head against a slab of granite.

All of us began pelting the Hunters with every rock and dart and arrow we could lay our hands on. I saw that of all the Hunters, the Man in Orange had gone completely untouched. Even though he wore no protective gear, not one of us had managed to slip an arrow past the plating of his ATV.

But Cat was ready to take him on. He pulled back his bowstring until his thumb rested against his cheek, held the draw . . . and then released. The arrow zinged forward through a gunpowdery haze.

At the final moment, the Man in Orange ducked, and it seemed like Cat had missed entirely. Then a thin line of crimson rose to the surface of his cheek: pearls of blood from lip to earlobe. The arrow had grazed the uninjured side of his face. He lifted a hand to inspect the damage. When he pulled his fingers away, they were slick with blood.

His bared his teeth, and they were pink and blood-stained. Like the wolf that had dragged June Bug away.

We stumbled to our feet and made it to the very top of the ridge, just managing to avoid a hailstorm of bullets that pitted the ground. We dove behind boulders. Hope was one rock away. I caught her eye.

"You okay?" I mouthed.

She nodded. It looked like she wanted to say more, but there wasn't time.

The Hunters were closing fast, no more than fifty yards away, drawing closer.

"Now!" Cat shouted at the very top of his lungs.

Emerging from the earth itself—from shallow pits *behind* the Hunters—hidden Sisters rose up and unleashed a flurry of darts. Scylla and little Helen and a dozen others began catching the Hunters in the backs of their necks. The Hunters went tumbling off their four-wheelers, and those who weren't struck by arrows were pummeled by swinging rocks we'd festooned with spikes.

"Don't let up!" Cat roared. We pelted them with every-thing we had until it was a horizontal rain of missiles.

The Hunters were in disarray. The Man in Orange

took in the situation with wild eyes and flared nostrils, blood dribbling down his chin. Then, with a snarl, he gestured to his troops. They turned their vehicles and began heading down the hill. A retreat!

He swung his eyes back at Cat and me a final time. And then he did something utterly unnerving. He smiled. It chilled me to the bone.

A spontaneous celebration erupted, and for the first time, Less Thans and Sisters hugged and congratulated each other. It was as though the act of fending off the Hunters—*together*—had torn down whatever walls existed between us, created some new and lasting bond. High fives and laughter overtook us. Hope and I found ourselves next to each other and shared a quick embrace. It was only for the briefest instant, but I was certain I could feel the beating of her heart against my chest. We pulled away, barely able to look at each other.

"Let's see who's wounded and get the hell out of here," Cat said. "These guys'll be back."

He was right. Celebrations were for later.

We rounded everyone up. Red had caught a bullet, but it only grazed his arm. Four Fingers suffered severe head trauma when Dozer threw him against the boulder. Dozer had no memory of his freak-out, or if he did, he didn't acknowledge it.

"What the hell, Dozer," Twitch said. "Why'd you go and hurt Four Fingers?"

"I didn't do nothing," Dozer responded, and left it at that.

But worst of all, we were missing one Sister.

We spread out and searched. Our joy at fending off the Hunters turned to grim reality when we found her, the girl named Iris, her body riddled with bullets. When I looked at Hope, I saw her eyes were filled with moisture. She turned away and gritted her teeth.

The grave was shallower than we would've liked, but time was not on our side. We cleared away pine needles and burrowed as deep as we could.

"We can always come back later and give her a proper funeral," Flush said as we stood awkwardly around the mound of earth. But we all knew that was a lie. Once we reached the new territory, we'd be done with this place. I hoped never to set foot in the Western Federation Territory ever again.

"Grab your arrows and let's clear out of here," Cat said.

"How about the guns?" Dozer asked. He reached for the assault rifle clutched in the stiff fingers of a dead Hunter.

"Leave 'em," Cat said. "They'll just slow us down."

"But that's our ticket outta here," Dozer said, his tone belligerent. There was no hint of the cowering LT who'd cried for help moments before. "That's how we'll win."

"We won just now because we used our heads," I

said, shooting a glance at Hope. "Because the Sisters knew how to use their weapons—and because Frank taught us how to use ours."

Dozer's eyes darted from Cat to me and back again. I thought his head was going to explode. "You're all crazy. Let's at least take the four-wheelers then," he sputtered.

Cat shook his head. "And lead the Hunters right to us? No way." He pulled the M4 from Dozer's hand, aimed it at a nearby ATV, and shot the engine to bits. Then he did the same to all the four-wheelers.

"If we can't use 'em, no one can." He tossed the rifle to the ground. "Come on. We don't have much time." He reached down and began collecting stray arrows.

We spread out across the ridge. The task was tedious and gruesome, but we needed the darts and arrows. Who knew how long before the next attack? As we worked, I edged toward Hope. I wanted to make sure she was all right.

I was nearly by her side when a strong, acrid smell tickled my nostrils. At first, I assumed it was the stench of death—all those rotting corpses surrounding us. But then I realized the smell was drifting toward us from somewhere distant. I lifted my head and tried to place it, as Argos began to bark.

All at once we realized what it was, and cried out in unison.

"Fire!"

50.

Drifting tendrils of smoke slithered on the ground like snakes.

"Run!" Hope screams.

Everyone tears up the hill: scrambling, falling, picking themselves up. Four Fingers still doesn't understand.

"Run?" he asks, a string of drool dangling from his lip.

The others pull him along.

"Stay together!" Hope yells, and the two outer flanks move inward.

In no time the smoke overtakes them. At first it is thin and delicate, like wispy tentacles, making the world a hazy blur. Following it is a hollow, rumbling roar so deep it shakes the ground beneath their feet.

"What's that?" Helen asks.

"The fire," Twitch answers.

At first, no one believes him. No fire makes that kind of noise. But this isn't just any fire. This is the Brown Forest: the biggest, driest box of kindling ever put on earth.

Something tells Hope this is no accident. This is the Man in Orange's doing, meant to consume the Sisters and Less Thans and burn them to a crisp.

Leave no trace.

The smoke thickens and they run faster. Behind them is the inferno, like a pursuing monster. Though they can't yet see it, they can imagine its dragon's mouth.

They make it to the top of the ridge and Hope glances down behind her. The smoke is suddenly thick and heavy, like an avalanche—an avalanche coming *up*hill, billowing past the trees. They cover their mouths and noses as best they can.

"We have to reach the end of the forest before the fire does," Hope yells.

"No way," Twitch says. "We can't outrace it."

"We'll have to."

"How about that stream?" Flush shouts. "We could lie there till the fire passes."

"The water's too shallow. We'd be cooked in no time."

Which is the worse way to die, Hope wonders: consumed by flames, or poached in a thin stream of boiling water?

A spark of light catches her eyes and she turns. Nearly a mile away are the first hints of flame, cutting through the thick white smoke. Jagged bolts of red and orange and black. A mesmerizing sight.

"Let's go!" Cat cries, grabbing Four Fingers and pushing him forward.

They're on level ground now, tearing through the forest like panicked rabbits fleeing the coyote's jaws. Hope trails the others to make sure everyone's keeping up—Helen especially. No one gets left behind.

But before she knows it, Hope's lost the others. Their shapes grow dim and she can barely make them out in the smoke. Then can't see them at all. Can't hear them either. There is only one sound: fire. Complete, engulfing flames.

Smoke burns her mouth, throat, lungs. It pricks her eyes, like a thousand needles jabbing her cornea. A throbbing, stinging agony.

Worse is the panic of falling farther behind, and in her confusion she stumbles and falls, slamming into the thick trunk of a spruce. Stars spot her vision. Dazed, she pushes herself to a standing position, prepared to start up again . . . and realizes she's completely turned around.

Utterly lost.

She no longer knows which way the fire is coming from and which way the others went. The smoke is all around her. Flames, too. She opens her mouth to shout for help, but all that comes out is a strangled yelp, immediately swallowed by the din of devouring flames.

The fire is closing in, the heat pressing against her like a smothering blanket. Furnace waves of air brush her face, tug at her clothes. Between the stinging smoke and blinding heat, she can barely open her eyes. She staggers forward, hands outstretched, waving weakly at the smoke.

Sound swallows sound until the fire becomes a living, breathing thing. No longer emanating from a single direction, but from many. All around her.

She stumbles to the ground and falls. The hot earth accepts her. *This is the end*, she tells herself, knowing it's only seconds before she's consumed by flames.

A lone figure materializes in the wall of fog: Argos, bounding forward with a series of insistent barks. He's followed by a person—a Less Than by the looks of it—but Hope can't tell. Whoever it is, he heads right for her, waving at the smoke, his silhouette wreathed by fire. Only when he's by her side can she make him out.

It's Book. He's come back for her. She has to stifle tears at the sight of him.

"Come on!" he says, extending his hand. She grabs it and they run, led by Argos, who seems to know exactly the best way out. She has touched Book's hand before, but this time as she grips it, it feels oddly different. It seems a thing of strength, of comfort, of *salvation*.

They find the others in a small clearing, where they're coughing and gagging and spitting great gobs of black mucus. Hope has never been so happy to see them in her life, and she gives a sideways glance to Book—a look of gratitude and thanks. He is staring off in another direction.

She's still shaking from being stranded in the smoke, and barely notices when a flaming ember torches her cheek. Then another lands. And another. The air is suddenly full of them, tiny red coals being borne along by the ferocious wind. They tattoo her skin and burn holes in clothing.

A red ball of fire explodes a couple hundred yards away—not from the ground but from the forest canopy itself. The fire is crowning, leaping from one treetop to another. There's not even the slightest hope of outrunning it now.

Hope realizes with a shudder their fate is obvious. Either they find some miracle path out of there . . . or they're cooked. The fire scorches their backs. They have to do *something*.

It's Book who comes up with the idea.

He rips off his shirt and begins tearing it in strips. The others watch, dumbfounded. No one seems to know what he's doing.

Except Hope.

She rips off her outer shirt and also tears it into long rectangles. "Come on!" she yells. "Help us!"

Others follow, not knowing what they're doing or why they're doing it, only that Book and Hope demand it. Book turns to Cat.

"Give me your arrows."

"How many?"

"All of them."

Cat doesn't hesitate. He empties his quiver onto the ground. Some still have Hunters' blood on them.

"Wrap those around the tips," Hope orders.

The Sisters and Less Thans look at her blankly. Most of them think she's lost it.

"Now!" she shouts, and they begin doing as she says.

When all the arrows are capped with tiny cloth coverings, Book and Hope begin moving through the haze, stopping at an edge of the Brown Forest. Before them, bathed in white smoke, stretches a wide pasture, free of trees but covered in tall prairie grass. The Brown Forest resumes on the other side.

Book looks to Hope and gives a nod. "You're the better shot," he says.

Without hesitating, she dips the arrow's tip against an ember and sets it aflame. She draws the arrow back, angles it, and sends it flying. It soars high above the prairie in a perfect arc, landing somewhere in the middle of that enormous grassy field. A small fire erupts.

Now it's Book's turn. He does exactly the same, lighting a second small blaze.

"If we ignite this whole prairie . . ." Book begins.

". . . then there's a chance it'll burn out before the fire reaches us . . ." Hope says.

". . . and we can dig in and hope the fire passes over." There's an ease in how they complete the other's thoughts. Like their minds are suddenly and perfectly in sync.

Cat's eyes open wide above his bandanna. "You really think this'll work?"

"It has to," Book responds.

The rest of the archers follow suit, sending flaming arrows into the pasture, landing more or less along the line Hope and Book created.

Soon, the prairie is ablaze. A dozen different fires stretch from one side of the clearing to the other. The flames spread, then join, pushed along by the firestorm's winds. Their idea is either the smartest of all time . . . or the dumbest.

The back-burn has to devour the entire pasture before they can even think of moving forward. In the meantime, the wall of flame behind them creeps closer. Century-old trees plummet to the ground with earsplitting crashes.

"Stay down," Hope commands, pressing herself into the dirt. Whenever she lifts her head and peers through

370

the darkening smoke, the prairie is still in flames. Have they misjudged? Is there too much grass? Will it take too long to burn out?

Meanwhile, the red flames behind them leap from tree to tree, emitting roiling spheres of black smoke. The sky is dark, the sun completely blotted out.

"How much longer?" Flush shouts.

Hope and Book both understand the need to wait. They also know if they hesitate much longer they'll be cooked to a crisp. When the rubber soles of Twitch's shoes burst into flames, they can wait no longer.

"Now!" Book and Hope both cry, and the Less Thans and Sisters take off in a mad dash.

They run as a clump, a force of bodies. There are no trees to dodge, no boulders to hurdle, just prairie grass six feet high in places. Their arms are machetes, hacking at the offending blades of grass, parting them as though stepping through a curtain.

With no warning whatsoever they emerge from the tall grass, finding themselves in the middle of a vast field. The earth before them is scorched and blackened, topped by thin ribbons of white smoke. Twenty yards away is the backside of a wall of flames, devouring the next section of prairie grass. But it's moving the other way.

They've done it. Book and Hope have come up with the plan that just saved their lives. The two exchange a

371

glance, and this time they don't look away.

"Hey," Cat says, and something in his tone whips them around.

The inferno is nearly upon them. The pasture they just ran through is an advancing army of fire and heat. It won't be minutes before it reaches them, but seconds. Any sense of self-congratulation is burned away in the charging flames. Panic swells in Hope's breast. All she can say is a single word.

"*Dig!*"

She flings herself onto the scorched earth, the heat scalding her knees and hands. She doesn't care. Like a dog digging a hole, she tears at the blackened dirt, carving out a shallow trench, even as the heat singes her fingertips and bites into her skin.

Once the others figure out what she's doing, they do the same, creating small cavities in the earth. Even Four Fingers senses their desperation and digs as frantically as the rest.

The wall of flame grows closer. The searing heat blisters Hope's back like bubbling tar. Trees fall, crash, explode. Embers zoom and soar, pasting their clothes and bodies. They shake them off as best they can, but the ash is coming down like snow. A spring blizzard.

Although Hope's trench is ridiculously shallow, it will have to work. She's run out of time. "Cover yourselves! Now!"

Just as she's about to fold herself into the narrow ditch, she notices Argos off to one side. Tail drooped, hypnotized by the flames, he seems incapable of movement.

"Argos!" she yells, but he doesn't hear her. She tries again. "Argos! Come!"

Nothing. He just stands there, slowly backing away, whimpering, his tail between his legs.

The wall of fire is nearly on them. And suddenly, as though emerging from the flames themselves, Book is scuttling forward and grabbing Argos up. When he races back to the hole, he rolls into a tight ball with Argos tucked safely against his chest.

A second later the fire hits.

51.

THE SOUND OF THE inferno was the most god-awful, thundering cacophony imaginable. I felt like I was lying atop an erupting volcano.

Worse was the heat. Once the wall of flame reached the edge of prairie grass, it was like a sizzling glove pressing down upon my skin. Bubbles of perspiration danced on my back like pebbles of grease atop a red-hot skillet.

Stinging embers tattooed themselves into my body. Lethal snowflakes. But to shift my position meant exposing my face—and Argos—to the passing flames. So the embers landed, hissing and spitting as they seared my skin, burned my hair.

Hell on earth.

All the while I cursed the decision to create this back-burn, to climb Skeleton Ridge, to leave Camp Liberty in the first place. If only we had stayed put. What were we thinking?

I have no idea how long we lay there, only that it seemed an eternity. I passed out . . . and was confronted with a familiar image.

The woman with long black hair.

She appeared through a fog of white, beckoning me forward. It occurred to me I might be dead and she was welcoming me to some hazy afterlife.

"You will do what's right," she said, her face creased with lines of worry.

I gave her a blank look.

She smiled a brittle smile and repeated it. "You will do what's right." Then, she disappeared as abruptly as ever.

"But I don't know what it means!" I screamed after her.

I felt moisture on my cheek and blinked open my eyes. Argos was licking me to consciousness. I wasn't dead. Raising my head, I saw a distant fire . . . and a series of still, dark mounds: bodies blackened by fire. Less Thans and Sisters.

I lifted myself from the scorched earth and shook the ashes from my clothes. When I ran a hand through my hair, a plume of black ash erupted. I was covered in the stuff. Argos had fared only slightly better. Although he was turned ebony from ash, I had managed to protect him from the burning embers.

I was turned around and couldn't tell who was who. All the still, dark mounds looked exactly the same. As Argos and I walked toward them, our footsteps exploded in clouds of ash and embers. Twitch's body was the first one we came to. I stuck out a hand and searched for a pulse. I couldn't find one. When he suddenly blinked and raised his head, I nearly fell back.

"We made it?" Twitch asked, his voice hoarse.

"Looks that way."

"And the others?"

"Don't know yet."

I helped him to his feet and we began walking from hole to hole. Some of them had managed deeper holes than others and their backs were badly scalded—Red's shirt was still on fire, so was Scylla's—but miraculously, everyone we discovered was still very much alive.

Except for Hope. We hadn't yet found her.

"Where is she?" I asked, pivoting in place, aware of the panic in my voice. "Where's Hope?"

Argos barked and I followed his gaze—to a motion-less mound in the charred landscape. I inhaled sharply at the sight of her. My feet were two-ton weights as I slowly approached.

It wasn't just the drifting smoke that made me feel as

if I was walking in a fog; it was the fear of what I was about to find. And as I made my way toward her—feet kicking up a cloud of embers and ash—it occurred to me that if she didn't survive, I wouldn't either. All my life I'd been searching for someone who understood me, someone who made me better, someone who believed in me.

Hope was that person. And without her . . . well, I couldn't bear to think about it.

I crouched down by her side, laying my outstretched hand on her shoulder. As my fingers rested on her warm skin, willing her to be alive, I remembered her body curved into me in the darkened tunnel; the grip of our fingers as we stumbled from the inferno. Things my body couldn't let go of. *Wouldn't* let go of.

But not just memories from the past—it's like my body could sense the future also. Sharing stories and laughter and tears. My hands running down her arms. The tips of my fingers exploring the hollow of her neck. Her milk-scented breath warming my cheek as we lay next to each other, counting the infinite stars above us.

A future that could only happen if she was still alive.

I shook her lightly. "Hope?"

She didn't stir.

"Hope?" I said again, my voice thick with desperation.

Still nothing. I turned away.

Then, I heard it.

"Book?" she asked groggily.

Her eyes blinked open.

A surge of relief shot through me and for a second I thought my knees would buckle. "Yes," I said. "It's me."

Her eyes batted away the smoke. "I'm okay?"

I was suddenly incapable of speech. Before I answered her, before I even uttered a single word, I hoisted her to her feet and pulled her into me, throwing my arms around her, hugging her like I'd never hugged anyone in my entire life. We stood there, embracing, our chests pressed against each other, our beating hearts mingling into one.

"You're okay," I said, whispering in her ear. "You're okay you're okay you're okay!"

She nodded fiercely, and I could feel her tears staining both our cheeks.

When I finally drew away, I looked into her face. Those eyes—those liquid brown pools that had drawn me in since we'd first met—called to me. Beckoned me.

So I kissed her. I leaned forward and slid my hands on either side of her face and brought it gently forward and kissed her—our lips pressing against each other in a kind of quiet desperation. We had kissed once before, but that was clumsy and hurried and maybe even accidental. This time, it was no accident . . . and we were in no hurry.

When we finally pulled away, my body radiated warmth.

"'Bout time," Diana said, and some of the others laughed.

For the first time I noticed them. We all stood in a clumsy circle, not knowing what to say. Somehow, against odds far greater than who we were, we were still alive, surviving Hunters and fire. It seemed nothing less than a miracle.

"What now?" Flush asked.

"First we get this crud from our lungs," I said.

"And then?"

"Then we wait for those flames to burn through that next section of forest."

"And then?"

I looked the others in the eyes. I looked at Hope. "Then we head east."

The water from our canteens was warm—in some cases downright hot—but it helped cut through the smoky grime that coated our throats. I looked around at my friends, at this motley collection, this band of brothers—and Sisters. I burst into laughter.

"What's so funny?" Flush asked, thinking he'd done something foolish.

"It's not you," I said. "Look at us. We're a mess."

It was true. Our clothes were blackened, red sores dotted our bodies where smoldering embers had branded us, and our skin was covered in soot. We suddenly began to laugh.

379

Red raised his canteen and offered a toast. "To Sisters."

"To Less Thans," Diana said.

"To prey," I added, and we all took long swallows of tepid water.

We stood there laughing and coughing, seven Less Thans and nineteen Sisters in a blackened wilderness of fire. I had never felt such relief, such gratitude, such *friendship*. Yes, it was freedom we were after—that's why we'd escaped from our camps—but at that moment, fire-tested and ash-coated, I realized what K2 had been trying to teach me all along: there was something else lacking in my life. Friends. Companionship. A bond. For once, I *belonged*.

And how much sweeter life was because of it.

We few, we happy few . . .

52.

THEY MARCH OVER SCORCHED earth. The underbrush is burned away, exposing bare, blackened rock. Hot embers glow like devil's eyes. When they come to a river, they lower their ash-covered bodies into the eddies. The water cleanses and cools them, leaving a sooty trail that snakes into the winding current. For Hope, it's like shedding a layer of skin. A former life is past; a new one set to begin.

The kiss was proof of that.

A drizzle wakes them in the morning: the hiss and sizzle of raindrops landing atop smoldering earth. The river is deep, but they're able to ford it by hopping from rocks to logs to get across.

Although no one says as much, they feel like

explorers on the verge of a new continent. What they'll find in this other world—the Heartland—they can't say. All they hope is that it'll be less dangerous than where they came from—a life of being hunted, of being tortured for someone else's purpose, of being treated like animals.

That next night, sitting around the campfire, Sisters and Less Thans together, Twitch begins a ghost story and Book gets up and drifts away. Hope is compelled to follow him.

She finds him sitting on a boulder and takes a seat nearby. For the longest time neither speaks. Every so often the laughter of others drifts their way, but other than that the night is utterly silent.

"What do you think it's like?" Book finally says.

"What's *what* like?"

"Heaven. Hell."

So that's *what he's been thinking about*, she realizes, wondering what this has to do with his secrets—the part of him she doesn't know.

"I don't believe in heaven or hell," she says.

"Then the afterlife, whatever you want to call it. How do you imagine it?"

"I don't."

"Not a bit?"

"Well, it's not angels with wings on big, puffy clouds, if that's what you're getting at."

382

For the longest time Book doesn't respond.

"You know how I picture it?" he asks. "I see it like a road. A long, dusty road in the middle of nowhere. And on this road are the people who've died before you. Like Frank and June Bug. And when you die, you walk awhile and eventually you catch up, and from that time on you walk with them, side by side."

Hope isn't sure what to make of this. "So everyone who's dead is walking on this road?"

"That's right."

"People you like, people you don't?"

"I suppose."

"What if you don't want to walk with certain people?" She can think of any number of people she'd just as soon avoid.

"You don't have to. It's the afterlife; you get to choose who you walk with."

"Hmm." Then she asks, "Is there someone you want to walk with on that road?" Book grunts but says nothing.

Hope thinks of her mom and her dad—and Faith—and the memory prompts her to reach out and put her hand on Book's. He doesn't move away. His fingers are warm beneath hers, and a rush of contentment surges through her. She could stay here all night.

"I know, you know," she murmurs. Her voice is quiet, subdued.

"Know what?"

"What you tried to do."

Book pulls his hand away. "I don't know what you're talking about."

"It's okay," she says.

"I have no idea what—"

"You tried to off yourself."

From the look on Book's face, it seems this is the last thing he wants to talk about. Hope can only imagine the nightmare images floating through his mind.

"How did you know?" he finally asks.

"The scars."

Book gets up and tugs at his sleeves.

"Is that why you go off by yourself sometimes?" Hope asks. "Because it's something you can't talk about?"

"Of course not. . . ."

"Because if you talk about it, it might help it go away."

His head snaps toward her. "What do you know?"

"About pain? More than I want to."

Book stands there, his arms hanging limply by his sides, and Hope wonders if she's gone too far, if she's crossed some invisible line. But the words are out there; there's no going back. Besides, there are things she wants to know. *Needs* to know.

"Why'd you do it?" she asks.

"Guess I was unhappy."

"*Everyone's* unhappy. Why'd you take it further?"

Book doesn't respond. A feeling of disappointment washes over Hope. She's tried to get him to talk, to open up . . . and she's failed. There are things about Book she'll never know. A sigh escapes her lips as she pushes herself from the rock. As she starts to walk away, she gives him a final glance . . . and sees moisture in his eyes.

Tears.

He angles away to hide them, but there's no concealing them. Hope's heart breaks, and she reaches out a hand and lets it rest on his shoulder. She feels an intimacy in the gesture . . . and knows that Book feels it, too. They are surrounded by quiet.

When Book finally speaks, his words are slow, muted, deliberate. In halting sentences, he tells her all about K2—how two unlikely LTs became the best of friends. Hope listens quietly.

He starts from the beginning, telling her about the first time they met and then the bargain they made. The *friendship* they made. Book has to catch his breath as he explains how they were recruited to go up the mountain. They were chopping down trees. By the third day everyone was tired and grumpy and ready to come back down. The Brown Shirts weren't paying attention to what they were doing and all of a sudden a rope slipped—one used to guide the falling timber—and the next thing Book knew a tree was dropping in the wrong direction, headed straight for him, a sixty-foot lodgepole pine.

Hope's hands are clenched, fingernails pressing into her palms. She has no idea where this is leading. Doesn't know if she wants to know.

"And I froze," Book says. "This monster tree was headed right for me and I couldn't decide which direction to go. *Should I jump to my left? To my right?* So I didn't move at all and the tree was coming at me and K2 . . ."

Even as he describes it, Hope can hear the violent *snap* of the tree separating from the stump, the whoosh of air whistling through branches. A part of her doesn't want to hear the rest. Dreads it.

"K2 saw what was happening and ran over and pushed me—he got me out of the way. He saved my life. And then the tree fell." Book pants for breath. "It landed right on him. Pinned him to the ground, the trunk right on his chest. He was alive but just barely. There was no way we could save him. I ran to his side and he opened his eyes and looked at me and . . ." Book is breathing heavy now, sucking air. ". . . and he said, 'Why didn't you move? I thought we had a bargain.' And then he died. He died because of me."

He gives his head a shake and Hope gets the feeling he's trying to dislodge the memories from his mind.

Not possible, of course. She knows that from Faith. It's what they have in common—what drives them both. Guilt. Survivor's guilt.

A long moment passes before Hope speaks. "Why didn't it work?" she asks, glancing at his wrists. "Cuts not deep enough?"

"No, they were deep enough. . . ."

"Then what?"

"Someone rescued me. Before I bled to death."

Hope gives him a quizzical look. In the dim starlight, she can see his chest rising and falling.

"For real," he explains. "Someone found me on the latrine floor."

"Who?"

"Don't know. But whoever it was, they carried me to the infirmary and saved my life." His voice is hoarse, his breathing heavy.

Hope wonders if Book has ever shared this story before.

"When was this?" she asks.

"About two years ago. I'd hoped these"—he gestures to the zigzag of lines on his wrists—"would be gone by now, but no."

Wind whistles through the trees. An eerie, haunting sound.

"I'm glad someone saved you," Hope says.

Book grunts. "Sometimes I wonder."

"If they hadn't, no one would have saved *me*." He looks over at her. "In the fire—you came back for me. You took my hand and led me out of there. You saved me. You saved all of us."

A half smile etches itself on Book's face. "I did, didn't I?"

Hope matches his smile with one of her own. "You did."

She looks at him with her wide brown eyes. He meets her stare and doesn't look away. They hold the look, neither saying a word, and it's like the first time they touched—that current of electricity passing through them. Hope feels her breath go shallow, her limbs tingly. It's a miracle she can stand at all.

Book steps forward and leans into her. For the longest moment they just stand there, separated by mere inches, inhaling the other's breaths, feeling the heat of the other's body. Neither makes a move.

Book slides his hands to her waist, then slowly pulls her into him, pressing his mouth against hers. His lips are soft and his breath tastes of cinnamon. Hope returns the kiss and the longer it lasts, the more passionate it becomes. She feels her heart slamming against her chest. They've kissed before—twice—but always with others around. This is the first time they're alone, and his hands run up and down her back. Her hands explore him with a hunger, an urgency, as though, finally, after all these weeks together, they're able to pour their pain into the other person, to take the other person's pain away.

By the time they pull back, Hope can barely breathe. A million stars press down on them, glimmering in the other's eyes. The reverie is broken only when they hear an explosion of voices from the campfire. Their eyes remain locked.

"I guess we should be getting back," Hope murmurs.

They don't move. The heat Hope feels is as intense as the fire they just escaped from. Book leans in for a second kiss, his hands easing around her neck, pulling her into him. For a long, beautiful instant that lasts forever and no time at all, they merge as one, the press of their bodies like melting wax.

When Book pulls back, Hope feels like the air is sucked out of her body. Sucked out of the sky.

"Shall we?" he asks, gesturing to the camp.

"You go on ahead," Hope murmurs. "I'll be there in a moment."

She watches as Book hikes the short distance to the others. Once he disappears into the dark, she leans against a boulder to catch her breath. She smiles to herself. It takes a long while before her heart rate returns to something resembling normal.

That night, when the others are fast asleep and the camp is a chorus of snores, Hope thinks about Book, about their kiss.

She feels a giddy, unbridled joy—a sense of happiness she's never felt before—but she also experiences a stab of anxiety. There's no guarantee they'll reach the Heartland—and even less assurance that all will be well if they cross to the other side. And there's still the question of her father, of how he's connected to Dr. Gallingham. One way or the other, she has to find that out.

At one point she glances over at Book. He is curled up in a tight ball by the fire, Argos pressed against his side, and for a brief instant their eyes meet, as if he's aware she's watching him, has been aware this entire time.

For once, it's Hope who looks away first.

53.

W<small>E WOKE WITH THE</small> sun and headed east. There was a new sense of camaraderie, and some of the group began to sing.

I felt something, too—a sensation I'd never experienced before. I didn't know what to do with it, where to put it. It was like a stray book in a library and I couldn't figure out what shelf it belonged on. All I knew for sure was I couldn't stop thinking about her.

Hope. A girl named Hope.

Then we finally reached the point where the fire stopped. Suddenly, there was grass and weeds and trees—life itself.

And that night, the woods parted and we found ourselves on the crest of a hill. Beneath us, in a valley not more than a hundred yards away, was a rusted chain-link fence, topped with coils of razor wire. On each side of it the trees had been razed, leaving a no-man's-land of stumps and weeds. An enormous scar in the geography.

As we stared at the fence that stretched in either direction as far as we could see, I wondered: Was it for keeping people in or others out?

"What now?" Flush asked.

"Now we find an opening," Cat said, walking parallel to the fence but staying hidden in the trees. His eyes remained focused on the valley below.

It was forty-five minutes before we saw a distant glow lighting up a cone of sky. The longest minutes of the entire trip. To be so close and yet so far seemed the cruelest of jokes.

We padded to a stop. There—on the other side of the fence—was the edge of a community. Houses, stores, a town square. Under the flickering glare of torches, a small band played in a gazebo, their enthusiastic strains floating through the air like smoke. Families sat on blankets while squealing children played tag and hide-and-seek. There was laughter; there was music. It was unlike anything we'd ever seen. Like we'd gone back in time—how we imagined the world pre-Omega.

We crouched in the woods, observing. Mesmerized. Some of the Sisters were moved to tears.

"There're no soldiers," Twitch whispered.

"There's no fear," Diana added.

It was true. There was no indication of badges or Brown Shirts or weapons. Just people—just regular people—enjoying themselves on a late-spring night. Mothers and fathers and children and neighbors, relaxing and playing. A far cry from anything we'd experienced the first sixteen years of our lives.

"So let's go," Dozer said, rising from his kneeling position.

Cat caught him by the arm. "Not yet."

"Why not? Let's go ask those people where the opening is."

"Not yet," Cat said again.

We sat there, watching, admiring, *longing*.

"Come on," Cat said at last, and began walking. But not toward the fence—*away* from it. Back to where we'd been.

"What the hell . . ." Dozer fumed.

But Cat just kept walking. We did our best to keep up. It made no sense, of course. We'd come all this way, survived all those hardships, in search of this very place and this very moment . . . and we were leaving it.

We marched back a quarter of a mile until the lights from the town were a distant glow. Cat stopped and faced us.

"There's a hole down there under the fence," he said.

"I saw it earlier. That's where we'll crawl into the new territory."

"Um, why don't we just go back and ask those people where the gate is?" Dozer said.

"Because we don't know they'll let us in."

It was a decent point. Although the people by the gazebo appeared friendly enough, for all we knew that fence was meant to keep us out. *No Less Thans allowed.*

"But once we cross to the other side," Cat went on, "we can find out where we stand."

"And if they don't want us?"

Cat shrugged. "I'd rather be on the run over there than here."

Although Dozer rolled his eyes and muttered something under his breath, the rest of us nodded. It made sense. And what would it hurt to stay on the side of safety?

"I'll go first and make sure it isn't electrified," Cat said. He was about to leave when I stopped him.

"We go together," I said. "All of us."

"I agree," Hope chimed in.

"Me, too," said Red.

It was unanimous. Everyone—even Dozer—agreed to join Cat down the sloping hill to the fence.

Cat angled his face to the skies. When a cloud pulled itself over the glowing moon, we scrambled forward.

Pine needles gave way to tall grass and the *swish* of

weeds brushing against legs. Fifty yards of no-man's-land and no sign of guards, no sign of lookouts. We were going to make it. After all this time. After all we'd gone through.

Forty yards became thirty. Twenty. Ten. And still nobody.

And then we were at the fence, falling in a semicircle around a swale in the ground. Draining water had left an indentation where the bottom of the fence no longer met the earth. A small but obvious opening.

Cat tossed a branch toward the fence. We held our breath. No sparks. Nothing. Then he extended the metal cap of his canteen. Metal touching metal. Still nothing. We exhaled.

Cat burrowed his head into the ground and tried to slither through the narrow opening. His legs churned, feet kicked. A moment later he pulled back out, his face streaked with brown.

"No good," he said, spitting out a mouthful of dirt. "Not big enough."

If Cat couldn't manage it, there was little hope for the rest of us.

"So let's dig," I said, and before anyone had a chance to protest I pulled out a knife. I figured we had less than a minute before the clouds rolled past the moon.

In no time we were chipping away, scratching and clawing at the hard earth, casting a small waterfall of dirt behind us. The sharp edges of the fence bottom scraped our knuckles raw, the blood mixing with dirt to create a kind of purplish paste. Our heavy breathing fell into a chant. There was an ugly beauty in our efforts.

"Let's try it," I said, when the hole seemed deep enough.

Cat needed no more prompting than that. He jumped back into the hole, squirming and prodding, until he managed to appear on the other side of the fence. He smiled, white teeth shining through a face smeared with dirt. Diana went next and she navigated the opening with no less difficulty. One by one the Sisters and LTs slid beneath the fence, twenty-four in all, until it was just Flush and me and Argos.

"I don't think I can do this," Flush said with a look of panic. Clammy perspiration dotted his face.

"Of course you can," I said. The others nodded their heads in support.

"I'm too big. Twitch barely made it through and he's a beanpole."

I placed my hands on Flush's shoulders. "Look at me," I commanded, and his eyes locked with mine. "You survived the Brown Shirts and the Hunters, and now you're telling me a little hole's going to defeat you?"

"Well . . ."

"You made it through the hard part, Flush. This hole's the easy stuff. Remember, you once ate maggots."

"I was hungry." He couldn't help but smile as he said it.

"So what I'm saying is, if you can do *that*, you can do *this*." My gaze shifted to the hole. "All we ask is that you try. You willing to do that?"

He nodded a trembling chin. And then, like a duck diving into the shallows, he lowered his head and began to slide his way through the makeshift tunnel. It was a feat that would have been utterly impossible a few months earlier.

But Flush had changed. We all had.

My focus shifted from Flush to the line of others on the opposite side. Pale moonlight cast a crisscrossing shadow of chain-link fence across their faces.

That's when it hit me. We'd made it. We had done something extraordinary. This group of misfits. Of Less Thans and Sisters. *We few, we happy few.* We had survived the most insurmountable of obstacles and made it to a new territory. To freedom.

And yet . . .

Flush popped up on the other side and people patted him on the back. A smile the likes of which I had never seen before plastered his face. There was genuine pride there. A feeling you only get from pushing yourself beyond all boundaries. Something *earned*.

"Thanks," Flush said, leveling his gaze at me. "I'm glad I did it."

I got what he was saying. Not just grateful he'd made it through the hole, although that was part of it, but grateful he'd come along on the journey. Grateful he belonged. Even grateful he was a Less Than.

That's the moment I understood what the woman with the long black hair was really saying.

You will do what's right, she'd told me, over and over, echoing in my dreams. Or my memories. Or both. And now I finally understood. *You will lead the way.*

She'd been guiding me all these years and I just hadn't known it.

"Come on, Book," Twitch said. "Your turn."

But I didn't move. And then I said the two words that surprised me most. Words I didn't know were still a part of my vocabulary.

"I can't."

Jaws dropped. Eyes grew wide.

"What're you talking about?" Flush asked. "*I* made it."

"Yeah, and he's a whole lot bigger than you," Dozer added.

After fires and deserts and Hunters' bullets, what was there about a little hole to be afraid of?

"It's not the hole," I said. "It's something else."

"Like what?"

I hesitated, if only because I wasn't entirely sure what I was going to say.

"The others," I said at last.

"What're you getting at?" Dozer asked.

"Is it fair we're here and there are Less Thans stuck back at Liberty?"

"They didn't come with us," he sputtered, suspicious and disgusted all at once.

I thought of the ones gagged and manacled in the bunkers. Thought of the ones, too, who'd be sold off after the next Rite, when they turned seventeen. "We didn't give 'em the chance."

Even in blue moonlight I could see Dozer's cheeks turning crimson. "We couldn't've done it with hundreds! We're not frickin' Methuselah or Moses or whoever it was! We had trouble enough with just us."

"Fine. So now we can rescue the others. Those hundreds."

"*We?*"

"Okay, maybe *I* rescue them. I know how to get back, what to avoid, what precautions to take. I'll lead them here."

Dozer laughed. A sarcastic scoff. "*You?*"

"No offense, but you can't rescue all of them," Diana said. "Not by yourself."

"Maybe not, but I've gotta try. They're dead otherwise."

No one could argue with me there. That's what the woman with long black hair had been telling me. *You will lead the way.* Not to the new territory, but back to where we'd come from all along. I still didn't know who she was—but after all this time I finally understood what she was getting at. It wasn't intended for me to save my own skin, but to help the others. What was the point of surviving, if there was only a handful of us?

Even if I was lucky enough to have Hope in my life, I'd never stop thinking about the ones we'd left behind.

"So you're going all the way back to Camp Liberty?" Hope asked, trying to make sense of what I was suggesting. "Through the Brown Forest?"

"Yep."

"Across the Flats?"

"That's right."

"Up the mountains?"

"I don't have a choice."

It was crazy—I knew it. We'd reached the Heartland. Had traveled halfway across the West to do so. But even more than that, I'd finally been involved in something that mattered. For the first time in my life, I actually belonged. And yet, by leaving, I was saying good-bye to all of that. Saying good-bye to Hope, too. For what?

But I knew the answer. To save the others. *To do what's right.* That simple.

I gripped the cyclone fence, my fingers curling around its metal strands like vines. "Thanks," I said.

Several of the others placed their hands on top of

mine. Twitch. Scylla. Flush. Red. Even Four Fingers.

"Thanks for what?" Twitch asked.

"For us. Thanks for being us."

To my surprise, Flush's chin quivered and tears streaked his dirt-covered face. Dozer was irritated beyond words and rolled his eyes. Hope looked at me, perplexed or hurt or both. And then there was Cat, sitting off to one side, shaking his head.

"You're crazy, you know," he said.

"I know."

"You'll never make it there alive."

"Possibly."

"We'll be safe and sound and stuffing our faces and you'll be tromping through the wilderness fighting off wolves."

"True. But I seem to remember someone who risked his life to walk across the No Water because it was the right thing to do." I pried my fingers free and took a final glance at my friends. At Hope. She could barely meet my eyes.

I started walking up the hill, Argos following at my heels. It was just him and me. Two of us, taking on Brown Shirts and Hunters, Crazies and wolves. It was a long walk up the slope, the dew-covered weeds brushing my legs.

"Wait," someone called, and I turned.

It was Cat. But instead of trying to talk me out of

going, he was crawling through the hole.

"I thought you told me I was crazy," I said, when he popped up on my side.

"You are," he answered, brushing away dirt. "But I'm crazy, too. And there's no way I'm going to let you have all the fun by yourself."

There was more to it than that, I figured. Something having to do with his dad, maybe. I didn't ask.

And then the most remarkable thing happened. Cat smiled. He actually *smiled*. I couldn't believe it. Emotion surged through me. Relief and joy and a sudden love of life.

He turned to the others and said, "Any of the rest of you Janes care to join us? It'll be the adventure of a lifetime."

"As if what we just went through wasn't?" Twitch asked.

"That was nothing. We're talking real fun this time. The chance to free several hundred Less Thans and stick it to Westbrook all at once."

"The Flats?" Flush asked.

"Unfortunately," I answered.

"Crazies?"

"Probably."

"Brown Shirts?"

"Definitely."

"Wolves?"

"I don't see how we can avoid 'em."

On the other side of the fence, the five LTs and nineteen Sisters looked nervously at each other.

"Then count me in," Flush said, and he dove into the very hole that minutes earlier had stopped him dead in his tracks. And then Twitch did. And Scylla and Diana and Red and Four Fingers, until gradually all the Less Thans had joined me and a handful of Sisters.

But not Hope.

My heart faltered at the sight of her on the other side of the fence, sitting in the grass, her eyes avoiding mine. But I couldn't blame her. I really couldn't.

There were fourteen of us: seven Less Thans and seven Sisters. We had changed over the course of these weeks. We were covered in grime. Our clothes were more tattered rags than anything resembling actual shirts and pants. The sun had weathered our skin, and we had become stronger, all muscle.

"Now what?" Twitch asked, brushing the dirt from his clothes.

I felt the eyes of the others and looked to Cat. His expression seemed to say, *This was your idea, pal. You're in charge.*

"Now we get back to Liberty and free those Less Thans," I said.

I took a final look at Hope and her eyes met mine one last time.

I turned and began working my way up the slope. The others followed, spreading out without needing to be told—a squad of seasoned warriors. A band of brothers—and Sisters—washed in a slant of moonlight, bows slung over our shoulders, ready to take on whatever came our way.

Whether we would succeed or not was anybody's guess, but we would try. We would give it our best shot. We would do what's right.

Just before we reached the crest of the hill, I heard a voice behind me call out, "Hey, wait up!"

I turned around . . . and smiled.

ACKNOWLEDGMENTS

No book is created by oneself—a first book especially so—and I am incredibly grateful to all the people who had a hand in the shaping of this manuscript.

To my agents, Victoria Sanders, Bernadette Baker-Baughman, Chris Kepner: thank you for your guidance, your wisdom, and—most importantly—your faith in me, even during those lean years when I didn't earn you a penny.

To my editor Alyson Day, copyeditor Renée Cafiero, designer Joel Tippie, marketing manager Jenna Lisanti, and publicist Gina Rizzo, and all the wonderful folks at HarperCollins who believed in this book and did editing and copyediting and book jackets and designs and marketing plans and on and on and on: please know that I am more grateful than I have words to say.

An enormous round of thanks to those readers who offered early feedback and got me on track when I went off it: Gracie Anderson, Kendra Carlson, Katie Caskey, Josh Hinke, and most especially Ryan Gallagher, who read more drafts than anyone and has never been shy in sharing his pages and pages of notes—and usually made me laugh in the process.

Thank you to friends Daren Streblow and Jessie Rae Rayle for answering my questions in fields related to their expertise and far removed from mine. Any mistakes that still exist are mine and mine alone.

Thank you to all my UMD students, current and past, for your daily bursts of creativity, talent, and inspiration, which, in turn, inspire me. You've touched me more than I can express.

Thank you to my family for all these many years of love and support—and for sitting through just about every play I've ever been in.

And finally, to Pat, who is my first reader, my best reader, my true companion, who teaches me to laugh, to mourn, to live today and live tomorrow.